What people are saying about …

The Preacher

"Stephen King meets Frank Peretti in Darren Dillman's new thriller, *The Preacher*. Dillman cracks the stained glass to reveal a church turned upside down by a single man, a preacher who is evil to the bone. Standing against him in the fight are the few in the congregation who find themselves in the uncomfortable, sometimes unbearable grip of spiritual acuity. What would you do if you could see the unseen? Awareness—in this case a view into a celestial battle fought in the hot air of a Texas summer—brings with it the curse of responsibility. In this riveting novel, Dillman will draw you in through that stained-glass window and make you choose."

Melanie Wells, author of *My Soul to Keep*

"Don't pick up Darren Dillman's new novel if you want to get any sleep. When I picked it up, I did not put it down, literally, until I had read every word. *The Preacher* is a very powerful page turner. I recommend it."

Linda Hall, author of the upcoming
Shadows at the Window

DARREN DILLMAN

David C Cook®

transforming lives together

THE PREACHER
Published by David C. Cook
4050 Lee Vance View
Colorado Springs, CO 80918 U.S.A.

David C. Cook Distribution Canada
55 Woodslee Avenue, Paris, Ontario, Canada N3L 3E5

David C. Cook U.K., Kingsway Communications
Eastbourne, East Sussex BN23 6NT, England

David C. Cook and the graphic circle C logo
are registered trademarks of Cook Communications Ministries.

Scripture quotations taken from the King James Version of the Bible.
(Public Domain.) And the *New American Standard Bible*, © Copyright
1960, 1995 by The Lockman Foundation. Used by permission.

LCCN 2008942919
ISBN 978-1-4347-6809-4

© 2009 Darren Dillman
Published in association with the literary agency of Daniel Literary
Group, 1701 Kingsbury Dr., Ste. 100, Nashville, TN 37215

The Team: John Blase, Steve Parolini, Jaci Schneider, and Karen Athen
Cover Design: Amy Kiechlin
Cover Photos: iStockphotos
Interior Design: Sarah Schultz

Printed in the United States of America
First Edition 2009

1 2 3 4 5 6 7 8 9 10

122708

For my parents

Acknowledgments

Many family members, teachers, and writers have provided encouragement over the years. Deep-hearted thanks to John Wood, Jim Harris, Neil Connelly, Vicki Soper, Shonell Bacon, Jackie Walsh, and to John Blase and the extraordinary human beings at David C. Cook. A tip of the cowboy hat (which I don't actually own, but supposing I did) to Steve Parolini for his editing and to Greg Daniel for his advice and hard work.

Satan doesn't knock on the front door and say "Hi, I'm Satan." He comes in the back door using the most cunning, convincing, persuasive language possible.

—Charles Stanley

Chapter 1

Waymon Taylor loosened his collar, tried to breathe, and slouched just enough to convey that he might not be so uptight over the whole thing. Lately, though, his patience had the half-life of a housefly, and his facades disintegrated like oil in the Permian Basin. The eldest of the group, with tendrils of gray metastasizing through his remaining curls of hair, he was the only black member on the pulpit committee. He'd never chaired the committee, though he'd served for twenty-six years as a deacon at Crown of Thorns Baptist Church. He took a seat along the side, two seats from the committee chairman, Rick Pettibone.

The service at First Baptist Church of Oxford had let out two hours before, and the building was empty, engulfed in the dead silence of a Sunday afternoon. Here, in a leather-scented conference room near the entrance, the pulpit committee convened in a church half the size of its own. Tall antique bookcases housed biblical translations and volumes from Martin Luther to C. S. Lewis.

Rick told a joke to Casey Atwood, whom he shared the golf course with on weekends. Casey's mustache was fine-tuned to perfection, the corners sharp as tended hedges, yet thick in the middle. His dark eyes were flat and slanted like those of livestock anxious to avoid slaughter, and he wore a garish Western shirt inundated with blue and black spurs. He sat in the seat in front of Waymon, his aftershave radiating toward the elder's nostrils.

Brother Atwood acted as if he were Doc Holliday. How much aftershave did he have to put on?

"You awake now, Matt?" Rick asked, laughing.

Matt "Meatloaf" Berringer raised his eyes and sighed. "Getting there." His shirt had that wrinkled just-out-of-the-drawer look, a breaded odor crawling away from it. "Pretty long trip."

"Amen," Luther Harris said. He swiveled toward Rick. "Us old geezers," he said, nodding to Waymon, "can't hardly make a trip like this anymore. I left my bones a couple states back."

"Across the bayou, on to the Missis'," Waymon said. "I don't believe the pulpit committee ever traveled this far before."

Rick looked away. A Duke graduate, he owned a chain of telecommunications stores. His blond hair was loosely parted on the side, and he rested his patched jacketed elbows on the table while interlocking his fingers. He'd chaired the committee for six months. Well liked by most in the congregation, Rick practiced a foolproof *How to Win Friends and Influence People* disposition, but once in a while a cocky demeanor slipped through his skin and he couldn't keep from making a smart-aleck remark.

"Everyone ready?" Rick asked.

Nods all around.

"What did you all think of Brother Tisdale?" Rick asked.

Casey rushed in. "Best preaching I ever heard. Spirit was working in there."

Several nodded.

"Billy Graham dreams of being that good," Scott said.

Guffaws from Luther and Stan; a twanged bellow from Casey.

"That's the most excited I've felt in a service in a long time," Stan said. The Sunday school superintendent sat to Waymon's left and sported a brown mustache and beard. His black cowboy hat rested on the table in front of him like a patient pet, and he wore an amiable smile, revealing a set of recently polished teeth.

Cowboys all around me, Waymon thought, determined to ruffle some feathers. *Old black man ain't got no place in the Wild West. If the Injuns don't kill him, the cowboys sure will.*

Luther spoke up. "I think he'd make a good pastor. Of course, I'm kind of partial to anyone with a few gray hairs."

"I thought he was pretty good, myself," Rick said. "I'd like to echo Brother Luther's sentiment. After all the talking I've had with him on the phone, and then meeting him yesterday, I think Brother Tisdale's the real thing.

"He's devoted. He loves the Lord. He's not necessarily looking for a change of scenery. He likes it here. He loves his flock. But he's widowed and said if the Lord calls him somewhere, he'll go."

"Amen," Stan said. "That's something we need to pray about."

Fingers drummed, knees swung, knocked against the other.

Finally, Rick turned to Waymon. "Brother Waymon, we haven't heard your two cents."

Waymon's throat tightened like an old dog's arthritic back. For a second he didn't think he could produce any sound. Finally, after a short grin, the words came out, smooth as water from the spigot.

"I recommend we don't invite him in view of a call," he said.

Six pairs of eyes protruded from their sockets.

"I know I'm the odd one out. There's just something about this preacher I don't like. I can't put my finger on it. I've seen a lot of 'em over the years. Maybe I've seen too many. He's a fine preacher. I just couldn't feel the Spirit moving in his words. He said the right things, but I didn't sense much compassion in his message." He studied the faces. "And there was something about the invitation. He acted like he almost forgot it, or he was afraid—"

"Yeah, the invitation could've been better," Luther said.

Rick looked around the room. "Anyone else feel like Brother Waymon?" He cleared his throat. "Any misgivings? Other comments?"

Half of them looked down at the table. Waymon focused on a Billy Graham title in the bookcase, awaiting the inevitable.

"Well, in that case," Rick said, "I recommend Brother Tisdale in view of a call. I move we ask him to come to Dallas and preach."

Waymon grinned. "No need to make a motion, Brother Rick. We're not in a business meeting."

"You're right, Brother Waymon," Rick said. He laughed it off. "I recommend it."

Chapter 2

They came in Lincolns, BMWs, Mustangs, Tahoes, Expeditions, old dusty pickups, and beat-up station wagons to hear Brother Tisdale preach.

The church's lawn was mowed short, the sides edged an inch inside the concrete walkway, its small Bermuda blades cut to steep short walls, bleeding a sour-sweet smell. The hedges were granny-groomed; no leaf or twig jutted out. The red and white roses in the flower bed extended and drooped like bowing ballet partners, with orange marigolds squatting between the bushes. Around the building, as the bed curved to the side of the auditorium, yellow marigolds joined the orange, and the petals of a dozen portulacas blushed a cherry red.

Inside, Andrea Cormieaux sat with her husband, Curt, and their six-year-old daughter, Elizabeth, on the right side of the pews, five rows from the front. Elizabeth had only recently begun accompanying them to the service, while their son Wesley, just three years old, remained in the nursery.

Elizabeth carried her mother's features: long, silky blonde hair tied in a ponytail, placid crystalline blue eyes, a gentle face, and aquiline, bony nose. At home she was cantankerous—especially when something new or foreign caught her interest. She had a habit of tuning others out, rarely coming inside when Andrea told her to, staying up twenty or thirty minutes past her bedtime, and lounging atop the monkey bars after being excoriated for sitting on them. But in public she acknowledged her parents' commands, knowing how embarrassed they became if she didn't obey and the penalties that awaited her after a silent trip home.

The choir, robed in maroon with gold collars, wandered single file into the loft from the side and remained standing, looking, for the most part, at the music director. After a couple minutes they started softly into a variation of "Have Thine Own Way, Lord," with synthesized accompaniment chiming from the speakers. When the last notes faded, they sat down and Stan Wilcox walked up to the podium.

"I'd like to welcome you to Crown of Thorns Baptist Church," he said.

Andrea's attention waned. She studied the beams of light that penetrated the stained-glass windows, how they broke from the prism and spilled onto the maroon carpet, each in its own path.

The auditorium was nearly full, and the air conditioner struggled to cool those on the far front rows. The church hadn't housed this many people since Easter four years before, when Jack Walker was still pastor. During the past three years attendance had fallen off a cliff under Brother Levin, who'd been gone for three months, run out of town like a losing football coach. Two weeks ago Andrea counted less than one hundred thirty, and rumor had it that more letters of membership were disappearing every week. By Andrea's guess, at least three hundred people were seated for today's service, and a few dozen more, dressed in proper church attire with black cowhide-covered Bibles clutched against hips like firearms, were still filtering through the doors.

Stan was saying something about numbers. Sunday school attendance had jumped to one hundred sixty. Or had he said one hundred fifty? Such details escaped Andrea when she drifted away. Drifting was something she'd begun when she was a child, and she hadn't always consciously drifted but rather had been pulled into the spiritual world around her.

"Brother Tisdale is here to preach on recommendation of the pulpit committee," Stan said. "Hopefully you met him when you came through the door this morning. After the service we will vote on calling him as our pastor."

Andrea glanced at the baptistery and at once knew it was empty. She had a feeling—no, more than a feeling—a knowledge that though she and Curt had missed the previous Sunday, there had been no water in it for three weeks. Three weeks without a baptism. She couldn't remember the last time someone had walked the aisle, professing Jesus as his or her newly proclaimed Savior.

Crown of Thorns Baptist had rarely been the main spiritual attraction in town. It had never attracted the same numbers as First Baptist. In Dallas the competition for members had a vacuum effect on stagnant churches like Crown of Thorns, although thirty years prior, during the two-year span of Horace Stringer, with attendance numbers surging toward a thousand, Crown of Thorns Baptist's auditorium had burst at the seams, pews packed end to end like seats at the Super Bowl, and the auditorium had demanded a face-lift. The old members—those who hadn't succumbed to coronaries, strokes, or Alzheimer's—often reminisced how Stringer's services had uplifted hundreds of souls, stirring dozens of raised hands and invigorated amens. In the wake of his success, Stringer had accepted a call to First Baptist Church of Houston.

Stan elaborated on Brother Tisdale's service to God in Oxford, Mississippi, said he was a widower, and told of his willingness to relocate to Dallas if he felt God's call.

"Now it's time to stand and greet our guests," Stan said. "If you're a guest, please remain seated so our ushers can find you."

Although the welcoming premise held good intention, it left Andrea feeling insecure and uncomfortable, standing, shaking hands with those who offered their own, and occasionally hugging someone she knew, like Carol Tinsley, who taught her Sunday school class, or Gretta Mullins, an older woman who made her feel at ease. It seemed ironic that the one exercise intended to relax the congregation and prepare their hearts for worship tended to spread tension—to divide people. Cliques were the sole beneficiaries of such festivities, and during the past year and a half—the span during which she and Curt had been members at Crown of Thorns Baptist—Andrea watched many visiting families sit in solitude, fingers laced in their laps, throats gulping. The few times Andrea had moved from her pew had been to greet such guests.

Curt stepped over and reached across, lending his hand to as many people as possible. Elizabeth stood by her mother, chewing gum in quick, snappy bites, gazing at the faces.

When they sat down, they sang three hymns, ending with "Power in the Blood." The offering followed. Andrea had handed in theirs during Sunday school, as she often did. The only time she put something into the plate was when they were late. Curt handed her the empty plate, and she passed it to the usher, who moved on to the next row.

A college-age woman sang a contemporary hymn during the offering. Then Brother Owen Tisdale walked up the steps, black Bible in hand, and took the podium.

He looked like an old farm boy: tall, maybe six feet two, slightly hefty, straight as a pillar, a full face, with dull, wide cheekbones and a straight nose. The irises of his eyes stretched as large as quarters and swelled with the clear blue fluid of a Caribbean lagoon. His forehead glared where he was balding; what was left was strawberry blond, with strands of gray jutting between. He had a gentle charisma, an almost grandfatherly presence, expressed through sighing and in the way he started to speak but held back, exhaling as he studied the crowd.

Andrea held her breath as she watched the preacher's face. His eyes locked onto hers. She felt as though she'd seen him somewhere before, but she knew she hadn't; she didn't recognize him. It was only a feeling.

He opened his Bible, divided it in half at Psalms, the midway point taught to children in Bible drills.

"The last time I was in Dallas was fifteen years ago for a pastors' conference," he said, grinning. His voice was deep and unrelentingly Southern. "And I have to say, honestly, it looks like the same ol' Dallas to me."

Laughter bucked from the pews.

"Which is a good thing," he interjected, then gave a brief laugh. "I'm blessed to be in Dallas this morning. I've only been here since yesterday, but already, I can tell you there are some fine Christian people doing the Lord's work here."

Amens rose from the crowd.

Brother Tisdale looked into his Bible. "I'll be reading from the Fifty-sixth Psalm this morning, so if you'd like to follow along, that's where I'll be." Another grin, though less becoming. He waited as hundreds of fingers thumbed through onionskin pages. "Starting with the first verse: 'Be merciful unto me, O God: for man would swallow me up; he fighting daily oppresseth me.'"

Nausea grabbed Andrea's stomach, squeezing it as if clenching its fist, and bits of a black void obscured her view like shots of a flickering black-and-white film. It couldn't be hot flashes. She had never had any like these. Perhaps it was hunger.

She hadn't eaten any breakfast, although she'd scrambled eggs, fried bacon, and buttered toast for Curt and the kids, hurrying to make it in time for Sunday school.

The nausea subsided, and she focused on the preacher.

"Mine enemies would daily swallow me up: for they be many that fight against me, O thou most High."

The darkness threatened, obliterating her view of the pulpit.

"What time I am afraid, I will trust in thee."

It climbed into her thoughts.

"In God I will praise his word, in God I have put my trust; I will not fear what flesh can do unto me."

Her vision swirled into a moving darkness, and her equilibrium swayed. Remnants of the church's interior faded fast, though preciously, like memories of childhood field trips. What light intruded was scant, amorphous. In front of her she saw a land without any ground, marked only by ivory-shaded outlines moving about, perhaps slithering, a clouded kaleidoscopic mass. Something hovered above her, and she wanted to duck, but she wasn't able to move; she couldn't see any part of her body: no limbs, no breasts. All she had was vision.

Like a stirring sea of blood, the church's maroon interior flooded back into view.

Andrea lifted her head as though she'd been dozing—something she'd done countless times as a child, especially during Sunday- and Wednesday-evening services. Why couldn't this be like any other somnolent sermon? She took in a good breath, not too deep, because she knew a really deep breath—combined with the pallid, distraught look on her face—would attract attention. She turned to see Curt sitting at her side, eyes glued to the preacher, apparently unaware of her lapse. On her other side Elizabeth was drawing pictures, songbook braced against her skinny thighs, paper sliding across the book's hardbound edges and corner. The smell of spearmint wafted from her delicate mouth with each chomp of the gum.

Andrea looked at the preacher.

Brother Tisdale continued: "Every day they wrest my words: all their thoughts are against me for evil." His voice, crisp and sonorous.

The nausea returned, and Andrea could see the darkness somewhere in the distance, lying still and inviolate.

The preacher's eyes caught her own as he looked up from his Bible.

The darkness squeezed its fist around her, pulled her back in. In the distance, something gleamed. She seemed to rise above the moving mass of ivory, floating, but she didn't think about leaving, because this vision was like a dream.

She saw that the gleaming structure cast a gold incandescence, and from it white bodily shapes. Two or three, bright as the moon, made of flesh, floated toward her. Their bodies had human features—arms and legs, hands and feet, a head. Within their hands, or dangling about their bodies, trinkets of gold glittered like golden stars, their beams cutting through the shadows. Dots of orange or gold—their eyes?—flickered as they moved closer to her.

From the ivory plane more shapes emerged, none as bright as those in the distance. Silver scepters danced about them, rotating from body to body. A red fire lit their eyes while others blazed a torrid blue. With them came the sound of rushing water pouring over a cliff, crashing against a canyon wall, rising in frequency as the two sides came upon each other.

In a matter of seconds their bodies met and were interspersed between, among, and upon each other. Blinding flashes of light forced Andrea to close her eyes, leaving her squinting when she opened them again. The amplified noise of rushing water raved, and she held her hands over her ears, cutting the sound in half.

A gentle force propelled her forward, guided her toward the holocaust. Bodies writhed on the ground below, impaled by fragments of radiant silver and gold. One of the lighter beings grabbed at the silver scepter protruding from its belly, jerking its head forward and backward, while another being, its body darker, clutched the gold surrounding its neck, embedded like some lurid necklace.

Andrea noticed the absence of blood. The wails and screams caused something of a sonic boom, which darkened the landscape, leaving only pieces of the vision.

One of the luminous beings—by far the brightest—stood several feet from his nemesis, and they faced each other, patiently, until the effulgent one released gold from its arm, showering it in a rainbow shape. Then the gold turned into silver and surrounded the dark shape in a tall, radiant rectangle that looked to be made of glass.

With that image embedded, the church's maroon interior faded into view. She heard Curt's voice, a soft whisper.

"Andrea," he said. "You okay?"

Her head drooped as if in prayer and her chin angled toward Curt's shoulder. Her eyes felt weak. How long had she been out? Her body stiffened with fatigue.

"Andrea," Curt said, eyes wide with fright.

Andrea looked around, saw the concerned looks of those in the pews near her. She sat up straight, opened her eyes wider, and took in a deep breath. A little strength returned. Tisdale's voice droned on, but she couldn't make out the words. Elizabeth went about her drawing, chewing her gum. Nothing seemed to irritate her: not stickers in the weed patch beyond the trailer, rusted nails in the alley, not even the nose-picking bullies in school.

Andrea rose from her seat, slowly. She felt Curt's hand touch hers.

"You all right?" he asked softly.

"I'll be okay," she said, a little briskly. As she neared the edge of the pew, she lunged forward with a quick series of steps that made

Curt jerk toward her as if to help, but gripping the corner of the pew, she gathered herself and stepped into the aisle. Curt sat back in his seat.

She again locked eyes with the visiting preacher—those blue eyes like a fire's center—and heard him say, "Shall they escape by iniquity? In thine anger cast down the people, O God."

Suddenly a deep sickness wrenched her stomach. She turned abruptly, focusing on the doors leading into the hallway, but her legs couldn't scissor fast enough, and she thought the vomit might lurch from her insides before she could reach them. She slowed, however, because she didn't want to attract attention and because she might trip over her own feet. She took a gradual deep breath, fought the pain, and after a couple steps up the small platform, made her way through the door and closed it gently.

Once outside the auditorium the panic simmered, and she breathed a deep sigh. But the nausea was still wrestling her insides. She hurried through the glass doors and ran, her heels clopping against the tiled floor, to the women's restroom, where she barged into the first stall, bent over, and vomited, pressing her stomach for the bad stuff to spew.

She didn't let her knees touch the floor. How would that look—a woman on her knees in a restroom stall? It seemed like the wrong place to repent. She remained there, bent over and gagging on her sickness, for the next five minutes. She cleaned herself up, wiping her mouth and face with a wet paper towel, and washed her hands.

She tottered out of the restroom. A gun to her head couldn't have forced her back into the auditorium.

Andrea walked down the hallway to the glass doors. Southern Baptist literature filled shelves along the opposite wall and covered a small table underneath. She noticed the title of one pamphlet: "Walking Daily with Jesus."

Through the doors and walls she could hear the preacher's voice, hardly condemnatory, its gentle Southern accent barely discernible from most Texans'. As she honed in on that voice, the nausea resurfaced, doubling her over slightly; it crawled away just as fast, scooting on its thin bug legs. Then, whether prompted by an overactive imagination or a recognition of seeming coincidence, she began to see a correlation between the preacher's words and her condition; it was almost as if his words festered her sickness. Was it the Scripture? Was he cursing her? *Superstitious thinking,* she thought. She was becoming like her mother: a witch's mind and a Christian's heart.

She wiped her moist forehead with her hand and waited, slightly stooped against the wall.

Light piano notes trickled through the door crevices: the invitation.

A moment later, the organ joined in, and the choir's somber rendition of "Have Thine Own Way, Lord," accompanied by the preacher's beckoning voice, prolonged the service another four or five minutes. Finally, Stan's Western voice bellowed from the pulpit.

The door to the auditorium opened, and Brother Tisdale walked into the hallway.

Andrea almost jerked back, her eyes wide with caution. If she'd been against the opposite wall, the preacher wouldn't have seen her— unless, of course, he somehow knew she was there. But she wanted to be certain Curt and Elizabeth could find her once they came through the first set of doors, so she stood directly in view of anyone in that first square of the hallway.

What is he doing out here? she wondered. *Oh, of course, they're voting.*

The preacher's head had been tilted toward the floor in front of him, but now, as he stood in front of the glass doors, he raised his blue eyes to Andrea. He grinned.

Andrea quivered. The grin appeared too warm, hardly a grin that meant well, and she felt, with some intangible fright, that the preacher knew this. She crossed her arms, giving off vibes of reticence, shuddering from unease as much as her nausea.

The preacher looked down again, made a small circle with his mouth, as if to whistle. Stan's voice quieted in the auditorium, and through the silence Andrea heard the mature whistled notes of "Deep and Wide," a song taught to toddlers and kindergartners. The preacher raised his eyes, but this time she looked away. He whistled through the song twice more. Finally, the auditorium door opened, and he was ushered back inside.

Another couple of minutes passed, and then the piano and organ pounded out the postlude and people filtered through the doors. Curt and Elizabeth were the fifth and sixth persons through, their hands intertwined.

Andrea thought about forcing a grin, but with her stomach shifting, it was better to reflect the way she really felt—somewhere between miserable and horrible. Miserable because of the nausea and vomiting, horrible because of the way the preacher had grinned at her. And besides, if she smiled and concealed her pain and sickness,

Curt might expect her well enough to cook dinner, among other things. So she gave a hollow, insipid look instead.

He laid a hand on her shoulder. "You feelin' any better?" Elizabeth was swinging his other arm and chomping her gum.

Andrea sighed. "Honestly? No."

"Stomach hurt?" he asked.

She moaned. "Almost didn't make it to the restroom in time."

"Well, you want to go get Wesley?" he asked.

"Yeah," she said, pushing off the wall. They took a couple steps together before she looked at him and asked, "What did you think of the preacher?"

"Brother Tisdale?" he said. "Sounded pretty good to me. We voted him in."

Chapter 3

The first thing Andrea did when she got home was call her mother in Lake Charles, Louisiana, where Andrea had grown up and where she had met Curt. They had gone to the same church, First Baptist of Lake Charles, but hadn't begun dating until high school, between her junior and senior years. Curt, two years older and already graduated, had been working for Southern Louisiana Natural Gas Company at the time. They married just after Andrea graduated, and seven years later, Southern Louisiana Natural was purchased by Southwestern Natural Gas Company. Curt, caught in a transition period of layoffs and reassignments, was transferred. So here they were in a small town just east of Dallas.

To Andrea, three years ago seemed like ages, when life was full of magic and the spells were unfolding in front of her on a daily basis. When her worries were limited to things like the hours Southern Louisiana Natural was cutting from Curt's schedule, the crayoned pictures of dinosaurs Elizabeth had drawn on her bedroom walls, and the rash on Wesley's bottom.

The simplicity of hearing her mother's voice or seeing how green the birch leaves looked on a postcard was all it took to summon the collage of memories. That, and the trailer they lived in just outside Mesquite, where nothing but tumbleweeds grew, often left her feeling daunted and abandoned.

It was nice living outside the city, away from traffic and busy intersections, and at least they had a yard and weren't jam-packed in a dead-end trailer park. But it didn't feel or seem like home, and when she thought about the years to come, she worried that it never would. The land was stomped flat and dry, the bushes withered and decrepit. She'd planted marigolds in front of their trailer the year before but nothing had risen, and they were having a hard time getting the Bermuda grass to do anything; a small patch would spring up, then curl as if sick, and finally crumple. They had watered it every day, something they hadn't had to do in Louisiana. All the tidy, delicate sprinklers spitting water on neighbors' lawns seemed like cheap toys or promotional gadgets. At least Curt had a good lawn mower.

Leaning back against her bedpost, the TV humming slightly, she picked up the phone and dialed the number.

It was after noon, almost one o'clock, so the only thing Andrea might have to compete with was a potluck at First Baptist of Lake Charles. Jean Lavoie never took naps unless she was traveling, and even then it would take a long, hot, fatiguing trip to force her onto a bed. The woman had too much energy. She'd just turned fifty-two and was constantly on the go, teaching piano lessons, an English literature class at the junior college, drudging up music for the church choir, and sometimes flirting with the detestable tarot cards and that cornball coven called the Southern Louisiana Order of High Magicians, which seemed to Andrea even more ridiculous than any of the Elvis-is-not-dead junk.

Her mother answered, and Andrea told her about the fainting spell.

"Did you hit your head?" Jean asked.

Andrea paused a moment. "Oh, no, it wasn't like that. It happened during the sermon. I started feeling weak, and I guess I blacked out."

"Are you feeling any better now?"

"I'm fine now," Andrea said. "It was just, when I blacked out I saw something." Her throat tensed up, and she swallowed. "Hallucinations, maybe. It was strange." To her surprise, she'd been able to finish this explanation without an interruption. How ironic, she thought. For once, her mother was silent.

"Can you describe them?" Jean asked.

"I'll try," she said. She painted word pictures of what she remembered: the preemptive darkness, the wavering landscape, the city of gold, the beings impaling each other. "I felt like I was there, watching it."

"The war," Jean said.

"Mother?" Andrea asked.

"Could you have seen a war in heaven?" the elder woman asked, almost to herself. "I don't know if it was *the war*. Maybe it wasn't in heaven. But I believe you saw angels fighting each other."

Please, Andrea thought, *not this again. Too much tarot and old women's Bible studies.*

"The bright ones you talked about are the archangels," Jean said. "I think the weapons you described have more to do with spiritual warfare and identity than the physical war we're used to seeing, although it doesn't sound too different, does it?"

"No," Andrea offered. Was this what she had called her mother for? "Mother, have you been reading Revelations again?"

"It's Revelation, honey, without the *s*," Jean said. "And no, I haven't."

"I don't know what I saw," Andrea said, "but when it happened, the furthest thing from my mind was heaven. It was closer to hell."

"We don't always know what we're seeing," Jean said. Now she sounded like the part-time English professor. "Sometimes I think the cards are lying, but usually I'm just not listening to my deeper intuition. Maybe what you saw isn't for you to know or interpret."

"Then why did I see it?" Andrea asked.

"Maybe something—a spiritual stimulus of some kind—made you see these things."

Andrea laughed. "Are you telling me I'm a spirit child?"

"You had a special connection—a gift—when you were younger," Jean said. "You have to remember."

Andrea couldn't peg exactly how old she had been, but when she was seven or eight, the Christians of Cajun Louisiana had proclaimed her a *traiter*, or healer, and Jean had driven her across the state performing supposed miracles: closing wounds with her hands, giving sight to the blind, vaporizing cancer. That was so long ago, she doubted its authenticity now and attributed it more or less to Southern mysticism. Even if she had possessed the power, the years had elapsed like passing cars.

"Bits and pieces," Andrea said.

"I think the spirit world pulled you back in," Jean said. "Or maybe something pushed you into it. Have you thought about that?"

Andrea hadn't enjoyed the vision. She didn't want to see it again.

"We're Baptists, Mother, not Mormons," she said, leaning her head against the receiver, sandwiching it between her ear and shoulder. "We don't believe in modern-day prophets, and we don't believe Jesus is the Devil's long-lost brother." She didn't know why she was being so spicy; perhaps, she thought, it had something to do with being closed in, cooped up, whatever you wanted to call it—the need to let out some steam and her lack of an adult to talk to besides Curt. How she hoped he didn't become just another redneck in Dallas.

"Your dad and I happen to know some very good Mormon people."

"You know what Curt says about them," Andrea said. "He says with all the weird stuff they believe, they *better* be nice."

For a second Andrea thought the line went dead.

"Andrea, what do you remember about your traiter powers?" Jean asked.

Andrea sighed, coiling the phone cord with her fingers. "It was like a movie or something."

"It's still in you," Jean said.

"How do you know?"

"My secret. God's gifts are forever. Keep your eyes open, okay?"

"I will," Andrea said.

"Don't worry about the visions. You'll know more about them soon."

When she and Curt turned off the lights and slipped underneath the comforter and sheets, Andrea noticed an ivory glow on the ceiling-fan light.

"Why is the light doing that?" she asked.

"Doing what?" Curt asked. "I don't see anything."

Andrea leaned against her pillow, slung her hand across her stomach.

"It's just the dark," Curt said. "Your eyes haven't adjusted yet." With that, he rolled onto his side and went silent.

Andrea closed her eyes, but the image of the glowing light followed her into the darkness, circling and weaving through a coarse, earthen tunnel.

An old man lay shriveled up in bed, coughing, gagging, at times shaking intractably, urinating drops of ungodly pain, writhing only as much as the constricted mobility of his limbs allowed, teeth biting down on his tongue, drawing blood.

A gray-haired woman with a few pounds to spare and concern plaguing her face led the small blonde-headed girl, the girl's mother, and the local pastor into the room. The lighting was poor. Light hurt his eyes, the woman said. The old man's shaking worsened, as if someone had dumped a bucket of ice down his back, which was burning with inflammation, the disks and cartilage worn away, the vertebrae corroded.

The woman's own hands shook. She moved them close to the man as if to touch him but retracted them as if she didn't quite know what, if anything, to do. Her eyes were bloodshot: taut with fear, dismay, panic. She fidgeted back and forth, speaking to her husband who lay dying, unable to hear, until the pastor gestured to the young girl to step forward.

The girl was seven. A white cotton shirt clung to her skin. Her nose was bony and a little long, but other than that, she didn't seem to scare the old man, who shook with Parkinson's. The girl brushed her hair behind her shoulders and looked up to her mother: a face full of hope. And faith. Her eyes a blue sea that could flood, storm, or part with the proper command.

"Okay, Andrea," her mother said. "It's time for you to help."

The girl circled around the bed, took bite-size steps toward the bedridden man. His hands were dark and curled up like talons, his face smothered with the same oil-slick complexion. His life seemed to flutter away in a steady stream like butterflies, yellow and orange monarchs, lilac and crimson, showing him the trail. The girl could see them, and she saw that he could see them as well. His time was near.

She edged closer, near the bed's seam. His face took on a blissful countenance, and his mouth and teeth rattled. His pupils dilated uncontrollably. The girl understood: it was like looking at the Grand Canyon for the first time, knowing you couldn't go down until tomorrow, even though it was so beautiful and rugged and consuming you wanted to explore it right away. She smiled and looked up to her mother.

"He sees it," the girl said.

Behind her, the pastor did his best to smile, to understand, to leave it in God's hands—which seemed to flow in a most serendipitous medium through those of this seven-year-old, while the gray-haired woman gave a modest, if not perplexed, grin.

"Go on, honey," the girl's mother said.

The little blonde reached over the mattress with fingers small as caterpillars, seeking the pain. Touching the old man's arm felt like touching a woodstove: simmering, dry, and wakening. Enough to wipe off the girl's smile; her face turned sad—a glum, painful shade of sad—instead.

She moved her hand to the old man's forehead, which broiled, then brought her other hand there as well, pressing against his temples with tiny fingers. The pastor gathered her mother and the other woman together and began praying in their small circle, eyes closed, hands roped into fists. The girl closed her eyes and held her hands on the man's forehead for several minutes. Then she sensed—and heard—bones popping in the old man's spine, knees, hands, and elbows: felt his pain draining as if through a channel.

His hands unclenched, as did his jaws and knees, relaxing as the tension dissipated.

The girl opened her eyes and saw the old man straightening into a supine position. He lifted his head close to his pillow, drew his knees up, moved his hands and fingers. He looked at the girl as if he'd just now noticed her and smiled a healthy elderly smile.

Chapter 4

Waymon Taylor knelt at the pulpit steps, the spot Baptists consider the altar. His knees were bent, and his head was bowed.

He hadn't turned on the lights; that way, he wouldn't draw attention, and no one would interrupt his prayer. The dimness gave the maroon interior a violet complexion.

It was a meditation, a vigil he'd kept for twenty-six years, when the utmost of matters needed addressing, each Tuesday and Thursday—T 'n' T, his mother called them—the days of the week when the Devil, thirsty for the hearts of men, worked overtime to destroy the Lord's flock. Since that special ordaining service twenty-six years before, when he felt the Spirit flow through the hundreds of hands that had been laid upon his head, he'd felt a responsibility to serve as protector of the church, and he'd labored to make each session private.

Next to him in front of the pulpit stood a short, stocky oak offering table with engraved letters reading This Do in Remembrance of Me. Sprinkles of light filtered through the stained-glass windows and seeped in from the cordoned sunlit section of the hallway.

Outside, sprinklers rattled and hissed, and old cars and burly pickups lumbered down the street.

He offered the prayers as thoughts, mostly, uttering fragments and phrases when he became unconscious and the Spirit took over. The church had voted 224 to 7 to call Brother Tisdale as pastor, and that was one of the primary concerns the elder deacon, hands locked, knees weighted against the hard steps, brought before God. Until a minute before, he'd felt warm and comfortable. Now he was cold, as the air conditioner had rumbled to life, sending him shivering with gooseflesh up and down his arms.

At that moment an alarm rang inside him. If he didn't hear anything, he felt something; if he didn't feel anything, his curiosity spoke to him, screaming that someone or some thing was standing behind him. He released the spiritual hold on his prayer, stood, turned around, and forced an old man's gentle grin.

"Brother Tisdale," he said.

"Brother Taylor," the pastor said. He was taller than Waymon remembered, clad in beige work pants and a dark blue knitted turtleneck sweater.

Waymon reached out his hand. "You remember me." The pastor's hand was surprisingly warm and strong—as every younger person's grip tended to be these days.

Brother Tisdale laughed. "Oh, my head is full of names, numbers, and faces."

"I bet it is," Waymon agreed, holding his smile. "I bet it is."

A cumbersome silence followed. Waymon slipped his hands into his pockets and straightened the expression on his face. "It's Thursday, brother, and you're down here already. Don't tell me you moved in too. You got a sermon in your pocket?" He stepped closer and feinted as if to peek.

"Oh no," Brother Tisdale said, more reservedly, harboring his humor. "I'm here on a skeleton shipment, let me tell you. All I've got is my wallet and my toothbrush."

They shared a brief laugh.

"Well, Brother Tisdale, if you need to borrow some clothes or if you need anything—"

"Bless you, brother," Brother Tisdale said. "Thank you. I think I have what I need. The Lord provides."

"Yes, He does," Waymon said.

"Except for fools, of course," Brother Tisdale added. "Why, they don't recognize His blessings."

Waymon nodded as if to agree, but instantly knew he betrayed his own true feelings. "You sure you don't need anything?"

"Yes, I'm quite sure. But thank you for your generosity."

The air blowing against Waymon was twice as frigid now. He fidgeted with his arms for a couple seconds, rubbing his bicep with the knuckles and fingers of the other hand instead of crossing his arms—that would be a sign of weakness, which, for some aberrant reason, he didn't want to convey to the new pastor.

"Sure is getting cold in here," Waymon said.

Brother Tisdale was silent. He looked at the carpet, casually raised his head.

"Come in here to pray frequently?" he asked.

"Only as frequent as things need praying for," Waymon said.

Brother Tisdale's forehead rocked a habitual nod. "I understand you've been at Crown of Thorns Baptist for many years, Brother Taylor."

"I reckon I have," Waymon said. He gave a half chuckle that felt awkward and imbecilic. Awkward because it was cut short; imbecilic because Brother Tisdale hadn't consented, but rather lowered his cold, stern expression toward the ground, as a principal about to punish a pupil. Even in the darkness, with the preacher's head down, Waymon marveled at the blue incandescence that appeared to fill those eyes.

"If I'm going to lead this church," Brother Tisdale said, pausing, raising his glare, "I have to know that everyone's in support of what I'm trying to do—and that is the Lord's work." His eyes turned a shade darker as he pronounced these last words. "The Lord despises a rebel."

Waymon nodded. "That He does."

"I understand seven members voted 'nay' last Sunday."

Waymon repositioned his feet, tried to steady his hands. "But brother, there were two hundred twenty-four who voted for you. In every Southern Baptist church I've been a part of—and even in the Missionary Baptist church I attended once upon a time—that's a mighty strong call. Church votes don't get any more convincing than that."

The air, blowing in a forceful torrent now, chilled Waymon from head to toe.

"Oh, I'm pleased about the call, Brother Taylor," Brother Tisdale said. "I guess, as much as anything, I'd like the opportunity to meet the ones who voted against me to learn more about where they're coming from and maybe about any special needs they might have. I don't suppose you would know some of those who voted in the minority."

Waymon tried not to squint, tried not to study the man. This was an awkward request.

"Well, Brother Tisdale, we carry our votes by secret ballot," Waymon said with a tact he'd learned to use over the years, one devoid of emotion and ridicule and filled with humility. "We do it that way so no one knows who votes for what, so everybody's secret is safe in his own heart. Been that way since I can remember." He finished this last part with a harmless smile, one he hoped—and even simultaneously prayed in his thoughts—the preacher would not take offense to. The pressed, melancholic look on Brother Tisdale's face suggested, in all its weary anticipation, that he already knew these things.

"I understand," Brother Tisdale said, upbeat—and, it seemed, empathic—kicking his shoes lightly against each other. Then, after swinging his weight to the side, but hesitant to leave, he added, "I also understand that a member of the pulpit committee was in some disagreement with the other fine men."

As the words died, an icy stream of air smothered Waymon, and he crossed his arms, shivering. He took a step away from the pastor, toward the hallway exit.

"I'm sorry, Brother Tisdale," Waymon said, in more haste than he'd planned. "I don't mean to bail on you, but this place is freezing my ol' buns off."

He met the pastor's cold, distrusting smile and, as quickly as his limber bones could creak, scampered away from the darkness.

Chapter 5

Andrea pulled apart the fluffy white kitchen curtains and looked outside. Elizabeth and Wesley were playing inside the fenced front yard, throwing around an assortment of miniature footballs, basketballs, and soccer balls.

She'd told them dozens of times before—even in her sleep, it seemed—not to unlatch the gate and go beyond the fence, but on occasion, for reasons that made sense to children, Elizabeth did it anyway. Andrea made a habit of looking out the window every ten minutes while she prepared supper.

She'd cut through two thawed chickens and basted them with the Cajun flavors her mother had taught her to mix. She placed the pieces in separate cooking bags, slid the pan into the oven, and sat down at the table to catch her breath.

Through the back windows, she saw voluptuous clouds, white and gray, rolling and bubbling in the sky like mashed potatoes. The kids would have to come inside soon. She took a drink of Diet Coke, watching the battalion of clouds invade what was left of the pale blue Texas sky, and lost herself in that picture.

When her mind came back to the kitchen, she rose from her chair and looked outside the front windows. Her heart took a jackrabbit leap.

In the yard, wearing a blue short-sleeved shirt and brown slacks, crouched to the height of her children, talking and commanding their attention, was Owen Tisdale.

A wave of panic washed over her: the intricate network of her insides knotted up, her breathing quickened. She hurried to the door, opened it, and, more eagerly and hastily than she intended, descended the steps and walked to her children.

Brother Tisdale noticed her and stopped talking, reserved in his introductory manners, his face full of gentility.

"Hello there," he said, getting to his feet. Dirt stained the knees of his slacks. "I believe I saw you Sunday morning. I'm Owen Tisdale." He reached out his hand and Andrea took it, hesitantly. She tried to smile, digging for a slice of amenity, but the humble housewife look came out instead, rearing its distrusting face.

His hand simmered.

"Andrea Cormieaux," she said, and stepped back. Her stomach tightened up a notch, and she had a flashback of Sunday's nausea. She thought it was gone by Tuesday, disposed of like a Raided yellow jacket's nest. She was wearing a plain white blouse and old faded red pants. Her frayed, disheveled hair was moist from the kitchen steam.

"Your children were kind enough to tell me their names," the preacher said. "Weren't you?" he asked them playfully.

"Preacher," Wesley blurted back. His light brown hair frolicked with the wind, which was picking up more each minute.

Elizabeth nodded.

"I was just asking Wesley and Elizabeth what they enjoyed most about church," the preacher said. "Wesley said he liked the toys, and Elizabeth said she liked the cookies and Kool-Aid."

Elizabeth blushed slightly.

The preacher gave a hearty red-faced laugh, which toned down once he collected himself.

"I've been trying to visit some of our members," he said. "And I've taken a special interest in meeting some of the new folks—like Wesley and Elizabeth." He smiled at the children. "I'm sure they'll want to be a part of our fellowship when they get older."

A mild growl of thunder came from above, where a moist thunderhead of gray and white puffs floated eastward, unraveling.

"Well, it looks like I've worn out my welcome," the preacher said, glancing upward. "I'm sorry I didn't get a chance to talk to your husband, Andrea."

She looked up at the clouds, lifting a hand to shield her eyes from the rays slicing through them.

"I don't know if they'll make him go out in this stuff or not," she said. "He works for the gas company."

"Hopefully, they'll let him come home," the preacher said. "But it's been a privilege visiting with you and your children." He offered his hand a second time, then turned to the children. "And it was especially nice meeting the both of you," he said in that playful grown-up facade, clasping their soft miniature hands.

Wesley and the preacher cracked smiles as wide as the Mississippi River, and Wesley laughed as the man kept hold of his hand.

"I can't remember when I met a more well-mannered, beautiful pair of children," the preacher said.

What Andrea would remember most from his visit was the alarmed—if not spiteful—look on Elizabeth's face as she quickly pulled her hand away from the preacher's—as if his palm had burned her—as the storm spat its first drops.

Chapter 6

Waymon barely had a chance to sit in his living room chair and set his cup of coffee down before his wife, Beula, who was sitting in the dining room with a clear view of him through the archway, said in a loud voice, "What's buggin' ya?"

His legs tightened up, especially below the knees.

He could only get out the "wh" sound of "what" before Beula called out again: "I said, What's buggin' ya? You ain't said much the last couple of days."

Though her eyes didn't let up on their vicious hold, she took a slow sip of her own coffee, giving him ample time to respond. He remained silent.

"Whew!" she said, drawing back from her cup. "That stuff wants to boil off my lips."

"Well, I'll call Ripley's if it makes a dent," Waymon said.

"Okay, smart butt," Beula cautioned, eyes glowering. Her weight jiggled as she shifted in her chair, which creaked at the legs.

She was the thinnest of her three sisters when Waymon married her thirty-seven years before, but after having their third child she'd put on forty pounds. During his midlife crisis, Waymon had begun to believe that those extra forty pounds were perpetually formed and chiseled, like Mount Rushmore and Stonehenge; they were immortal. He'd looked many a *Playboy* and *Penthouse* in the eye, wrapped in plastic along the high eye-level bookstore shelves, luring him, and he had walked away every time, settling for the same life he'd always known, the one where he went to work, went to church, watered the yard, filled the car with gas, paid the bills, and made love to his aging, nagging, weight-gaining wife, for better or worse.

Beula, five years younger than Waymon, was sixty years old now and hadn't stepped inside a church since their children had left home. Waymon counted the days until she might shed the weight. Sooner or later old age would take it off, he reckoned. She'll be skinny as Momma before long. But he feared in a couple of years he might not have much of a sex drive. *"I will repay," saith the Lord,* he thought. *Remember the years the locusts took away.*

He grabbed the cup of coffee, brought it to his mouth, its steam drenching his face, and blew on it. He took a sip.

"Honey!" Beula said, ruining his imagined consolation.

The cup rattled in his hands and a couple of hot drops streamed over his lower lip.

"You gonna tell me what's botherin' you, or are you gonna go to your momma's again like some poor little black boy?"

"Dadgum it!" Waymon said, wiping the drops from his chin with the back of his hand and setting the cup back on the table.

"Come on, honey," Beula said, in a more enticing, empathic tone. "I know a bug done crawled up your butt and bit you. Someone been pickin' on you at church?" Her eyes narrowed. "Tell me, honey."

"I can't tell you, Beula, because then you'll go off and tell everyone you know," Waymon said. "And that's exactly what I don't want."

The room was warming. In a week or two it would be summer, and as far as Waymon could tell, it looked like it would be a hot one. Beside the front door sat an old stereo-cased, twenty-five-inch Quasar television, which he hadn't turned on since Tuesday, three days before. Above it was a painting of Jesus shepherding a flock of sheep in a rugged, mountainous setting. In his loose white garments, bare feet, and heavy beard, Jesus looked like he was about to break a sweat. Waymon smiled at that thought.

He rose from the chair and took another sip of his coffee.

"Coffee's good," he said. "Can you save me some for later?"

"Will do, hun," Beula said, flicking him away with her hand and crawly fingers. "You run off to your momma's now."

"I will," he moaned on the way out.

In his old age, he had fallen in love with big cars.

He figured he couldn't afford to get blindsided or rear-ended in some boxy import from Korea or Yugoslavia. Aside from the luxury—he'd never had a car with power windows—the strong, resilient body of his Mercury Cougar, which he'd only been able to afford in his retirement, made him feel equally secure and protected from all directions, even as he rolled through downtown Dallas.

He didn't like to run the air conditioner because of the strain it put on the engine. But even in late morning, the air seethed a blood-warming ninety-eight degrees; he'd called the bank, and the automated weatherman had told him the temperature in his deep, giddy TV-game-show voice.

He parked in his mother's narrow, empty driveway. In the front yard five feet from the sidewalk, a yucca towered eight feet into the air, the tip of its spear in golden bloom. In the flower bed, red and white petals stretched from a plethora of begonias, and rose purslane spread over the dark, damp soil. Two angel's wings cacti guarded the bed—one on each end; his mother told Waymon they were meant to keep the kids and cats and rodents out, not necessarily in that order.

As a child he'd been taunted by his classmates about the house's ugliness. It was small and squared, surrounded by siding that flirted with peachy tan during the heat waves, and bordered with maroon panels on top and around the windows and doors. The siding had been blue for decades, but ten years ago Waymon had painted it light brown, rendering a more amicable face. The roof was flat.

The screen door was all that blocked Waymon's entry. He guessed it was locked, as it normally was, and a light tug confirmed his intuition.

"Momma," he hollered softly.

He waited.

Scrawny as a paper doll, Mozelle Taylor limped toward the front door in purple pants and a golden-beige blouse. She leaned into the screen, focusing through her small, rectangular glasses. Her eyes brightened and her gaping mouth formed a smile.

"Hi there!" she said.

"Hi, Momma," Waymon said, stepping inside and hugging the old woman. "You getting around okay?"

"As much as I need to," she said. "What you been doin'?"

"Not a whole lot, really. A little aging. A little praying."

She laughed. "You ain't kiddin'. When you get old, you need it more, and you got more time to do it."

"Ain't that the truth?" Waymon said. "I think it's one of them physiological reactions. Your body starts falling apart, and you start looking up to heaven."

Laughing, Mozelle motioned with her hand and said, "Sit down."

She grabbed a burnished mahogany cane by the coffee table and padded toward the kitchen.

"You want some coffee?" she asked.

"Well, I—" he mumbled.

"You do?"

"I might take a cup if you've got some made," Waymon said in a loud voice.

She shuffled into the kitchen, limping noticeably, the time-release result of hip replacement surgery twenty years before.

Waymon took a seat on the sofa. A small lamp table separated it from Mozelle's recliner, where a heavy white afghan impaled with a crochet hook on one of its final rows hung on the arm closest to the lamp. The blinds were pulled open and thick ten-foot beams of sunlight shot in from the front windows over the television, warming the room.

"You can turn the TV on if you want," she said.

"Oh, that's all right," Waymon said. He glanced into the guest room across from him. A dresser rested there on the plush carpet. His father killed himself in that room forty-five years before, a shot to the head. The family had been there when it happened, had grieved together. Waymon felt the old man's fist ramming into his eye socket, and he jerked.

Mozelle came back into the living room with a cup of coffee and set it down on the table in front of him. The spoon swirled around a half turn.

"I put some sugar and cream in it for you—the way you like it," she said, and took her seat in the recliner, resting her arm on the afghan. In the light her face was highlighted: lips sharp and thin, eyes black and droopy. "How's Beula?"

"Beula's fine," he said. "Still lashing me for one thing or another."

"Well, I guess that's what wives is good for."

"Who you telling?" Waymon said, lowering his brow. He grabbed his coffee, blew into it as he stirred, and took a sip. "Oommhh, Momma! You still make the best coffee!"

"It's just now I can afford the best, seeing I ain't got nothin' else to buy," she said.

"I hear you," he said.

The boards in the back of the house crackled and creaked.

"And when Henry was still around," Mozelle said, "you could kiss away twenty dollars a week for his beer or whiskey, or whatever he felt like drinkin' at the time."

"I know, Momma," Waymon said, nodding. "Not a day goes by, I don't thank the Lord for turning my head the other way."

"Good for you, honey," she said.

He looked at her, and she met his gaze.

"That took a lot of strength for you to walk with the Lord all them years, Momma," he said.

"A lot of strength for both of us. Them was hard times."

"Yeah," he said, staring into the cup.

As the seconds beat away, Waymon felt his heart drumming beneath his breastbone, seemingly with its own body, mind, and spirit, and he suspected his mother's was beating to the same cadence, though hers was weaker and full of years. And he thought he felt the Spirit right then, flowing between them, moving invisibly in their thoughts and souls, even in this small aging house in downtown Dallas, where vandals and crack dealers were more apt to prevail.

"Your church call that new pastor?" Mozelle asked.

Waymon took a quick sip, more from nerves than thirst. "Yeah, I'm afraid so."

"You don't act like you think much of him. What is it you don't like?"

"Oh, I don't know," Waymon said. "He's a character, all right. His preaching's fine. Good speaker. I guess that's what Baptists want these days is a good speaker. But there's something about him, you know?"

He pondered whether to spill the details. He didn't practice gossip—he'd seen it bring more than one church to ruin—and although he could foresee changes taking place at Crown of Thorns Baptist, he didn't believe the cancer of negativity was the way to go about it. But this was his mother, wise in church affairs, who had been reading the Bible, praying, and attending church her whole life.

He decided he wanted an opinion. Not only that, he needed support. Guidance.

"I was praying in the sanctuary—I guess it was Thursday— and he came up behind me, and we started talking. Ain't nobody interrupted my altar prayer in twenty-six years. But we get to talking, and before I know it, the S. B. wants me to tell him who voted against him. Now what kind of preacher wants to know that?"

"I don't know," Mozelle said. "Sure sound funny to me. You didn't call him an S. B. while you was talkin' to him, did you?"

"No, no. I got more sense than that. I tried to be polite. I mean, he's new in town, and for all I know, maybe they do things a little backwards where he's from."

"Well, I guess he's gonna have to learn a new way of doing things," she said.

"Yeah, well, I just hope it ain't the other way around," Waymon said.

Chapter 7

Owen Tisdale had been called lots of things in his lifetime: the Man with Many Faces, Fallen Angel, the Black Indian, Serpent, Devil.

They'd riled his darkest spirit, summoned his ugliest face when he'd first heard them centuries and decades before, but he was indifferent to them now. However, he preferred the labels of *brother* and *pastor,* or even what the poor folk called him, *preacher,* and each time he heard those titles, especially when they were pronounced with generous reverence and cowardly admiration, vials of laughter exploded inside him, because he knew how simpleminded these pieces of walking flesh were and how easily fooled they were.

Especially these idiot Texans. They were really stupid. And what was worse, they thought they were smart.

All they cared about were George W. Bush and the Dallas Cowboys. Bush this, the Cowboys that … King, country, and football.

Rednecks, Owen thought. *If only they were smarter. I wouldn't have these fools in my home for half heaven's angels.*

Owen was certain that through the counseling and healing he'd performed, he'd alleviated more suffering, calmed more hearts than the average, or even above-average, pastor. He loved the facade, the game of charades. Although Crown of Thorns Baptist paled in comparison to the spiraling tabernacles of Los Angeles—some of which drew as many as thirty thousand people—Owen avoided the spotlight. Through the centuries, after many defeats and small battles he'd won, he had developed a patience and a penchant for nipping away at the kingdom of God. Besides, legions of ordained servants were doing his work on larger fronts. No, he didn't have to worry about California.

He lived instead for another day of deception, for the need to feed his spiritual bad boy, to get out of Dallas and raise some good old-fashioned hell, just as he had in his youth. He was hardly old and elderly. There were so many parties to crash he couldn't count them, an endless surplus of alcohol and absinthe. And who was there to stop him?

A mile back the sign had read TERLINGUA, POP. 320. He'd reached the west Texas town in five hours, gunning his red Porsche Cabrera to 120 miles per hour. He turned onto a dirt road and parked next to a corral post, away from a small lot with cars and motorcycles.

The bar's Old West saloon facade faced the road. Silver cinderblocks and a black metal door comprised the back. A decrepit sign above the back door read The Brass Nipple, under which it read *Chicas Calientes!*

"Flesh and trash," he said to himself, as he stepped out of his car. "Flesh and trash."

He dug his left upper canine into his lower lip, drawing blood. He wanted to feel pain—its hot fangs and the pulse that transmitted it to the brain; he reveled in it, leaning his head back as if in a hallucinogenic stupor.

In my house are many chambers, Owen thought, licking the blood off his lips. *In my house are many chambers. Many chambers, many chambers, legions of chambers shelving millions of souls and bloodless flesh writhing the way I want to see it and taste it and broil it. In my house are many chambers, all for me.*

He felt a little uncomfortable in his blue slacks and long-sleeved Western shirt, because he'd been wearing formal attire for several years and was getting used to its rigidity. He pulled his sunglasses snug against his eyes, popped a piece of bubblegum into his mouth, and began chewing. Ten feet from the back door, his gum lost its flavor, and he spat it onto the dusty parking lot. It rolled, wrapping itself in the shrapnel of rock grains. Across the street, a chicken scurried in circles inside its pen near a tin shack. A barge of a bell was clanging a block away.

"Stinking Catholics," Owen said, scratching his crotch.

The black door was just as heavy as it looked—he knew it would be. But with the touch of his lean index finger, it creaked open like the restroom door of a dirty filling station.

He stepped inside a dim, musty room and pocketed his shades. His dress shoes clacked against the floor as he walked a couple steps and passed through an arch into the dressing room. Above, a single lightbulb flickered as if from a power surge. Rows of lockers lined the walls; a couple of pine benches, coarse with splinters and darkened wood, stretched beside them. A dampness redolent of skin, sweat, and blood sagged in the air.

He trudged toward the center. On the other side of the room another arch led to a corridor that took a short series of curves leading to the bar and dance floor. It was past this arch that he saw a woman in a G-string standing against the wall, eyes closed, breasts bare, head tilted back. Her white skin shimmered against black hair. Sweat trickled down her forehead.

Unmarked, Owen sensed. *Fresh meat. No Holy Spirit within a mile of her. There are many chambers in my house. Fresh meat.*

He ambled toward her.

Beyond the walls music reverberated, rattling the lockers.

The dancer looked up. Jerked. "Who are you?"

Owen shook his head, the questions stopped.

He inched toward her, pulled his hands out of his pockets, looked over her body. She straightened up. He placed his palms on her belly, smooth and moist, pressed against the slope. He pulled her head toward him and kissed her. Her mouth tasted like spearmint.

He pulled away, and she opened her eyes, looking at him.

He smiled.

In my house are many chambers. And women.

The Red Hot Chili Peppers' "Blood Sugar Sex Magik" was stomping from Peavey speakers above. The dance area was propped three feet off the main floor and slivered in a rounded L shape, with silver poles gleaming at each bulbous end. Six men and a woman leaned on pervert's row, another four sat at the bar, and five or six were sitting at tables against the back walls, lusting for lap dances. On stage, a dancer slid down the pole, flinging her head back, flaunting her brown breasts as her buttocks bounced against the stage floor, littered with dollar bills.

Owen drew a bellicose look from a lean Mexican sitting near the entrance, holding a portable microphone in his hand. A heavy mustache badged the Mexican's lip, and he wore a tawny Western shirt buttoned at the collar. He was moving toward Owen. A bald biker at the bar turned his head slightly toward Owen, then went about his business.

"Hey!" the Mexican said. "What you doing in there?"

Owen took a hundred-dollar bill and floated it toward him.

The Mexican looked at it as if it were a dead rat, then gestured toward the locker room. "You better tell me what you doing in there."

"Better be nice to me, Pancho," Owen said. "That way, I won't have to ram my fist through your throat." Owen looked content. And he felt content too.

The Mexican dropped his mouth; his face went grim. He backed up a step.

"No quieres mi dinero?" Owen asked.

The man clutched the bill with a look of contempt. Smiling, Owen put his hands in his pockets and took a seat in front of the dance stage.

A Hispanic girl with braided dark hair approached Owen with a tray. "Can I get you something?"

"How about some of that Warsteiner?" he said.

"Okay," she said. "That's it? Need some ones?"

Owen smiled. "I don't carry change. Only big bills. But thanks for the service."

In my house are many chambers. Do you know who I am? I know everything about you.

She swallowed and hustled to the bar. She was back in seconds, her eyes large and attentive. She set the bottle of beer, already opened, gently in front of Owen, watching his eyes as she did.

He held up a hundred-dollar bill. "You know your master." She would have dropped the bill if he hadn't kept hold of it. "It's yours."

She grasped it faintly, placed it on her tray, and sauntered away.

The dancer, a cocoa-skinned Mexican, strutted toward him. Black moles dotted her body and a sword-shaped birthmark stretched from her belly to her sternum.

In my house are many chambers. Nectar sweeter than your flesh.

She stood there in all her full-frontal glory, grinning modestly, aroused from the tickling sensation Owen had planted in her mind. She danced for him, slowly. She would do anything he asked; she would go to extremes that only he might imagine.

Bask with me in paradise. Offer your flesh, and I'll exalt your soul. In my house are many chambers.

He sucked on the bottle's mouth, guzzling the beer.

The dancer turned her back to him, bent over and looked at him upside-down, her face between her legs, her hair hanging to the floor in a tangled web of blackness.

In my house are many chambers. You can have whatever you want.

He tilted the bottle of beer again and drank steadily.

The intro to Rage Against the Machine's "Killing in the Name" thundered from the speakers, and Owen leaned his head back, dazed and medicated, with a euphoria he hungered for, and tossed his burdens behind. The dancer gyrated more wildly, exotically, the muscles of her belly pulling tautly on both sides. She swung a leg over the rail onto the small sliver of counter, resting her foot next to his drink.

Owen caressed her calf, moved his hand up to her thigh. She leaned her head back, sucked in sonorous breaths.

The owner, a brawny old cowboy with a glass eye, pulled him off.

"Perv," the owner said, slinging Owen to the ground. The bouncer stood behind him.

The dancer stepped back onto the dance floor.

Twenty pairs of eyes were glaring at him; the other few were tending to games of pool and lap dances. He started to get to his feet, but the owner slugged him, the man's knuckles popping against Owen's upper lip. A spatter of blood flew from Owen's mouth, and he fell to his knees, hands scraping the floor.

"No one touches my girls," the owner said.

Idiot Texans, Owen thought, grinning at the floor. *In my house are many chambers, and I'll throw these wasps in the furnace. They eat the toughest steak and pork, but my meal is too coarse for them.*

He rose to his knees, wondering for a second if the owner was going to kick him with the sharp toe of his boot, but he slowly got to his feet. Blood streamed from the corner of his mouth down the side of his neck, parallel to his carotid artery.

The owner tossed him a clean, white folded handkerchief. "Here. Clean yourself up and scoot back where you come from."

Owen made no attempt to catch the handkerchief but instead watched it uncoil from his shoulder to the ground. The beginnings of a grin formed on his beaten Southern face.

The owner made a move for the handkerchief, but Owen held his palm out. The man flew backward off his feet with the blunt, prodigious force of a car wreck, slamming into the wall. He hit the floor, his knees buckled, his cowboy hat rolled down the groove between his shoulder and collarbone, and his real eye rolled back into his head.

I'm bringing hell to you, Owen thought. *In my house is a fun house, and I'm the killer clown.*

The bouncer punched him, and Owen's head spun around as he crashed into the dance stage. Bent over, he gulped down a mouthful of blood.

Your groin hurts, he thought. *I'm stabbing you in the groin.*

The bouncer crashed to his knees, clutching his groin and crying out like Linda Ronstadt. One of the poles on the stage, shaking and bobbling, unhitched, became airborne, and impaled the man in the chest, plowing him against the wall.

Owen looked around. Behind the bar, Cheech Marin's dumber twin lowered a black sawed-off shotgun, then dropped it completely. The women scattered, running for the doors, but his dancer stood in the spot he'd left her, staring at him obsequiously.

Owen swung two fingers desultorily toward the liquor bottles behind the bar: they exploded. Thick, curvy glass fragments blew like shrapnel into the nearest exposed flesh, and clear, peachy liquid flowed along the shelves. The place smelled of burnt bourbon.

Heading toward the door, Owen said, "Starting to look like a bar."

As he opened the door, he pointed his index finger quickly, effortlessly, at the bar, and a flame reared its neck and head like a cobra, hissing as it spread to the beer, its blue base whipping side to side along the floor. He passed through and let the door slam. Then a deafening blast rocked the building, sending misshapen shards of glass and serrated chunks of concrete and boards flying through the air, disfiguring the vehicles in the parking lot. A few charred hands, arms, and feet landed near them.

The flames scorched Owen's back, but he made no moves to avoid them. This body was only flesh; it was expendable. Immersed in their insensate outskirts, he walked with the flames instead, witnessed their infinite consuming beauty. How they danced and licked! He reminisced and ascertained that hell wasn't so bad after all and that while he was here, intoxicated with sex and blood and the facade of a Christ servant, treading among so much dirt and flesh, he might as well bring a little more of it to the Lone Star State.

"Don't mess with Texas," he said, pacing to his car.

Chapter 8

Waymon laid his Bible on the table before setting his cup of coffee next to it.

The Adult IV men's Sunday school class was small in number and space. The room was warm, and dust particles wafted in the air. Luther looked much older than Waymon—like a seventy-year-old—a prime candidate for the mega-estate nursing home in Arlington, yet he was sixty-four, a year younger than Waymon.

"It sure is warmin' up," James Robertson said from the head of the table, opening his Bible and lesson book. Beside his cup of coffee was a chocolate doughnut, pieces of syrupy chocolate hardened at the bottom edges like rat droppings.

Don Bilbo's eyes bulged at the doughnut.

"Where'd you get that?" Don asked.

"I swiped one from the youth department," James said.

"Them kids don't need all that sugar, anyway," Waymon said. "Makes them act funny in church."

"Nah," James said, rolling the doughnut over on its side like a wheel, studying it. "I think these were last Sunday's, and they warmed a load in the microwave so they could get rid of 'em."

"I hope they didn't give none to my wife," B. L. Sherwood said, his massive arms toiling above the table. A field foreman for Texaco, his fifty-year-old hair was thinning and graying at the same time—the sun did that to people in the oil field. "She'll go on another chocolate binge and start buyin' and eatin' up the stuff like it was goin' out of style." From the looks of B. L.'s knobby, ruddy face, Waymon surmised the man had chewed out more people in his lifetime than former Cowboys coach Jimmy Johnson, and he still hadn't figured out why men like B. L.—the crudest, brawniest of rednecks—went by initials instead of first names. Were their first and middle names so god-awful they couldn't be spoken? He could put up with him in Sunday school, he supposed, but he sure wouldn't want to work for him.

Waymon opened a packet of Equal, poured it into his coffee, stirred. Don sneezed into a handkerchief, and Waymon saw a yellow green pudge of snot stuck to the white cloth like that Crazy Jelly Putty kids buy at Kmart, only seeing Crazy Jelly Putty didn't make him gag. He took a sip, anyway, pretending he hadn't seen anything. The coffee tasted burned and bitter, the worst he could remember. He thought about getting up, going over to the pot, and putting the hit on it with about five scoops of creamer, but he noticed Luther watching him.

"Like my coffee?" Luther asked, in an old-man-like way that was almost as bitter as the coffee, but not quite as senile. "I made it."

"Yeah," Waymon said, in a voice less than enthusiastic. He could put on a facade about everything else, but he didn't lie about coffee—until now. "Fine brew."

"You ain't supposed to lie in church, you know," Luther said.

"I need something to wake me up, anyway," Waymon said.

"Y'all let me know when you're ready to start," James said. "We'll be in First Thessalonians this morning."

They continued stirring and drinking.

Finally, Luther said, "Who's bringing the message today?"

"I believe Terry Fouts is," James said.

"The association director?" B. L. asked.

"Yeah, that's him," James said.

"I was under the impression Brother Tisdale was gonna preach," Waymon said.

James and Luther looked at him as though he hadn't met his quota of shock treatments in the nuthouse. Confounded, Waymon waited for someone to say something.

"That'd be kind of soon, wouldn't it?" B. L. said.

Don blew another snot ball into the other side of his hanky, and Waymon's insides sank from the two separate stimuli.

"Well that's what I thought," Waymon said, "until I saw him down here Thursday when I was praying."

"Thursday?" Luther said, and looked at James.

"Stan Wilcox said he got a hold of him Wednesday, and Brother Owen told him he had to wrap up some things in Mississippi," James said. "He said he couldn't be here until this coming Wednesday."

Waymon felt like someone who'd reported a UFO to his friends, foolish and garrulously juvenile. He looked at his coffee and raised its dark contents to his mouth.

Chapter 9

Vicki Ainsworth, the Crown of Thorns Baptist secretary, held a master's degree in English, but she might as well have had a doctorate in public relations; she knew all about being polite and gregarious—she made a living at it. That, and proofing the church bulletin.

Smiling, draped in a denim dress with overall straps, she leaned her tall, stocky frame in the office doorway of Craig McManes, the music director, who sat in front of his computer, hand on his mouse, jaw open, watching the screen and clicking.

"Craig," Vicki said.

Craig jerked from his seat as if shocked by a Taser. The noise he produced sounded like "whoo-a-huh."

Vicki dropped her head, laughing.

"I'm sorry, Craig," Vicki said as she took a step inside. "I didn't mean to—"

"It's okay, I was spacing," he said, smiling an embarrassed smile. "Typical Monday. Maybe I'd be a good study for that attention deficit thing, whatever it's called."

"Hey, you think *you're* bad. You should catch me at closing time." She stepped in front of his desk, offering a proofed copy of the bulletin. "Anyway, I didn't find anything except for the date and Rubob on the inside."

Craig swiveled in his chair, took the copy and studied it. "Rubob?"

"Ruth and Bob Woods," Vicki said.

"Oh, Ruth and Bob." He broke into a laugh.

Vicki laughed again, holding her stomach.

"Stop it," she said, bent over, cheeks flushed crimson. "You're gonna laugh me to death."

"You're the one who marked it," he accused.

"I swear we have too much fun in this place," she said.

He turned the bulletin over, studied the back page. "Watch out with that swearing. I'll tell on you."

When they settled down, Vicki said, "I had another call from a boy wanting to pick up an application for RA Camp." Vicki turned the last word into a question and waited for a response with a cautious grin.

"Oh yeah," Craig said, pensively, squishing his lips to one side of his face. "RA Camp. Best time of my life, minus the bugs and spiders." He took in a deep breath. "I looked through the drawers the other day and still didn't find anything."

"That's the only form I don't have."

"Hmm," Craig said, clicking his cheap pen compulsively. "Maybe we used them all up."

"The only other place I can think of, although I doubt they'd be in there, is in Brother Levin's office," Vicki said.

"Now Brother Tisdale's office," Craig said.

"Okay, music guy," Vicki said. "The pastor's office."

"I don't know where else they'd be. I'm probably hiding them subconsciously." He winked.

"That's no excuse, buddy," Vicki said, turning and walking to the door. "I'll look in Brother Tisdale's office. He's supposed to be in later this week, you know."

"He might even stop by Wednesday, although I bet he'll be tired from the move," Craig said, shrugging his shoulders. "If you don't mind looking in there, go ahead. I'm going to Hastings to look for some new music. Don't work till you drop or anything."

"You should've told me that a year ago," she said.

She walked to her desk, took a drink of the Diet Coke she kept under the counter by the computer, and proceeded to the door of the pastor's office. It was the first office one encountered when entering the lobby. The door was locked, and it took an odd, laboring jiggle to get the key to work. It was also heavy as a bull.

She walked inside and turned on the light. It was just as Brother Levin had left it: wrecked and banished, furniture scratched, chairs with gaping cuts, saturated with dust. It looked more like a storage room than an office. Vicki crept toward the desk, turning her head to look for cobwebs or any other medium that might house a crawling or flying poisonous thing.

"This place could use some custodial care," she said, unsure if Craig could hear her.

"Amen!" he said. "I'm out of here."

"Okay," Vicki said. "No rap music now!"

"All right, just this one time," he said. "Don't do any cleaning. You'll probably stir up the dust and catch something." As he left, the small jingle bells hanging from the glass door handle clanged as the door opened and closed.

A crumbling pile of books covered much of the desk. Behind it, a large coffee-colored stain stewed on the carpet, and something khaki and fuzzy was spreading across its surface carrying with it a dank, rotten smell. Vicki turned her head, covering her nose and mouth. A smattering of books with cracked or breaking spines sloped along the shelves. Vicki kept her hands to herself—she didn't remember it being this messy.

What was going through Brother Levin's mind? she wondered.

She stood behind the desk, seeing the room—and perhaps the world—as the pastor saw it. A sharp, deep lesion winked like a closed black eye past the shelf on the left, glaring as though the wall had been stabbed.

Vicki bent down and opened the first drawer on the right. A spate of dust spewed up into her face, irritating her eyes, and half choking her. She leaned back, took in a breath, and brushed the dust in the air with her hands. In the drawer lay several thick folders. She sifted through them. Some contained church financial printouts, budget outlines, expense forms; others were bloated with counseling files scribbled with bad penmanship. She shuffled through them for a minute, then shut the drawer.

The drawer below rivaled the first, and again the dust whooshed up, but she closed her eyes and held her breath this time until it settled. Expense forms and business meeting fact sheets were stuffed between folders. She quickly pushed in the drawer and went to the left side of the desk. Except for a few rusted paper clips and a midget pencil, the top drawer was empty.

She got down on her knee, opened the lower drawer, and looked through an inch of scattered papers.

"Well," she said to herself, sighing, "there doesn't seem to be much in here."

"Well maybe you haven't looked everywhere," a deep, soothing voice said from the other side of the desk.

Vicki's heart seemed to have jumped through her chest and motored away on jackrabbit legs, sprinting with increasingly innate *whumpum-whumpum* drumming. She'd recognized Brother Tisdale at "maybe," but the picture of his gentle, Southern face, full and inviting, had done little to compress her fright. She sat behind the drawer, staring at the carpet with eyes big as golf balls, one hand on the drawer's rim to steady her balance, the other on her heart, trying to gather her own breathing. When she decided she wasn't going to faint, she looked up at him.

"My goodness, you scared me," she said, barely able to finish the sentence.

"Oh, I scare everybody," Brother Tisdale said in his confident storyteller's voice. He picked up a book from the pile on the desk, turned its dusty pages. "Big mean ol' preacher. Nobody wants to see me. Afraid I might think something bad of them." He tossed the book back onto the pile, glanced at Vicki, and looked at his shoes. "Yeah, they usually wait until one of the kids gets a girl pregnant, or someone has an accident, or their momma or daddy's dying. Then they come see me."

Vicki floundered to her feet, shifting the bulk of her weight onto her good hip—something she'd developed a skill for when she wasn't sitting on her caboose typing and talking.

"Oh, I'm so sorry," he said, moving closer to Vicki, placing a comforting hand on her shoulder. "I must have scared the dickens out of you."

"More than that," Vicki said. "I think you scared three or four dickens out of me."

"I don't know why I didn't holler at the door," he said. "I really am sorry."

"Oh, it's not your fault," Vicki acquiesced. "I didn't know when you were coming in. It's been just Craig and me for the last few months, and I usually hear the bells on the door when he comes in. I guess I'm just jumpy." A little laugh bubbled from inside her. "I'm telling you, I need some help. Look at me—scared to death by the pastor."

Brother Tisdale acknowledged her humor, laughing cordially, allowing his cheeks to flush.

"Just wait until Halloween," he said.

"Oh please," Vicki said.

"I have this wonderful mask," he said, smiling.

"Don't we all?" she said, taking a couple steps toward the door. "I was just looking for some applications for RA Camp, and I guess we're all out." She stopped in the middle of the room and swiveled, looking again at the walls and texts. "Looks like someone's gonna have his hands full with this place."

"Ah, it's no big deal," he said. "I've seen worse."

Chapter 10

As she walked with Carol Tinsley down the hallway, listening to the older woman talk away, Andrea could hear the piano prelude in the auditorium, the keys of the baby grand drumming away in a playful, resplendent melody, conjuring up an image of happier times, of children and youth running inside a smaller, friendlier church.

She wondered if she could make it through the service this time. When Carol had told her a guest from the association had preached the Sunday before, it had left her feeling foolish, because she'd missed that service fearing some supernatural infection had spread from Brother Tisdale's Scripture reading. She told Curt that she'd had some strange waking dreams when Tisdale preached. She'd also told him of the preacher's visit to their trailer but left out any indication of her discomfort.

Her experiences at Crown of Thorns Baptist—and Dallas, in general—left her feeling naked and empty. Sometimes she felt like one of the homeless people she saw downtown, the ones layered in Confederate-looking garb who held cardboard signs saying "will work for food." She'd never felt this down about anything, not even when she'd given birth to Elizabeth and Wesley and her hormones had taken a plunge.

Why were these people so cold toward her? Did they take her for white trash? Lord knew, sometimes she felt like it. Was there something in her voice, in her Southern Louisiana manner, or in her appearance, that made them feel uncomfortable toward her? Or was this just the way they were in Texas?

"When we moved here years ago, it was the same for me," Carol said. Silver strands glimmered from her wavy, medium-length hair. Once in a while, when the sun caught her just right, her beady hazel eyes sparkled like emeralds. She led Andrea with a gentle step. "I didn't know anybody, and hardly anyone came up to talk to me, and if they did, it was just 'Hi' or 'How ya doing,' you know?"

Andrea nodded.

"I felt like I was all alone. I even blamed God."

If there was a bull's-eye of commiseration on Andrea's heart, Carol hit it. Why couldn't others in the church be as amiable as she? Wasn't that what being a Christian was all about—reaching out to the forlorn, the empty and sick and brokenhearted?

At last they reached the door to the auditorium, but Carol paused before entering.

With small but nimble fingers, she took hold of Andrea's shoulder, looked the younger woman in the eyes, and said, "Hang in there, honey. Sometimes that's all God expects of us." She sighed. "It hurts me to see such a sweet young woman worrying." And with that, she squeezed Andrea's shoulder lightly and gave her a hug. Andrea's eyes welled up.

They walked down the steps into the auditorium.

Andrea paused, then located Curt and Elizabeth, who were sitting where they always sat: on the right side, five rows back. She slid inside, patting her eye with her thumb, and took a seat beside Curt, with Elizabeth sitting on his other side.

Andrea didn't care for Curt's mustache and beard, but at least they were well trimmed, and because his hair was so thin, his facial hair was barely noticeable. But she loathed the rugged, spiky feel against her lips when she kissed him. Throw on a pair of shades and a baseball cap, and he'd be ready for the major league.

"Any problems with Wesley?" she asked, trying to hide her emotion.

Curt shook his head.

"What did you and Carol talk about?" he asked. "Womanly things?"

"Curt," she warned and pushed him gently in the side.

"You gonna be all right?" he asked.

"Yeah," she said, smiling.

The choir filed into their loft. Craig McManes sauntered to the pulpit, asked everyone to turn to page ninety-four, and led the singing of "At the Cross." And the service proceeded as it had dozens of times before, a somnolent procession of century-old hymns, stiff handshakes, hammered smiles, and the offering.

Andrea saw Brother Tisdale sitting in the front row: a view of his back and right side. Once, before the third hymn, he turned to the side, smiled, and caught a straight glance of her, his teeth emitting a resplendent white.

She caught her breath, looked down, and turned the pages in the hymnal. She hardly looked up after that, not until the special music started, and even then she gave only a couple glances, afraid that the preacher might see her. She couldn't bear his looking at her, or talking to her, or talking to her children, or preaching—it made her feel dirty, although she didn't know the exact source of it.

When the special music ended, Brother Tisdale walked up to the podium, Bible in hand, microphone pin tacked on, wearing polished black shoes and a freshly pressed black suit. For a second he studied the audience, then gently smacked his lips before speaking.

"A pastor once went to visit an elderly woman," he began in his soothing vernacular. His face hardly labored at all; preaching came naturally to him. "She was in her late seventies and lived in a nursing-home apartment complex. She answered the door, asked the pastor inside, and he sat down in the living room. Just then the phone rang. The elderly woman answered it in her dining room and began talking. She stayed on the telephone for quite some time, and the pastor became a little restless." Tisdale's eyes roamed from side to side, front to back, as he roved behind the pulpit, making eye contact with every person, it seemed. "On the small table next to him was a dish of peanuts. He reached into it, grabbed a couple, and began eating them. Then the old woman came into the living room and sat down on the sofa. She said, 'I'm sorry to keep you waiting. It isn't often that I get a phone call.' The preacher responded by saying, 'Oh, it's quite all right. I hope you don't mind my eating some of your peanuts.' The old woman said, 'Oh, I don't eat peanuts. They hurt my teeth. I had some chocolate peanuts, and I sucked the chocolate off and put the peanuts in that dish over there.'"

Waves of laughter undulated from the congregation, continuing for almost a half minute.

Afterward, Brother Tisdale said, "Let us pray."

Some bowed their heads; most closed their eyes.

"Father," Brother Tisdale said, "we thank You for the opportunity to come to Your house and worship You in a way we believe to be true and loving."

Andrea's insides stirred.

"We ask that if anyone here doesn't know You as their personal Lord and Savior, that they might come to know You as such today and may begin living a full life in Your Son, Jesus Christ. We ask all these things in Jesus' name, amen."

Andrea fought a tide of nausea, internal pain, kaleidoscopic dizziness.

Upon opening his eyes, Brother Tisdale immediately opened his Bible. "Please turn in your Bibles to John, chapter six. I'll be reading out of the New American Standard version. For those of you who are hard-set on the King James Version, I apologize." His warm smile drew a few chuckles, and with that note hanging in the air, he told another joke.

"A preacher was sitting in his office one day when the Devil walked through the door. The Devil was a handsome fellow, not at all like what the preacher had expected. No horns, no goatee, no shimmering green eyes. They started talking. Then they got into an argument. Not a nasty one—the Devil was very cordial. But he said, 'In the battle for human souls, I've always relied on two truisms. The first is that man wouldn't know God if He appeared in the flesh right under his nose. The second: Man wouldn't believe the Bible even if it were easier to understand.'" Laughing faces turned toward one another in the congregation. Brother Tisdale looked at his Bible.

"Starting with verses one and two of the sixth chapter. 'After these things Jesus went away to the other side of the Sea of Galilee (or Tiberias). A large crowd followed Him, because they saw the signs which He was performing on those who were sick.'"

Something was stabbing at Andrea's stomach, right in the middle near her navel, piercing her with each pulse.

The preacher read: "Therefore Jesus, lifting up His eyes and seeing that a large crowd was coming to Him, said to Philip, 'Where are we to buy bread, so that these may eat?'"

Back into the darkness and upon that oblique, roving landscape, she heard the waves of many rivers, saw the bright shapes wandering about, moving back toward the golden city. Except for the brightest. The ground dissolved both him and the one enclosed in the cubicle, effacing everything except for the being's afterglow, which remained on the surface.

She looked above her: no sky, no moon, no stars. Then the darkness took her.

When she returned to consciousness, she found her chin had been tucked slightly under. She lifted her eyes toward the preacher, tuned in to his words. Immediately her head throbbed at the temples and her back muscles suddenly spasmed.

Scripture or not, she fought the words and rode out the stabbing pains as long as she could.

"'One of His disciples, Andrew, Simon Peter's brother, said to Him, "There is a lad here who has five barley loaves and two fish, but what are these for so many people?"'

"'Jesus then took the loaves, and having given thanks, He distributed to those who were seated; likewise also of the fish as much as they wanted. When they were filled, He said to His disciples, "Gather up the leftover fragments so that nothing will be lost." So they gathered them up, and filled twelve baskets with fragments from the five barley loaves which were left over by those who had eaten. Therefore when the people saw the sign which He had performed, they said, "This is truly the Prophet who is to come into the world.""

Andrea had had enough. If she didn't leave now, she might go into convulsions. Maybe into a coma. Neither Curt nor anyone else had taken notice of her unconscious flight this time. She turned toward him.

"I'm feeling sick again," she whispered. "I'll meet you in the nursery."

"Okay," Curt said, eyes narrowed with consternation.

She rose and left swiftly, avoiding the preacher's face and eyes, tuning out the remaining words of Scripture, thinking of the potluck and the food that was being prepared and sorted and apportioned at that moment. She made it up the steps and through the doors without any problems, then stopped for a drink of water before entering the restroom.

The queasiness bogged her down, but she felt that, despite what had happened last time, she wasn't about to lose her breakfast. She went into the restroom and splashed some water on her face. When she came out she followed the hall that circled behind the auditorium and passed the library before coming to the nursery, where she worked for the next half hour, changing diapers and playing with the children, including Wesley.

Brother Tisdale preached about the multitudes and masses. Curt listened. Elizabeth drew pictures, humming in a barely audible intonation as her head swiveled, the back of her golden pony tail sloshing back and forth over each shoulder, the ballpoint pen scraping across the paper against the songbook.

"In today's world, things—and especially people—are hardly ever what they appear to be," the preacher said. Even most of the children and youth were listening, and he peered into their hearts, searching for their desires. "And more often than not, we take these same people, objects, or circumstances at face value and forget about what the Bible has tried so hard to teach us.

"Look at the world. Look at the material items it has to offer. Money can buy a lot of things, but it can't buy your health, it can't buy salvation, and more often than not, money leads to spiritual ruin. Sports figures pretending to be role models are prosecuted for rape and murder. World leaders are exposed for harassment and adultery. I'm telling you today, as your brother in Christ, as someone who has fallen into the same traps of humanity over and over again, as someone who struggles with temptation every day just as you, there is no end to the evil seed of appearances and deceptions. We have only God to show us what is right and wrong.

"What the disciples saw were five loaves of bread and two fish. What Jesus saw was an opportunity to minister to the physical, mental, and, finally, the spiritual needs of five thousand people who were not only hungry for food, but hungry for Christ."

During the invitation, eleven people came forward, including two families. Three made professions of faith, one rededicated his life, and seven joined the church.

Curt slipped into the nursery. Elizabeth had teetered at the drinking fountain and said she needed to pee, so he had let go of her little hand and warned her of the spanking she'd get if she didn't meet him at the nursery within the next five minutes.

In the nursery, a heavyset woman with glasses was changing a baby's diapers in the corner facing him. She was talking in a baby voice and could manage only a smile for Curt. Wesley was in the opposite corner playing near a cardboard stove with a girl who looked his age. And in the middle of the room, Andrea was helping a little boy put a light saber in Anakin Skywalker's hand. Curt made his way toward her.

She looked up at him. "Oh, is it over?" She rose to her feet.

"Yep," he said. "How you feeling?"

"Better, I guess. It comes and goes. It only does that when I'm in church."

The used-diaper smell filled the small room. Thankfully, Wesley—who would be four years old in two months—had been potty-trained for more than a year. The nursery hardly seemed like a place of sanctuary.

"You feel well enough to eat?" he asked.

"I think I'll be all right," she said. "As long as he doesn't start preaching again."

"You don't like him?" Curt asked.

"How can I know?" she said. "I haven't made it through half a sermon. I know everyone likes him, but ..."

He waited. "What?"

She exhaled a breath of dismay. "I don't know what's wrong with me."

Behind the other parents and children who'd assembled at the door, Elizabeth peeped inside, rearing her blonde head with the humble look of obedience.

"We didn't bring all that food for nothin'," Curt said. "Let's go eat." He grabbed Wesley, swung him up onto his arm, and led the way to the fellowship hall.

In the hallway, trailing a step or two behind Curt and Wesley, Elizabeth walked alongside her mother.

"Mom, why did you leave during church?" Elizabeth asked, looking up with blue eyes, which Andrea met with her own.

"I wasn't feeling very good," Andrea said.

"Why not?" the child asked, almost portentously, like little Pearl questioning Hester Prynne about the scarlet letter on her breast.

Andrea looked down at Elizabeth. For a second she almost forgot she was her child; she averted the hold of her eyes.

"I just wasn't," Andrea said.

They went through the entrance of the fellowship hall, Elizabeth first, with her mother following behind, hands on Elizabeth's delicate shoulders, guiding her through. Once inside, they latched onto the end of the line behind Curt and Wesley.

Elizabeth looked up at her, then toward the line.

"Is it because of him?" the girl asked, pointing toward the

other end of the line toward those who had paper plates supporting mountains of food. A man turned at that end and stood in the aim of the girl's finger.

Brother Tisdale.

He balanced a plate full of food and was walking to the table with paper cups and tea and Cokes and Kool-Aid. He wasn't smiling.

Andrea slapped the girl's arm down.

"Don't point, Elizabeth!" she quietly chided.

But when they reached the paper plates and plastic forks, spoons, and knives, Andrea weighed her daughter's words. Did Elizabeth know something about her sickness that she didn't? Had she, through the thin walls in the trailer, or perhaps in the car, overheard her talking to Curt about the preacher?

The smell of food made Andrea think of something else. Ahead, Curt was preparing a plate for Wesley as well as loading up his own. Dishes of chicken enchiladas, lasagna, and chicken and dumplings, as well as large bowls of salads, crowded against each other on the table. It was difficult deciding which to spoon onto her plate and to estimate how much of it she would actually be able to eat. Her tuna casserole was already half gone, evenly split across the middle of the pan, as if by a sword. She scooped up some lasagna, slung it onto her plate, added some salad, and moved on.

She looked at Elizabeth's plate: fried chicken and mashed potatoes.

"Elizabeth, get some vegetables," she said.

"I don't want any vegetables," Elizabeth said in a high-pitched voice.

Andrea glowered at her, and Elizabeth reached for the large broccoli spoon.

By the time they arrived at the dessert table, only two pieces of Andrea's chocolate cream cake remained. Elizabeth grabbed one. When they sat down, Wesley dug into his food, picking up pieces of chicken and cheesy pasta with his fingers and shoving them into his mouth.

"Is that good, Wes?" Curt asked.

"Mmmm," Wesley said.

Andrea looked across tables, searching for people she knew. She saw Vicki Ainsworth, the nice, bubbly secretary who had taken her to lunch a few times; Waymon Taylor, a sweet old man; and Carol Tinsley. They were busy talking to their spouses and friends—and trying to swallow at the same time. She turned to Elizabeth, noticed her plate, studied her features.

Her daughter mimicked the girl in her own childhood photos. Curt's hair was somewhat auburn, and Elizabeth didn't seem to have any of his features. Because she was so bony, her nose peeked out a little, and she had Andrea to thank for it. Andrea often glimpsed into her daughter's future, playing the prophet, hoping Elizabeth would mature into someone with a good heart and Christian conscience. Did she possess the strength to oversee that process? Could she raise her right, in this terrorist world of sex-starved kids who gunned each other down over teen politics and basketball shoes?

"Eat your broccoli, honey," Andrea said.

"I will," Elizabeth moaned.

Andrea took a drink of her tea and saw, out of the corner of her eye, sitting near the end of a table two rows away, Brother Tisdale pushing something on a fork into his mouth. Deacons, elders, and church officials surrounded him. He was looking right at her. Andrea broke eye contact. Suddenly, the nausea catapulted back, and she no longer felt hungry. She would find a way to hold down what she'd chewed and swallowed. But the food on her plate would go to waste.

Chapter 11

Owen Tisdale was the first one through the door for the finance committee meeting.

He'd skipped the missions committee's meeting three days before because he had little time to support missions that worked against his own.

He perked up with two cups of coffee before the first committee member—its chairman, Rick Pettibone—showed up in a tie and slacks. He'd seen a lot of Rick: his clean-cut blond hair, blond mustache, and eyes that were nowhere near as blue as his own. *Take away his Duke degree, telecommunications business, and material possessions, and you'd have one sorry sad sack,* Owen thought. A whole country of self-proclaimed Christians spoke against the world and its resources, yet how many were willing to part with them? How many could give them up, their beaming luster, omnipotent horsepower, the smell of cash, multistory mansions, and the security burnished onto their coats.

He knew centuries before there had been One able to do this, One who wasn't right in the head, who claimed, even as He lay starving in the desert or nailed to a cross, that He had no use for anything tangible—only the Spirit that fed Him. The thought of it lay embroidered in his mind, stabbed in there like a sharp tumor, at times pulsing, metastasizing. No, he couldn't think of that; he couldn't dwell on the past.

Owen knew how to read people, and he read Rick to the hilt. Thoughts and feelings. Front to back. And what he read told him what he'd already known: Beneath Rick's suave, intellectual-posed gregarious exterior, burned a banal redneck. He could see Rick's mind, his past, photographed on reels of microfilm in the human library, unwinding as he extracted them, searched them. How easy this game was, and oh, how much fun! He saw a little boy with straight blond hair hanging down to his eyes—always the finest haircut. He couldn't have been more than ten years old. Rick was shooting lizards with BB guns, same as any other kid in Texas, blowing their tails off, watching them wriggle away, then blowing those racers and mountain boomers to bits with Black Cats and M-80s, getting excited every time their intestines blew from their abdomens.

Rick appeared calm and polished now. No doubt, his parents were enamored of his success and his active role in church.

From a chestnut brown leather notebook Rick extracted a small stack of papers bound by a paper clip. He pulled the top paper out from underneath the clip and handed it to Brother Tisdale, who'd already seen it as it lay concealed in the notebook.

"Here's a copy of our finance report," Rick said in what Owen took as his best authoritative voice. It was almost queer—like that of a new member knocking on the doors of membership. Rick pointed at the graphs and charts. "Here's our monthly expenses. Annual. And cumulative."

"Hmm," the pastor said, impartially.

"We're sixteen thousand in the red," Rick said. Owen's eyes raised to meet Rick's, then dropped back down to the charts. "But it was as high as thirty thousand about a year ago. It was a bad time for that because several of our bonds matured last year. But the state convention bailed us out. They made a few payments and saved our bond rating."

"Little slip in the bucket, isn't it?" Owen said.

"Yeah, afraid so," Rick said. "It put a bad taste in everyone's mouth. When the oil field companies started moving, so did our members. Then, for some reason or other, Brother Levin started taking all this time off. He was hardly ever here, and when he was, his sermons didn't have the same punch, so then even more members left."

Luther wandered in with a cup of coffee, slumped over, eyes glazed and half closed. Rick looked at him a bit uneasily, as if Luther had just caught him looking at a dirty magazine.

"You ain't spillin' the beans without me, are you?" Luther asked.

Owen turned toward him. "No, we're just simmering them a little bit. They haven't even started to boil."

"Well, I reckon we don't need none," Luther said. "Last time my wife got ahold of some, she turned our dining room into a concentration camp."

"Is that right?" Owen said, laughing like a fat Santa.

"I was just giving Brother Owen a rundown on where we're at," Rick explained.

"Well good," Luther said, patting the pastor on the shoulder. "These young'uns need a rundown once in a while."

Soon the other members of the finance committee trickled in and were seated, each glued to the finance report in front of them, as well as to a summary of important fiscal decisions—purchases and other related allotments—decided upon at various business meetings. Like Luther and Rick, most of the others had also sat on the pulpit committee. Casey Atwood. Stan Wilcox. Scott Bukowski. Only B. L. Sherwood hadn't, primarily because of the oil field and its roundabout, unpredictable hours and emergencies. You never knew when a derrick was going to stop pumping, or when a well was going to dry out, or blow up.

B. L. hobbled inside, wearing mud- and gas-stained jeans and a blue shirt for a uniform. A dotted scab decorated his forearm, another thick one tattooed his forehead like a fungus. His mustache was rippled a golden-khaki color where the sun had parched it and stood out over his lip like the blunt, dying bristles of a dead lawn. He also wore a ketchup-colored sunburn. He'd dipped more Copenhagen in the past twenty-four hours than he had in the previous week.

Stan worked in the warehouse of an oil-field supply company, but in a few minutes he had managed to change into casual clothes: jeans and a short-sleeved shirt. He looked at the finance report as though it piqued him a great deal, although he knew, in his mind as well as in his heart, that numbers mattered little when it came to instilling the Spirit back into the church.

Casey had trimmed his mustache since the last pulpit committee meeting, but it hadn't seemed to help much. It looked rough. He wore pretty much what Rick wore—without the tie.

"Brother Owen, the only thing that's kept our heads above water has been the interim period." Rick said. "We invited guest preachers from the area. They knew what kind of shape we were in, so they declined payment."

"I admit I haven't known too many preachers who would do *that*," Owen said, baiting chuckles.

"A few of us deacons got in a sermon or two," Luther added.

At this, Rick seemed a little annoyed, perhaps more at the thought that Luther was bragging than at the interruption.

"Did you?" Owen asked.

"We had Luther and Waymon," Rick said, "and some of our other deacons who have been here awhile."

"Brother Taylor preached," Owen said, showing sudden interest.

"Oh yeah," Luther said, with excitement. "Brother Waymon isn't the smoothest—I don't guess any of us part-timers are—but he's got the Spirit. You know it's in him. And I'm telling you, he about run the ol' Devil out of town with his last message."

"Did he?" Owen said, nodding.

"He sure did," Luther confirmed.

"Oh yeah," Rick confirmed, turning a bit red in the face. He looked like he wanted to gag Luther in one of those Hannibal Lecter masks so that he could retake control of the meeting. "Waymon can preach, all right. So if you ever want a weekend off, Brother Owen, you know who to call."

More chuckles. Owen laughed hard, drawing redness to his face.

"But, you know, I think we'll be okay now that we've got a pastor," Rick said, looking down at the notes in his binder.

"Amen," several said in unison.

"We ought to get back up to normal speed, normal attendance in a couple months, maybe sooner, if it's the Lord's will," Rick said, looking at Brother Owen. "I really think we'll be out of the red in no time. I really do." Rick always allotted time for input, but everyone else expected him to keep on trucking. He looked at Owen. "Brother Owen, did you have something you wanted to discuss?"

Owen perked up. "Yes I did, Brother Rick." He looked across the table, eyeing the members. "I've been in Dallas just a week or so, but I can honestly tell you, from my experience as a pastor, and from getting an overview of the present condition, that right now is the most crucial time for this church. We need to let people know about our church. We need to let people know we have a home here where they can come and worship and be a part of God's family."

"You're not talking about advertising, are you?" Rick asked, bordering on an interruption.

This more than peeved Owen, who did well to hide it. "I'm talking about faith. If we do our best to reach out to lost souls, the Lord will reward us. Like He says in the Scripture, 'I will repay.'" He looked down briefly at the finance report, then gently raised his head and sported his grandfatherly grin. "I realize this isn't the best time to talk about spending money we don't have. The graphs tell us we're over budget—no doubt about it. Our church is going to grow—I guarantee you, it will. I've never been part of one that didn't. But unless we deliver the message, reintroduce ourselves to the community, and give people out there some hope, we'll be closing ourselves in our own closet and our numbers might only modestly increase."

Scott Bukowski nodded.

"I guess that's something to think about," Rick said, opening his eyes a little wider.

"We don't have to decide on this today," Brother Owen said. "I can understand your reservations about spending. None of us wants to get further into debt. But I wanted to give each of you a general idea of the direction I'd like to see us take. And maybe next time we meet, we can discuss some figures."

Chapter 12

The next Sunday, before the service, Owen Tisdale sought out the visitors, just as they sat down, and struck up a basketful of conversations.

Seth Weimer, a small pale man with red hair permed in the back, at first appeared demure as a doe and slow of thought, apparently amazed, as most visitors were, at the preacher's accommodating efforts. But Owen had contrived his social etiquette from Mississippi and devoted fervent minutes to each individual while, somehow, as though holding back the big hand on the clock, found a way to fit them in before the start of the service.

Before long Seth was rambling in an effeminate manner, spouting off about his "roommate," the jewelry business he owned in the mall, and how he'd been raised in the piano-gutted Church of Christ.

Soul's weaker than his body, Owen noticed. *Has a heart attack when an old woman doesn't like her golden ring and wants her money back. Closet case, socially. Morally. Might be able to use someone like him.*

Owen also took an interest in Dan Bearden, a physician's assistant visiting from a sister Baptist church.

While Owen was shaking hands with these people, he observed a notable empty space in the row nearest the hallway, the one where Curt and Andrea Cormieaux normally sat with their daughter, Elizabeth. *She isn't here,* he enthused. *The damned blessed one, the blonde-headed Cormieaux.*

His sermon, on the Beatitudes and their modern applications, sang a genteel chorus to the souls who opened wide, with a dawning voice that drew everyone closer into his spiritual grasp. It may have been his best yet.

Halfway through the sermon a tall man who was bald on top walked in and took a seat in the back row. Ten walked the aisle: three professions of faith, five new members, two rededications. Many more walked to the front and knelt at the steps, delaying the service another ten minutes, trying Owen's patience for church rituals. He despised the conglomerating procession, the tautological pattern that Baptists, like Methodists and Catholics, followed Sunday to Sunday, and even on Wednesday evenings. The hymns remained unchanged, the handshakes patterned. The smiles, the laughs. The invitation. It made him sick to his own fleshy stomach, straight down to his bowels and appendix. But he had to take his losses; he couldn't keep God out of His own house. He knew people walked the aisle because of their faith in the message, not because of his delivery; he played no part in actual salvation, and therefore had no problem serving as the cog that occasionally supported the wheel. The only part he had subjective control over, the part he could change up and add flavor to, was the sermon.

Afterward, at the door, Seth Weimer's face was beaming.

"I loved that message," the little man said, shaking the pastor's hand.

"Well, God bless you," Owen said.

"I'd like to think about joining."

Brother Tisdale looked away briefly, as if in thought. "You know, Seth, this might be a good place for you. With all—"

"Well, I feel like it would be," Seth said, "but I'm a little hesitant about changing denominations."

Owen wrapped his arm around the smaller man. "I'd be glad to talk with you about it. It won't be any problem. A soldier for Christ is a soldier for Christ."

Owen shook a dozen more hands before Dan Bearden walked in front of him, face red, his handshake so firm it left people thinking they'd come out on the short end of a rock-paper-scissors tiff. Dan was also thinking of joining, and because of this, Owen put on a smile and hugged him, and Dan was out the door.

The tall man remained in the back row, waiting. Owen drifted toward his guest.

"It's not every day a celebrity visits Crown of Thorns Baptist," Owen said.

"I wouldn't say a celebrity," the tall man said, rising from the pew to shake hands.

They introduced themselves. The tall man's name was Donald Hayes. He was a retired judge who'd lived his entire life in Dallas and was now president of Texas Baptist Seminary, the largest such institution of the Baptist Convention.

"You're taller than you look in the paper," Owen said.

"To be a judge in Texas, you got to be six foot five," the judge said. "I just made the mark."

"You here to talk about the Lord?" Owen asked.

"Oh, I enjoyed your message," the judge said. "You mind if we sit down and talk a while?"

"Not at all."

In Owen's office they sat drinking coffee.

"You follow the convention?" the judge asked.

"I can't boast," Owen said. "I'll look at the newsletter sometimes. Maybe read an article in the *Baptist Texan.*"

The judge viewed the reference books on the shelf. "You might have seen the latest happenings. The liberals are trying to hijack the convention. Trying to get an Atlanta evangelist into the presidency."

"I saw that," Owen said with interest.

"It's only natural that we've got to counter them. They'll rewrite the Ten Commandments if we let 'em."

"They'll do more than that," Owen said. "They'll take over the seminaries, start planting their ideology into the heads of the next preaching generation."

"Could you tell me a little about your pastoral philosophy?" the judge asked. "Where do you believe the church should go?"

"I believe in God's love and mercy," Owen said. "However, I also know in my heart we need to make an ethical stand. Draw the line with homosexuals and abortionists. They're fragmenting society, and they'll cripple the church."

"Amen," the judge said, measuring Owen's expression, nodding. "I believe that's the line God wants us to tow. The election's coming up next year. I figure a preacher from a small church, one like yourself, someone with faith and vision, could sneak up off the radar and steal the presidency before the liberals knew what hit 'em. Are you interested?"

"Let's pray about it," Owen said.

Chapter 13

Andrea sat between her mother and father on a thin, hardened pew that seemed to be a hundred years old. She looked up into her mother's face, and her mother tried to smile, but a grimace of grief and anxiety formed instead. Her mother squeezed her hand—a little too hard. There was no singing tonight.

She didn't know why.

She was seven years old—she knew that much—and she'd been raised in this church. She knew its smell of old decrepit oak, blighted panels, and dusty pews, and she'd memorized the dark pinstripe patterns in the navy blue carpet. She'd been going to Sunday school inside these very same walls since she was three, listening intently to each lesson, and looking at the pictures that accompanied them: pictures of Jesus and giants and slingshots and shepherds and fisherman and the Red Sea, and the supernatural tales that went with each. She raised her hand at the teacher's questions and answered them correctly, and she'd made friends with the six or seven children who came regularly with their parents. It was a small church—a small building and auditorium and close-knit group of members—and everyone seemed to treat each other as family. The grown-ups had been especially nice to her—and to most everyone else, it seemed.

But something was different about tonight.

It was Sunday night, and the pews were packed with more people than usual—at least for an evening service. The faces Andrea glimpsed around her revealed fear, apprehension, and turmoil.

Her father put his steely arm around her and clutched her opposite shoulder. She looked up at him, and he looked down upon her with the blue eyes she'd inherited from him and grinned circumspectly.

Troy Conyer, a burly man about six foot five, leaned over their pew from behind and said to Andrea's father, "Calvin, you know we can beat him. My boy's a member. Your daughter's a member. We gonna let the kids vote?"

Her father glanced at her, then looked at her mother. "I don't know, Troy."

"I don't think we should," her mother said. "Let's keep them out of it."

Troy shrank back into his pew.

Andrea ignored most of the announcements, as she often did. Someone at the front of the church—not in the pulpit, but in front of it—said something about calling an official order of business. Boring, Andrea thought. Senseless phrases like "I motion" and "second it" preceded and followed one another for the next couple of minutes.

A couple of voices, a man's accusation and a woman's defense, whisked across the air with a cutting derisiveness. Then a woman across the aisle, Donna Kincaid, stood up and began acting funny. Her face was red, and she was starting to cry. The women beside her soothed her with soft hands and voices, but she withstood her own self-inflicted torment, saying, "My family's already been through one church split. I don't want to go through it again."

Andrea's mother bent down to her, grabbed her hand, and said, "Come on, honey. Let's go outside and play." She stood and led Andrea through the center aisle toward the side doors, where a handful of children her age were being sent by their parents.

Donna Kincaid's husband grabbed her hand and pulled gently on her arm, consoling her, and she sat back down, buried her face in her hands.

The preacher, Brother Hebert, rose from the front pew. He appeared poised and docile. "This meeting is not scriptural. I don't know which of you are behind this, but it's not going to work. The blood of the Lamb thwarts the Devil every time."

Troy Conyer stood up. "We didn't come tonight to hear any more of your BS!"

"Why don't you sit down, Troy?" Cliff Akin yelled back from the second row.

"Are you gonna make me?" Troy asked.

The two men rose to meet, but Cliff didn't get out of his aisle before Troy—a good three inches taller—planted his three largest knuckles in his face. Cliff's head snapped back, and he tottered to the floor amid the pews.

Andrea's mother tried to turn her away, prodded her toward the exit. "Come on, Andrea," she said, her voice frantic.

But Andrea turned her head to see what she would remember most from the meeting: Troy walking toward Brother Hebert, yelling and pointing his finger at the man in the navy blue slacks and tie; the preacher flashing his palm toward Troy; Troy jetting through the air, as if *by an ethereal blast, slamming into the concrete side of the auditorium, and falling to the ground; the slight, stoic grin on the preacher's face.*

Calvin Lavoie gave his grandson a gentle push in the swing, then took a couple steps back.

"Grab ahold, Wesley," Calvin said. "Grab ahold and pull." He was approaching sixty, and the potbelly above his belt bulged like a basketball.

It had rained the night before, and the patches of grass were still wet even though the sun had come out. Clouds scurried like puffy blankets in the distance, racing toward the horizon. Wesley smiled as he followed the old man's orders, pulling back against the ropes, kicking his legs toward the sky and sunshine. Beside him, Elizabeth hung from the monkey bars, pulling her way from ladder to ladder, gum hanging halfway out of her mouth. Curt stood nearby, between the bars and the slide, watching, making sure she didn't fall awkwardly. He'd helped her up there just seconds before.

"Watch me, Grandpa," she said, silky golden threads whipping behind her shoulders.

"I'm watching, hun," Calvin said. His blue eyes shifted between the two children as though they were playing tennis.

"Are you sure?" Elizabeth asked.

"I'm sure," Calvin said.

"Well, you better be," Elizabeth said in her playful bully demeanor.

Jean leaned back and chortled. "She sure told you, Grandpa."

"Elizabeth, you be nice," Andrea warned.

"Oh, she's just playing," Jean said, just above a whisper. Her short hair was tinged with trifles of silver, her eyes light blue with a stream of green visible when the sun struck them.

"I know, but she needs to show some respect," Andrea said in a half-agreeing tone. She'd learned early on she had to be firm with the girl, who, if given enough slack, would pull you to the dirt and drag you on your knees, laughing while she did. "I just hope she doesn't say anything like that to her teachers."

"You don't think she'd say that at school, do you?" Jean asked.

"I don't know," Andrea said, shaking her head lightly.

"I don't think she would," Jean said. "She's pretty cunning, though, isn't she?"

Andrea rolled her eyes and exhaled. "Oh, Mom, you ought to see the things she does."

"I know. You were the same way."

Andrea gave Jean a bug-eyed look. "I wasn't that bad, though. Was I?"

It was Jean's turn to roll her eyes. "Ohh," she said, sighing.

"I was?" Andrea asked.

"You played with matches, drew pictures on the walls, threw rocks, spilled bleach all over your bare feet, brought tarantulas into the house. And you seemed to catch temper tantrums instead of colds."

Andrea didn't know what to say; the shock kept her quiet.

"It's never easy growing up," Jean said. "Truth is, you never stop. Just when you think you've grown up, something terrible happens, and you feel like a child again, all vulnerable and paranoid."

"You don't still get like that, do you?" Andrea asked.

"Well, I haven't in a while," Jean said. "But you never know how you're going to react to something catastrophic. If something happened to any of my children or grandchildren, I don't know … I'd probably become so mean and bitter no one would ever take a piano lesson from me again." They shared a laugh.

"I don't know what I would do, either," Andrea said. "Go crazy, I guess."

"Daddy, come get me," Elizabeth said, hanging from a bar by her fingers, wiggling her legs and feet.

"Just swing over to the ladder," Curt said.

"I can't," Elizabeth pouted. Curt stepped toward her and helped her down. Then she moved toward the empty swing, sat down. "Grandpa, you have to push me now too."

"I can push you," Curt said.

"No, I want Grandpa to," Elizabeth said.

"Grandpa's pushing Wesley," Curt said.

"So. He can push me, too."

"It's not a problem," Calvin said, before Curt could tell her not to talk back. He sidestepped to a spot behind her, pulled her back in the swing, and gave a thorough push. "No problem at all."

"Mom," Andrea said, "remember what we talked about on the phone a few weeks ago?"

Jean puzzled for a moment. "Oh yes. The Sunday you had that bad spell."

"Yeah," Andrea said. She got a little sick just thinking about it; her stomach did a quick tiptoe dance. "Well, I've been having some dreams since then. About when I was little."

"What kind of dreams?" Jean asked.

"About church," Andrea said. "The split we had. You know, the one with Brother Hebert."

Jean reeled from the sound of the name. She nodded. "I remember that man."

"All I remember is we left and joined a new church," Andrea said. "And what I remember from my dreams. But I don't know if I can trust them."

"Believe me, Andrea," Jean said, "if they're *your* dreams, you can trust them."

"I don't know," Andrea said.

At the swing set, Calvin was close to breaking a sweat. "Ol' Grandpa's getting tired," he said. "I'm gonna have to rest a minute."

Elizabeth didn't argue, nor did Wesley.

Curt took Calvin's place as the elder man joined Jean and Andrea.

"You about had enough?" Jean asked him.

"I ain't got the stamina I used to," Calvin said.

"I'll second that," Jean said coquettishly.

"Mom!" Andrea said accusingly.

"Yeah, you behave," Calvin said. "What you gals talkin' about over here?"

Jean looked at the ground. Andrea took in a deep breath.

"It's not women things, is it?" Calvin asked, with the same look Van Helsing gave before entering the vampire's crypt.

"No, honey," Jean said. "We were just talking about our old church in Lake Charles."

"What was that whole thing about with Brother Hebert?" Andrea asked.

Calvin offered a grim look that said *Oh no, put that spider back in the jar.* A bitter look from what otherwise was a sweet face. And what came out of his mouth sounded bitter too.

"That was some bad stuff," he said, wrinkles cutting into his face like arroyos.

"He tore that church apart," Jean said. She looked at her husband. "Didn't he, honey?"

"Oh, he did more than that. He just ... was everything you don't want in a pastor. Even bad preachers don't do what he did."

Jean looked uneasily at her grandchildren. "He hurt a lot of people. And when we tried to talk to him about it, he almost acted like he *wanted* to hurt them."

Andrea stood thinking. "Then why did the church call him?"

"He was a great preacher," Calvin said, looking at the earth, measuring the dampness of a patch of grass with his boot. "State Convention recommended against him, but no one listened—not after his first sermon. He was too good to turn down. And those are the ones that spoil the church."

"What else did he do?" Andrea asked.

"He did whatever he could to run that church into the ground," Jean said. "He went over budget."

"Ran us into the red," Calvin said.

"He cut all of our good programs, like visitation," Jean said. "And there toward the end, he went on all kinds of trips and was hardly around anymore. Your dad never really cared for him. Did you, Calvin?"

"Not particularly," he said.

"What did you not like about him?" Andrea asked.

After a deep breath, Calvin said, "Just … the way he shook your hand. The way he smiled."

"Fake?" Andrea proposed.

"Well yeah, I guess," Calvin said nodding.

On the swing set, Elizabeth soared to the height of the overhead horizontal pole, yelling, "Higher!" with each forward swing, while Wesley was blurting "Yeah!"

"His sermons were awfully good," Calvin continued. "But after a while there wasn't much spirit in the service. Everyone got to hating everybody, getting in each other's faces and screaming till they got so red they couldn't breathe."

Andrea studied Elizabeth, then looked at her parents. "What was that final church meeting all about?"

Calvin and Jean exchanged uncomfortable looks.

"She means the night we split," Jean told him.

"Yeah, I know," he said. "A lot of us deacons got together and talked about everything Brother Hebert was doing, and we decided we needed to call the church together and vote on it."

"You were going to fire him," Andrea confirmed.

"Yeah," Calvin said. "We were gonna ask the church to vote on it."

"Didn't he have some supporters?" Andrea asked.

"Oh yeah," Calvin said.

"He had some staunch supporters, all right," Jean said. "Cliff Akin. That man had a mouth on him. And Theresa Norris. I don't know if you remember her or not."

"Just a little," Andrea said.

"It takes strength to stand by a preacher when he's in trouble,"

Calvin said. "But it takes a lot more to stand against him. It's not as simple as voting him out of there. That's one thing we learned during that whole deal."

"So what happened?" Andrea asked.

Jean and Calvin waited, tossing oblique glances at each other, as if to confer who was going to explain.

"Everyone was full of hate," Calvin said. "Brother Hebert had his cronies like Cliff Akin and R. A. Roberson riled up. We announced we were calling a business meeting, but Brother Hebert had gotten wind of it somehow, and they were ready for us. When we tried to call a vote, they stood up and did everything they could to stop it."

Jean's face beamed suddenly. "Troy Conyer punched Cliff Akin's lights out," she said chuckling. "I never will forget that. That was the best part of it all." The smile on Jean's face soured, as did the brief glow on Calvin's. The wrinkles dug back in.

"What happened next?" Andrea asked.

"It was hell after that," Calvin said.

Jean turned to Andrea. "We still don't understand what we saw," she said. "We talked about it so much the years after that we just decided to bury it and not let it worry us anymore." She shook her head.

Calvin cleared his throat. "Brother Hebert shoved Troy, and Troy went flying through the air and hit the wall. All of us saw it. No one knew what to think. People started fighting. It was a mess. It wasn't a church anymore. It was a madhouse."

Like the dream, Andrea realized.

"What happened to Troy?" she asked. "Was he okay?"

"I think he had a concussion and a couple broken ribs," Jean said, looking at Calvin for confirmation.

"Yeah," Calvin said. "He bruised some bones in his back."

"That's when we left?" Andrea asked.

"Yep," Jean said. "We got out of there and started our own church."

"What happened to Brother Hebert?" Andrea asked.

Calvin turned to Jean. "He moved on to another church somewhere, didn't he?"

"Yeah, I think he went out of state somewhere," Jean said. "Alabama or Mississippi or somewhere."

"So you decided it was better to leave than to stay and fight," Andrea said.

"It should never have come to violence," Jean said. "But that's what you get when you have a preacher who's a dictator. Some of them are just control mongrels. Of course a time like that is tough for a preacher, but instead of showing some composure and letting the church vote, he took the cowardly way out.

"After that, we didn't know if we wanted to be in church anymore. That night didn't leave us for a long, long time."

Calvin shook his head.

On the swing set, Elizabeth's shouts waned and her swinging height had plateaued well below the horizontal pole's. Wesley swung in tiny arcs, eyes closed and chin tilted, drool streaming onto his T-shirt.

"I remember you leading me out of the auditorium," Andrea said.

"Troy and some other people knew we could outvote him if we used our children," Jean said.

"And you children were members, Andrea, so there wouldn't have been anything wrong with it," Calvin said.

"Yes, but that didn't feel like the right thing to do at the time," Jean said.

"No, I guess not," Calvin said. "But the things that man did …. We were desperate to get rid of him." He took a deep breath, biding the silence.

"He must have had everyone brainwashed," Andrea said.

"He did," Jean agreed.

"He did some things that just …" Calvin said, looking into the past, shaking his head. He looked up at Andrea. "I sometimes have nightmares about that last night. I swear that man was the Devil."

Chapter 14

Owen Tisdale stood waist-deep in the water wearing swim trunks and white T-shirt, looking out over the transparent visor of the baptistery into the congregation, which was full. The water lapped cool against his skin. A cockroach-sized microphone was etched in the visor, catching the most diminutive of waves.

The service had yet to begin, and members of the choir stood outside the loft by the piano and organ, holding their folders, watching.

Brother Tisdale cleared his throat, which felt coarse as a grated dirt road. That, and the tickling sensation in his sinus passage, left him swerving a touch off-balance.

"In the Bible Jesus says, 'No man may enter the kingdom but by Me,'" he said. "And in Romans and Ephesians we learn that once we are saved through His grace, He will never leave us. He told Peter, 'My grace is sufficient for you.' Ephesians 1:13 says 'By your faith you are sealed …'"

A skinny boy wandered down the steps into the water, shaking in his T-shirt, crossing his arms. He appeared starstruck by the razor-blade eyes in the audience.

Slimy piece of meat frozen in the headlights, Owen thought. *I'd drown the little fool if it were just me and him.*

Owen tried to smile, took the boy's hand.

"Justin, upon your—" he started to say, then sneezed twice in a row, as if one bucked as a retort of the other, nasty sneezes, full of phlegm, "—profession of faith." Another sneeze, followed by a cough: pastor's worst nightmare. "I baptize you—" Sneeze. "In the name of the Father—" Sneeze. "The Son and Holy Ghost." Then, plunging the boy backward into the water, he said, "Buried with Christ—" Two machine-gun sneezes. "In baptism." Then pulling him back up, "Raised to walk in the newness of life."

Justin's eyes bulged with shock and bewilderment. Owen ushered him back toward the steps and came just short of another sneeze. He looked back at the congregation as another boy prepared to enter the water.

"I tell you, there's just something awful in this water," he said in the Southern vernacular, baiting chortles and *ha-ha-has!* He baptized the next boy in the same manner, addressing the Trinity prior to submersion, wrestling the sneezes.

After the third and final baptism—a man in his midthirties—Owen led the church in prayer and made his way over to the steps and ascended, then disappeared. Back onto firm ground, he fell to his knees, doubled over to the side, and heaved a half gallon of the bad stuff inside him. His face succumbed to the redness of asphyxiation, his fingers blue with hypoxia.

"Screw You, Yahweh," he said, looking about him, though not exactly up. "You know what You can do with Your church."

His throat constricted, and he reeled onto his back, clutching his

Adam's apple. The force released, and he sucked in air like a vacuum cleaner.

"I should have kicked Your sorry butt when I had the chance." He looked around him, rose to his feet, and staggered toward his Sunday suit.

His voice gave out on him during the service. One-fourth of the way through the sermon, he fought back two sneezes, drowning the tickling between his eyes with a drink of water as he instructed the congregation to turn pages in their Bibles. Other than that, the message flowed as it always did, facile and mellifluous in tone, structure, and content. Five people, alive in Christ and content to serve, stepped forward during the invitation.

Afterward, when he'd finished shaking hands, laughing at bad jokes, and kissing butts, Owen went into the fellowship hall, where Seth Weimer and Dan Bearden were sitting down on the edge of a table, talking. They stood up when they saw Owen.

"Can you gentlemen stay for a while?" he asked. "Or do you have something else you need to attend to?"

"I can stay," Dan said.

"I've got plenty of time," Seth said.

"You guys want a Coke?" Owen asked, eyes opening wide in consideration.

Seth glanced at Dan. "Yeah."

"If you're offering," Dan said grinning.

Owen sauntered toward the kitchen and veered beside it along a short corridor, where the Coke machine stood. No need to deposit any coins; he pressed the large red Coca-Cola button and heard them tumble to the bottom—three of them. He bent down, lifted the shutter, pulled them out. He trundled back to Dan and Seth and handed them each a Coke.

"Let's go back to my office," he said.

"Okay," Seth said.

They followed him through the hallways, some dim as an old manse, passing a few people outside the choir room, past the final stairwell and into the office complex. He unlocked his door and led them inside.

"Have a seat," Owen said.

They sat down, opened their Cokes, took sips.

"I asked you to stay today because I believe you both have a lot to offer," Owen said, looking back and forth from his drink to Dan and Seth. "I want you to know I'm just as new to this church as you are. I'm getting to be an old man. They tell me gray hair is a sign of wisdom, but I don't know if I believe that or not."

Seth laughed far more than the humor warranted, nearly spewing Coke from his nostrils. Dan laughed equally intensely. Caffeine and good will, Owen had learned, goaded the flesh.

"We're all getting there," Dan said. In his early forties, he was five years older than Seth.

"I guess everyone does, sooner or later," Owen said. Owen set his drink on the desk. His grin diminished but didn't disappear. "I've been pastor long enough to know that every church has cliques. I've never been in one that didn't. Some of the members here at Crown of Thorns have been attending for twenty to thirty years, and they might not acquiesce so easily to new faces—especially not when those faces start trying to get involved with church affairs." Owen realized what he was saying—and the tone in which he was saying it—might appear a little spooky for Dan and Seth, so he loosened up in his chair, sagged to one side, and laughed. "Have I scared y'all off yet?"

Seth laughed his effeminate laugh. Dan puckered his lips, shook his head.

"Good," Owen said, "because I believe we need some new members to help us go in another direction." He licked his chops. "Would either of you be opposed to serving on some committees?"

"No," Dan said.

"Not at all," Seth said, shaking his head. Curly red tendrils bounced behind his neck.

Why do I torment myself? Owen thought. *Hell will rain icicles before I let this wuss in.*

Chapter 15

Andrea was cutting up another chicken. She would fry it tonight. Curt had come home a little after five—early for him—and she found herself in a hurry to quarter and batter the limp bird in front of her.

The meat was slippery, and she had a hard time holding on to it, digging her fingers and nails into the pink flesh with each slice. She'd already cut away half of the chicken, had just chopped the wing off the other part, and was working on the leg and thigh. She tried cutting the pieces in two, squeezing the ends with her opposite hand and bearing down on the center with the blade, but the gristle, rugged and wiry, didn't want to give.

She gritted her teeth and gave it another try, muscles flexing in her forearm, but instead of cutting through poultry bone and joint, the knife slipped from the wedge of gristle and sliced deeply into her other hand between the thumb and index finger.

She cried out, dropping the meat and blade, which clanked into the sink.

The revelation of blood and pain cinched her breath. Dark drops squirmed from her thumb, seeming to move with a will of their own. She hadn't bled like this since her brother had hit her in the nose with a stuffed tiger when she was eleven. Her blood streamed down the drain, mixing with chicken blood, one happy mess of socialized serum. It was coagulating well enough, appearing in considerable volume, even as she held it under the water at full blast. This cut wasn't going to go away, not without serious pressure, not without a couple of gauze strips restricting its flow.

Curt came into the kitchen. He'd replaced his uniform with a T-shirt and pair of jeans. He saw the knife. The way she was holding her hand. The blood.

"What did you do?" he asked.

"Cut my ..." she managed to blurt.

He moved awkwardly toward her, readying his own hands, staring at the mess between her thumb and index finger. His eyes looked behind her, around her. He stepped past, yanked several paper towels from beneath the cabinet to her right, wadded them up, and applied them to her hand.

"Here," he said. "Hold it on there tight." He started to turn away but changed his mind. He gestured toward the dining room table. "Sit down for a minute, honey."

She didn't feel like doing anything except maybe falling to her knees and crying like Elizabeth. She wanted to roll her eyes and look away, wanted to flee this pain.

"Here," Curt said.

She opened her eyes to see him standing next to her, holding a couple of Tylenol in his open palm. A glass of water waited on the table.

"Thanks," she said, taking the tablets with her good hand. She shoved them into her mouth, and a couple waves of water washed them down, drowning the butterflies fluttering inside.

"Keep that there a minute," Curt said, nodding at the glob of paper towels, now dotted and splattered with red, some areas darker than others. "I'm gonna go see if we have any gauze." He disappeared into the hallway leading to their bedroom and came back, gauze in hand, just as Andrea's mind returned to the pain.

She looked at the clump of towels, drying with red.

"I do the dumbest things," she said to herself.

"Well, what does it look like?" Curt asked.

Warily, Andrea picked apart the sticky paper towels. When the last filmy layer came off, it revealed an inch and a half cut, maroon and darkening, that appeared to be pulling on both sides.

"Um … ouch," Curt said, facial muscles constricting.

"Honey—" Andrea whined.

"You might need to get that stitched up," he said, staring at it with the curiosity of a boy who'd just killed his first deer.

"I'm not going to the ER for this," Andrea said. She didn't know why she had made such an argumentative statement, but that same voice emerged in crises like these, even if this was a rather small one. And then, although she had no idea how such a lie could spring from her mouth, she said, "It's not that bad. And we really can't afford it."

"Andrea, I've seen cuts on the job," Curt said. "That's a bad cut. You can't just put a Band-Aid on it. It's not just gonna go away. You have to get it stitched." He walked away but quickly returned to the table.

They rarely argued, but when Andrea's health was concerned, Curt could get pretty ugly, even frantic. What appeared as common sense to him sometimes seemed horrifying to her.

"This isn't Louisiana, honey," Andrea said, straight-faced, glaring at him. And where did she get the courage? At least it partially eclipsed her mind from the pain. "We're not going to get a bill for twenty dollars. This is Texas. They charge an arm and a leg for doctor's visits here, and I can just imagine what the ER would charge."

Curt's hand fell to the table, and he returned a Texas glare he'd picked up from coworkers. "Honey, when it's your health, you don't care what it costs. You go get help, and then you worry about the costs afterward. That's how it is."

"Is it?" Andrea asked, patronizingly, with a thespian's smile lighting her face. Then she said in earnest, "You almost sound like the people you work with. The rednecks you've been complaining about."

Curt looked down at his shoes and swallowed.

"Quit being stubborn, Andrea, and just go to the stupid ER," he said.

"Quit being hateful, Curt," she said.

"I'm not being hateful," he said. "I'm being the opposite." He turned away briefly, shook his head, and turned back toward her, grimacing. "And you wonder where Elizabeth gets it."

They slept on their own sides of the bed that night. Curt laid his hand on her shoulder just as she turned out the lamplight. He rolled over and in five minutes gave in to a light snore.

Andrea stared into the darkness for a few minutes, trying to forget about the slice on her hand underneath the gauze—and whether or not it would heal properly. A wide scar would only tell her what Curt had been trying to tell her: It needed stitches. At worst, it might become infected. Then she would have to visit the doctor.

Thoughts like these plagued her with worry, but she felt better once she lifted her knees into a fetal position, and soon drifted off into another time and place, with a whole other realm of possibilities.

She smelled the old oak and darkened teak. Everything in Northside Baptist Church of Lake Charles had been antique: the carpet, piano, baptistery, hymnals, pews, pipes, and pillars; and, of course, many of the ladies. But the people had been magical, of the warmest hearts, and it had been home. Andrea had never imagined going anywhere else to worship God, learn about the Bible, or play with her best friends, and the thought of leaving seemed a sacrilege.

She floated away from the small auditorium, through a corridor she remembered fondly. Something propelled her back into the sanctuary, an extraneous force that desired her to bear witness. This gave her a view of the melee from a few rows back, centered, from above.

People were standing up. Some were shouting, pointing fingers, spitting out their words. A few were pushing each other. Someone stepped in between them, only to get pushed out of the way into a pew.

To the right, sitting against the wall, slumped over and unconscious, Troy Conyer was being tended to by a few people. Her mother was one of them. Above him, a patch of blood painted the wall: a smear of maroon against the coarse white. Troy's wife, Jan, was trying to get him to respond, shaking his shoulders, nudging his chin. The woman shrieked with hysteria. Jean consoled her, telling her he was all right, but Jan didn't appear to be cognizant of anyone else's voice.

At the fifth pew on the left-hand column, Connie Sparkman and Pat Richardson barked in each other's faces. Pat's daughter Melanie stood near her, blushed face matching her ketchup-colored hair, and behind Connie, her own son Phillip tried to ward off the grudge spat, making futile attempts to tug his mother away.

"Brother Hebert is the only decent person in this church!" Connie said. Her volume blended with the static, but Andrea could hear her.

"Are you crazy?" Pat asked. "There are a lot of good people in here."

"Not tonight there aren't," Connie said. "Look around. They're a bunch of animals. Hypocrites! Look at Brother Hebert. He's the only one with any integrity!"

"What?" Pat asked. "He's the bastard who started this whole thing! He's responsible!"

"He's no more a bastard than that whore of yours!" Connie said, pointing at Melanie, who recoiled from Connie as if from the Wicked Witch of the West. Pat sucked in a stabbing breath. "And you better keep her away from my son from now on!"

"Why you …!" Pat reached up and clawed Connie's face. Connie grabbed hold of Pat's hair, kneed the slightly heavier woman in the stomach, and together they tumbled to the rotten wood of a pew, spinning onto the floor.

Andrea turned and looked behind her.

In the back row Bill Ragle, a seasonal attendee with a mound of a belly, was giving Earl Peterson his two cents worth. Earl was a wise old man, scrawny—even in the overalls he wore tonight—who tended to mouth off about apparent corruptions like the one in front of him.

"Brother Hebert's a crooked man if I ever seen one," Earl said.

Bill turned to him, and his belly brushed the skinny man, nearly knocking him down.

"You're the biggest jackass I ever seen," Bill said, "going round talking garbage about folks when all they's trying to do is help."

"What do you know, Bill?" Earl said. "You only come at Christmas and Easter. For all I know, that man's the Devil."

"How can you cuss in the Lord's house?" Bill asked.

"This ain't His house," Earl said. "Hasn't been the Lord's house in several months." Earl walked away, sidling through the aisle.

Andrea felt the old traiter power brewing in her bones, thumping along her veins, especially those in her hands, and she wanted to help. A cathartic need to exert the forces possessed her; she had to expel those committing atrocities within the church, within the holy walls.

If she had the power to do it, she would cast it away.

What's making them do this to each other? she thought. She'd never seen grown-ups hit each other. The hate wasn't wedged in their knuckles or razor-sharp fingernails; it seethed in their words, minds, and blood—and in their hearts. Where had they contrived it? What had infected them?

Andrea redirected her view toward the front, where her father stood talking to the preacher and two other men.

"Come on," her father said, "we need to pray about this. This isn't the Lord's will."

"The Lord's children ain't supposed to act like this," one of the men said.

She didn't recognize Brother Hebert, she didn't remember all the faces; it had been nearly twenty years.

"*This is about as close to blasphemy as you can get,*" the other man said.

"*Come on,*" her father said, looking at each of them. "*Let's join hands and pray.*" He held his open palm toward Brother Hebert. "*Come on, Brother Hebert. Let's stop this.*"

His face reflected the worst epiphany.

Above, Andrea couldn't believe what she saw, even in quasi-dream.

Brother Hebert grinned. He began laughing.

Her father looked at the other men.

"*You people are so stupid,*" the pastor said.

Andrea's father clutched his throat, stumbled backward into a pew, crumbled into it. His face boiled with red, his ventilation cut off. Friends swarmed around him, trying to help.

Brother Hebert pivoted and walked through the door near the choir loft.

Andrea's father regained his breath but held his hands on his throat.

Several among the pews were still bickering. Connie and Pat rolled under the decrepit benches, pulling hair and scratching skin, while their children tried to pull them apart. Andrea yearned to heave a bucket of ice water on this fire, but fires like these didn't go away overnight; they carried lifelong ramifications. The traiter willed the violence away, and strangely—though she wondered, as she always did when she had these dreams, if it were real or unreal—the activity lessened. She wished the physical harm to a halt, but it didn't stop. She willed those who'd succumbed to hate to purge that bitter disease from their hearts, to forgive each other and embrace their brothers and sisters.

Most of all, she willed the preacher to go away.

During the brief transit between the dream world and the physical, Andrea sensed she was falling from something, but from what or where she had no idea. When she became fully alert with both intrinsic and extrinsic functions, she clutched the sheets with enough force to rip their cotton threads, and jerked forward from her fetal position on her side of the bed, nearly falling off. All she saw, at first, was the blurry darkness roving with the flagella of dust.

Her chest and stomach were tight, and sweat trickled down her belly. The sartorius muscle above her knee twitched; so did the trapezius below her neck, between her shoulder blade and spine. She rolled onto her back, closed her eyes, and inhaled a couple of deep breaths.

Crazy dream, she thought. She opened her eyes. *Too real. I was there. The old church. I saw what happened. Brother Hebert choked Dad. I don't know how ... but he choked him. I know it happened. How do I know?*

Moisture wriggled across her body like little bugs, stinging in places. Suddenly, she thought of the cut on her left hand, between her thumb and index finger. Surely the sweat would burn the wound; it was long and deep—Curt had been right about that. He'd also been right about her being stubborn; she knew now, after her mother refreshed her memory, that Elizabeth took that trait from her.

She pulled off the comforter and sheet, swung her legs over the side of the mattress, and stood in the darkness. With her right hand, she felt for the gauze wrapped around her cut. It had unfurled during her sleep and was damp. When her eyes had adjusted, she walked toward the doorway, hand in front, guarding against collision, bracing for what she couldn't see. She made it unscathed into the hallway, bare feet shifting across the thin carpet. Every so often Elizabeth left a jack or some other sharp object in the floor, waiting to stick into a passerby's flesh. Andrea hoped, however cognitively as she could in the twilight hours, that her little girl had picked up all her pernicious gadgets.

She made it to the bathroom, turned on the light.

She stood in front of the mirror, looking at herself. Hair badly disheveled, gown crinkled from drying sweat: a sad sight for a twenty-five-year-old blonde, she reckoned. She had a deprecated view of subjects these days and didn't bother to think that every woman stirred from her sleep looked that way.

She perused the gauze on her hand: droopy, warped, and wilting, stained with blood. She squeezed the thumb and index finger together. Little pain, not sore like earlier. She unwrapped the gauze in a motion that reminded her of stirring spaghetti, looping it over and under, until crusts of dried dark blood crumbled to the floor from the last layer. She dreaded pulling off the end, hoping it wouldn't stick to whatever scab lay beneath, but amazingly, as she tugged the elastic fibers, it rolled off almost effortlessly, damp but not stuck. What she saw, she could hardly believe: The wound had closed, no scab had formed; it had healed completely; all that remained was a light brown scar, and in a few days that would go away too.

Andrea took a deep breath, looked at her face in the mirror.

Gaping mouth. Dilated pupils. A look of fear and bewilderment. She looked around her, then back at her hand. She squeezed the finger and thumb. No pain. No soreness. It had healed in a matter of hours.

Chapter 16

Owen did his best work while feeding the faces of others.

Saturday evening, before his fourth Sunday as Crown of Thorns Baptist's pastor, he took Dan Bearden and Seth Weimer to the Steak Stockade. He had just finished a lengthy phone conversation with the judge. Fitting Dan and Seth into their chairmanships had been easy; he snapped them into place like Lego bricks.

The prior Sunday he'd talked it over with Kevin McBride, the previous chairman of the nominating committee, and they'd come to a mutual agreement to allow Dan, a new member with a fresh perspective, to take over.

"I'd like you to remain on the committee," Brother Tisdale had told Kevin. "I don't want you to think anyone's trying to push you out. In fact, if you want, you can keep the chair, no questions asked. It's not up to me, anyway. I just thought it might be good to let our new members get more involved with some of the decision making. Give them a chance to contribute, you know."

Kevin nodded. Brother Tisdale knew the man hadn't agreed;

insurrection brewed inside him, however temporary it might have been. Owen gave a tender smile.

Dan's first move had been to nominate Seth Weimer to the finance committee. Once it was approved by the committee, it would only take a few minor tweaks to catapult Seth to the chair. They would bring it up at a business meeting, and someone would move to accept, and someone else would second it. In addition, he'd nominated three new members: Jay Ingebritson, a pot-bellied weekly newspaper editor, to the finance committee; Justin Harkins, personnel director for Texaco, to the nominating committee; and Vince Dumars, a black construction worker, to the newly formed building committee.

Vince's nomination threatened the chemistry Owen wanted; the man was built like a brute and headstrong, but Owen gambled that his humble aura, whipped by prejudices and employers' lashings, would force him to stand down against any perceived discrepancies or corruption. His selection was necessary to make an honest selection in the eye of the congregation—one that emphasized diversity and openness. The old guard would never let him run the church—not as he saw fit, anyway. They were like lumps in a bowl of Cream of Wheat. They needed some smoothing over.

On the other wing of power, the fiscal side, Owen had talked to Rick Pettibone about relegating the finance committee chairmanship to Seth. He cornered Rick after the service and asked him if he had any qualms about relinquishing his title.

"If I thought it would help the church, I'd gladly give it up," Rick had said, face tightening. "At the same time, I've always felt called to that committee. I run my own business and—"

"Oh, I understand," Owen said, patting the nervous man with his hands, trying to calm him. "You've done a terrific job. You've blessed this church with your knowledge and leadership. We love you." Owen paused. "We want you to stay on the committee. We'd just like to give a couple of our new members an opportunity to delegate."

Rick's face had reddened, and he'd walked away.

Brother Tisdale still had a lot of work to do. He would ask new members if they wanted to greet and handle the offering plates, and if they said yes, he'd give the veteran ushers the same old line he'd given Rick Pettibone and Kevin McBride. He would do the same with Joanne Gilcrease, the pianist whose pretentious playing was starting to irritate him. Ruth Baum, the organist, had wanted to play piano for a long time, anyway, and Owen had heard that Stacy Kingsbury, a college student majoring in music education, could play either instrument. He'd bear the good news to Joanne, the even better news to Ruth, and the rewarding light of opportunity to Stacy. He guessed at least one of them would go home crying. *Another unhappy contributor*, Owen thought. *Them's the breaks.*

He hadn't encountered any problems with Sunday school superintendent Stan Wilcox, nor with Craig McManes, the music director; he didn't see any need to replace either of them. Lisa Etheridge, the pretty youth director fresh out of seminary, was an unknown. So far, Owen had been unable to gauge her; she'd kept a distance. He could see the Spirit within her, but it was a great deal weaker than what she perceived it of being. Owen, in his modern era of patience and munificence, wasn't sure what he was going to do with her. He didn't have to remove her. Not yet.

Chapter 17

Waymon's hands were shaking. He held them under the table, locked together over his knees, to hide his anxiety. He knew quivers and shivers came with getting old, just as diabetes and heart disease followed heredity and obesity, but he wasn't about to lie to himself—not even if his body was on the downturn. He had to be forthright, at least to himself: He didn't like the recent changes at Crown of Thorns Baptist Church.

He'd been questioning his feelings, his perceptions, relative to his years of service. Elders were frequently resistant to change. Sometimes changes were healthy and needed to be effected, even if it meant steering one's boat into uncharted waters. An internal debate had been brewing in his mind. In his heart. Which was why he hadn't raised the issues. Not yet, anyway. In past decades he'd seen young deacons lose their heads after speaking their minds, securing their own graves through political ostracism. Ironically, he'd only witnessed the act of church discipline once: under Brother Levin. And that hadn't been pretty. Not long after, members of notable power had springboarded their own platform calling for

Brother Levin's resignation, and just like that, church politics had sown and reaped aplenty.

If church strife wasn't enough, Waymon's aging flesh was declining. Besides depression and bickering, gas and bloating incessantly plagued him, emanating inside his bowels like nocuous chemicals. It had been worsening in past weeks. He chewed calcium carbonate tablets like candy, and just before the meeting he'd downed almost half a bottle of Pepto-Bismol.

The preacher was fifteen minutes late.

"Are we gonna wait on him any longer?" Brock Hennington, a broad-shouldered man, asked in a blunt voice. Like B. L. Sherwood, he worked in the oil field, measuring and testing wells and derricks.

"I say we just go ahead and begin," Carol Tinsley said, "and if he shows up, more power to us." The others laughed in agreement.

"Amen," Waymon said.

Brother Tisdale hadn't shown up for the last meeting of the missions committee. Waymon knew the pastor had graced the finance committee's palaver; he'd overheard Rick Pettibone talking of the changes Tisdale wanted to make in the budget, of views and goals he had laid out before the committee members.

Some of the changes were already taking place.

A new member named Dan Bearden had taken over the chair of the nominating committee, and he was already busy recruiting members—most of them new, like himself—to the various committees. Waymon had met him once or twice. The man's eyes were cold blue and rigid even with the smile he added, and his handshake was firm enough to crunch your knuckles into broken leaves. And to think such a person was recommending people to positions of prominent authority and responsibility …

Seth Weimer, another new face, had assumed a seat on the finance committee. Waymon meant to ask Rick Pettibone about it last Sunday, to find out whether he'd stepped aside or bolted from the committee altogether, but Rick hadn't been in church. Waymon couldn't remember when the proprietor had missed a Sunday. He only knew that Seth Weimer had somehow ascended the political ranks. Waymon took note of Dan and Seth talking to Brother Tisdale as if the three had formed a fraternity or tied some furtive kind of political knot.

The metamorphosis of new leadership possessed a ubiquitous nature—it spread to every cobwebbed corner and corridor. The faces and hands of ushers had changed. The service itself was undergoing a gradual face-lift. An ostentatious contemporary format replaced the traditional, with the words to hymns flashing on high overhead monitors and a half dozen singers accompanying Craig McManes. Tisdale had broken up many of the Sunday school classes. Men and women were paired now in the same class, although some of the older classes like Waymon's flouted the restructuring and continued to meet.

Recently, Waymon saw a Crown of Thorns Baptist television commercial. The witty piece centered around the Bible, although it was at first referred to as "The Handbook," something everyone needed to read to get through life in one piece.

Cleverly done, Waymon had thought. *How much money did it take to contract it out? How much more money does it take to air it? Who approved it? I don't remember the church voting on it.*

At the end of the ad, an amethyst sign with white outlines flashed toward the screen's center, accompanied by an adjacent white cross, along with the narrator's voice: "CTBC: A Real Church for the Real World."

More like a Real Worldly Church, Waymon thought. *What's with this CTBC business? Sounds like a television station.*

Waymon sat with resentment but pressed on, conducting the meeting of the lone committee he chaired. He wondered what could be more important than missions. Wasn't that what Christianity hinged on—reaching out to the hungry, those in despair? What did Jesus do during his thirty-three years on earth? Thinking of this eased the noose of his resentment.

"We got a call from the women's battered shelter, or is it the battered women's shelter?" he said to the ring of laughter. "I'm sorry, I get them confused sometimes." He scratched his curly hairs, dry and itching on his scalp. "Thing is, they're just about out of clothes. At least the kind you can wear without getting stopped by the police. Is it all right if we give them some from our clothes closet?"

Everyone consented.

Chapter 18

Vicki finished proofing the church program for Sunday's services and, for one of the few times that day, left the desk to hand her work to Craig McManes in his office. When she came back, Brother Tisdale was waiting, collar loosened, hair losing its thin texture, his tall frame reaching far above her like a daunting skyscraper. For the first time in his tenure, he wasn't wearing a tie. His blue irises swam with a gelatin of coarseness.

She had seen his moods swing like a pendulum in the past week. Apparently, the honeymoon period was over. She and Craig had engaged him in what she took for jovial Southern conversation, frequently talking for thirty minutes at a time while the screen on her computer blackened and went into sleep mode. Lately, however, the pastor's speech shot out in terse machine-gun raps.

He stood over her desk. He wasn't smiling.

"Vicki, could you look over these," he said. It wasn't a question. He handed her a memo and a letter, gazing into her eyes as they made the exchange. Why was he looking at her like that? Did her eyes hold a message for him? "I'll need those in a couple hours, if you don't mind." He wrestled a smile, then went back into his office and closed the door.

Nothing dealing with finances seemed to cross her desk anymore, as it had during the interim and at times during Brother Levin's reign when he'd been careless. She was wearing out the seat of a new chair, nesting for long hours in front of the computer, answering the phone, and jabbing the hold button so she could check if Brother Tisdale was busy. Anymore, she was half afraid to take a break, fearing Brother Tisdale might order her back to her desk. When she absolutely had to leave the chair, bones stiffening and creaking, she wandered to the corner opposite Craig's office and checked the fax machine, her remaining solace.

She perused the papers in her hands. The letter would be the first item church members saw when the bulletin arrived in their mailboxes, with a picture of Brother Tisdale embedded like that of a newspaper columnist. As she read it, Vicki acknowledged the same generous tone, amicable and loquacious, he had used with her during his first week in office. In the letter, he welcomed new members, explained that he had moved into his new house, situated himself in Dallas, and ignited a fireworks display of optimism for Crown of Thorns Baptist's future.

The other item, a memo, would only go out to deacons and committee members. It was reasonably short and to the point but, like the letter, full of hope. It read:

Dear CTBC Deacons and Committee Members,
First of all, let me say how sorry I am not to
have been able to attend some of your meetings.

Some of you have gone out of your way to accommodate my schedule, and I feel it is you whom I may have disappointed the most, and I apologize with all of this aging pastor's heart. My time has been consumed by unexpected events and business emergencies. I've been terribly busy moving in and putting the finishing touches on the overall transition from my home in Oxford. As soon as I bought my new house in Dallas, a nice young couple expressed an interest to buy my house in Oxford, and we've been ironing out the details with my real estate agent, and finally closed the deal just a day or two ago.

I have also spoken to some of you concerning our church's future. Our building is quite old and has had little or no remodeling in the past thirty years. In addition, its location may not serve the same purpose it did when Dallas was a young growing city and Mesquite a booming suburb. I realize I haven't been here but four weeks, but through talking and meeting with many of you, and from meeting those in our congregation, as well as fellow pastors of sister churches, I think we have to seriously consider where, in terms of location, our church would best be suited for the future. If we would be better equipped to carry out God's plan for Crown of Thorns Baptist Church elsewhere, I believe we should take on that responsibility. Building a new church requires the commitment of David and Solomon and a strong arm of faith, but believe me, if we follow God's plan for us, He will make up the difference. For now, I would ask each of you to pray about this matter, as well as any others you can think of regarding our church's welfare, and that the Lord might answer us in due time.

Your pastor and brother in Christ,
Owen Tisdale

There were no mistakes—grammar, spelling, or otherwise—in the letter. The paper itself was of a fine quality bond. Vicki thumbed it down, took a deep breath, and closed her eyes, hoping that when she opened them she would be back in the friendly office environment she had known for years. When she opened them, however, she saw that her hopes were as thin as the onionskin pages of her Bible.

Chapter 19

Curt lay on the bed, on his stomach, half hypnotized, half asleep. His jeans were still on but his shirt was off. Dressed in her ivory gown, wearing a couple sprays of Coty musk, Andrea sat on him, rubbing his back. The tender smile that lit her face came from two sources: seeing that the wax-on/wax-off motion with which she squeezed Curt's muscles relaxed him, and remembering the look on his face when she'd shown him her hand the morning after she sliced it.

He had never taken the Lord's name in vain until then.

"My God," he'd said, looking at her with the blank face of an inbred. "How did it …?"

She laughed at the image of his goon-faced curiosity. All the stories her mother had told him of her childhood miracles had resurfaced in that moment, and he spent the next two or three days brooding over the possibilities.

He appeared to have accepted it—unless, of course, he had dismissed it entirely—and had begun asking for backrubs before bed. When she complied, it numbed him into a trance. He fell asleep, and she ended up pulling off his jeans and muscling him onto his side of the bed. He hadn't been popping his back or neck or complaining of any discomfort since.

A fiddle from a Dixie Chicks song was playing from the small radio in the middle of the headboard.

Curt's shoulder jerked gently, and when Andrea moved her hand between his spine and shoulder blade, she felt the muscle there twitching. The muscle on the opposite side of his neck was doing the same, as was a large one in his lower back. Occasionally a bone popped as the muscles around it relaxed. She hoped she was helping and not hurting, and deep inside, beneath her secular perceptions, she knew she was. But the questions and unfamiliarity she had of life, herself, and her relationship and responsibilities to both remained a significant wound, her own spear in the side.

When she went to bed that night, her dreams spoke of youth, health, and remembrance.

She lay in the hospital, legs straddled and elevated. Beads of sweat slivered down her forehead and face. She was hyperventilating, sweating as if stuck inside an oven, breathing as if there wasn't enough air. She and Curt had already decided to name the child Elizabeth; the sonogram had determined it was a girl. And from what Andrea felt, it was going to be a big girl.

"Ohh!" she groaned, fighting the buildup of fluid in her eyes and what felt like a bellyful of watermelon. "Can't you give me something?"

"Honey, they're doing what they can," Curt said from her side. He had been holding her hand—the one opposite her arm with the IV—but

now she let go, determined to squirm and fidget. She didn't want anyone to hold her hand, not when she was in this much pain; you can't stay still while you're dying—or at least not when you feel as if you're dying.

The pain, digging and stabbing, the scalpel of flesh and bone.

Vague voices of nurses, doctors. Something about pushing and breathing.

Curt's voice: "You gotta push, Andrea. She isn't gonna come out by herself. Come on, honey. It hurts everybody."

Andrea closed her eyes, looked into the depths of blackness where everything—even the pain—stood still, and thought she might lose herself there. She felt the tears near the corners of her lips. One slipped inside her mouth, and she tasted it, the salt on her tongue, and the pain reared its head like one of the beasts in Revelation.

Lord, it's too much for me, *she thought.* Please, God, give me something I can handle.

"God, please make it stop," she pleaded.

Then, as if the sky opened and billowy clouds smothered her with precipitous sap, the pain evanesced. The pressure remained, pressing from her belly across her lower abdomen. But the stabbing had retreated.

Her breathing slowed, and with her free arm she wiped the perspiration from her forehead. She looked up at the nurse.

"What'd you give me?" she asked.

"We didn't give you anything, babe," the nurse answered.

She began to relax, but she heard Curt's voice, seemingly closer than before: "Honey, are you pushin'?"

The mass in her belly pulled her flesh with it toward the smaller opening. Aside from the bucket of water that had gushed out earlier, however, she didn't sense the blood that streamed out in rivulets, dampening, staining the clothes that had been white minutes before. She constricted her deadened muscles, tensing in her lower abdomen, and pushed with what reserves she had left.

After five minutes of this, the baby emerged on her own, bathed in her mother's blood.

Oxygen opened up her arteries, her lungs expanded and inflated, giving her the first breath of life. She blossomed into being. As if in summation, she screamed her first voice in the world, crying of her entrance, her existence.

Chapter 20

As had been the case every year of his life, Waymon didn't know where else to go to push the world off his shoulders. So he went to his mother's.

Inside, the TV was off. Above it the blinds were closed, but still, tendrils of light trickled in. She had been reading—she liked mysteries. A Mary Higgins Clark paperback was sprawled on its open belly along the arm of her recliner, tanning in the haze. A glass of iced tea perspired on the lamp table. It was noon. Hot, dry, and humid. Waymon, decked in denim overalls, settled for a Coke; despite his protests, Mozelle fetched it from her refrigerator, serving him as she always had.

"You don't have to wait on me, Momma," he said. He started to get up. "I'm old enough to get it myself, don't you think?"

"Well, I don't have anythin' better to do," she said, heading toward the refrigerator. "You've always been a blessing to me." Her voice was nearly drowned out as if coming from a tunnel. She came back and handed him the drink.

"You think so?" Waymon asked, expression bordering between smile and frown. "Man ..."

Mozelle gaped before sitting down. "Always did have to clean your mouth out, though."

"It's deeds that count," he said. "Not words."

"I hear ya," she said, sitting gently.

"Like this dadgum governor of ours," he said. "Frying more folks than McDonald's does burgers."

"Yeah, well, they's bad people, anyway."

"They're charred people now," he argued.

He paused to open his Coke. Took a drink. Looked into the guest room. Caught the traces of magnolias embroidered on the bed's quilt. He had stood at the dresser, glaring at the nickel his father had given him. His father stood behind him. *That's yours,* he had said. *Ain't nobody tell you what to spend it on.* He felt his father rubbing up against him in his jeans. He didn't know what to think. He twitched, caught his breath. *Anytime I want it, you gonna give it.* His father never went further than this. Waymon never quite knew what the old man was talking about, either. Only, the thought of the elder man pressing against him from behind infected him with nausea.

He quickly turned to Mozelle, as if having forgotten something important. "So how you been?"

"I been okay," she said. "Got this little achin' in my hip." She slapped the thigh of her bad hip. "Givin' me some trouble." She looked away.

"You call the doctor?" Waymon asked, face glowing. It was difficult hearing her complain of pain, even though she'd complained before and nothing had been wrong. He couldn't stand the thought of his mother suffering.

"No, I ain't callin' them," she said. "All they do to old people is stick needles in 'em."

"Some of them needles are good for you."

"Oh, I'd just rather put up with it, I guess," she said, laughing it off. Her eyes looked tired.

"I'd rather you didn't," he said. And now the thought of his mother dying frightened him, stirring in his mind the possibilities of fear, dread, and depression. Her smile dissolved into his look of concern, and she took a drink of her tea.

"How the church goin'?" she asked.

Waymon leaned back into the sofa's backrest, buoyed by its malleable cushions.

"I don't know," he said, each note falling.

Mozelle's face morphed into a frown. "What do you mean you don't know?"

Waymon laughed from her sudden change of expression.

"What are you laughin' at?" she said, trying to hold the frown, but failing.

His own face sobered up a bit.

"I tell you," he said, shaking his head twice, gradually, in a swaying motion. "Guess I'm just getting old."

"Well what about me!" Mozelle quipped. "You still got better sense than most folks."

"I don't know," he said. "These young folks are a lot different than I ever was."

"That's the Devil's 'I' standin' in the way of your service," Mozelle said. "They ain't no different than you were at that age. Not most of 'em, anyway. You gonna get some bad butts in any church, you know."

"Yeah, I guess so," he said.

"So what's botherin' ya?" she asked. "You as bad as you were a few weeks ago." Waymon fidgeted. "Quit actin' like a dummy and tell me what you really feel."

For a second he reminisced of his youth, reminded of the old woman as matriarch, of her power and the discomfort that came at suppertime if he'd acted up in school or church.

"Well, I figure you know most of what's on my mind," he said, focusing on the hands in his lap. "This pastor done some pretty unscrupulous things right in front of my eyes. Like he's laughing at me or something. Didn't I tell you about him?"

"You told me," Mozelle said.

"You don't suppose … you reckon a preacher—even a good preacher—can do Satan's bidding?"

Mozelle sipped her tea. "I seen him *own* preachers, boy, and I ain't talkin' up a storm. Devil's more powerful than any of us know. But so is God. When God came here on this earth in the flesh, He still beat the Devil every time they fought. Knocked his butt out."

Waymon laughed. He turned serious again, perturbed by the philosophical possibilities.

"But can the Devil corrupt someone who's doing the Lord's work?" Waymon asked.

"You know God can do anything He wants," Mozelle said. "Now, the Devil can do anything he wants, as long as God don't jump in and stop him. Or unless God gives someone the power to stop him."

The tandem of Mozelle's dark eyes and his awareness that they were discussing the Devil made Waymon break eye contact and look away at the TV, which he wished had been turned on that second, drowning out the silence. Just talking about such likelihoods sent cold tremors along his spine, even in the heat. He reckoned it was time to check his mother's air conditioner.

Chapter 21

Owen Tisdale indulged in house calls.

He sat on the brand-new sofa at Jim and Carrie Sherwood's home, occasionally drumming his fingers along his Bible or knee. Judging from the smell, the rest of the furniture was fairly new as well. Something had been cooking in the kitchen. Pasta, meat, and sauce: spaghetti.

Jim's father, B. L., had asked the pastor if he wouldn't mind talking to Jim and Carrie's son, Matt, about salvation, seeing as the boy wanted to profess his faith, walk the aisle, and get baptized—not necessarily in that order.

Skinny and awestruck, Matt slumped over the seat in bad posture, fingers interlocked. Either he wasn't getting enough calcium or his body wasn't taking it up properly.

"Matt, I understand you've made a decision," Owen said, knees angled slightly toward the boy's.

"Yes," Matt said carefully.

"What have you decided?"

Matt glanced at his mother, then tried to look into the

preacher's eyes, past the intimidating suit.

"I want Jesus to come into my heart," Matt said.

"Have you asked Him to?" Owen asked.

Another glance at his parents, this time at his father, who looked on with timid support.

"Yes," Matt said.

"And did He?"

The boy's lips hung an inch apart as he looked to his parents for help. "I think so."

"Good," Owen said, feigning concern, eyes heavy. He floated his hand on the boy's shoulder, which felt like a plastic ball joint. "You know, Matt, you don't have to do this. No one's making you walk down the aisle on Sunday. Do you understand that?" Matt nodded. "How old are you?"

"Seven," Matt said, eyes frozen, as if looking inside the mouth of a great white shark.

Owen swallowed. *Seven,* he thought. *Elizabeth Cormieaux is seven. This turd won't walk the aisle. One less runt in the baptistery.*

"Matt, you have plenty of time to make this decision. We want you to be sure so that in the future you don't have any doubts. Does that make sense?"

Matt nodded. He looked down at his clammy hands.

"You think he needs to wait?" Carrie asked.

"I don't think it would hurt," Owen said. "I think he'd be better off having a firm understanding of what it is he's doing and committing to. It's something people Matt's age have to ask themselves. But let's give it some time." He put his arm around Matt and massaged the other side of his neck, smiling. "Okay, bud?"

A streak of a smile formed on Matt's face, then burned out like a shooting star.

⸺⬦⸺

The youth were having a lock-in at the church. Owen dropped by after meeting with the judge at Texas Baptist Seminary. He wore jeans and a T-shirt and smiled and laughed as much as he could.

They sat on the fellowship hall floor. Lisa Etheridge, the youth director, looked the part in jeans and a beige T-shirt and as she spoke she swayed side to side and her breasts bounced. Owen stared. *The things I could do with her,* he amused himself.

Chance Bateman, a slender wide receiver on the Mesquite High sophomore football team, sat near the front next to Kimberly Stogner, his girlfriend of three months, a blonde whose body was more alluring than her face. She lay on her stomach with the bare midriff of her belly touching the cold floor, elbows propped up to her cheeks, listening to Lisa talk about self-esteem and peer pressure.

"Does it matter if someone calls you a Jesus freak?" Lisa was asking. Her eyes were green, a touch hazel. Her curves spoke in waves. Her hair, dark and silky, streamed behind her neck and terminated in a short ponytail at the large vertebrae. She often painted herself with heavy makeup, but tonight her face was clear and eclipsed the light from overhead.

Owen watched her. He could sense that she'd never been touched before.

"Feeling good about yourself radiates from inside," Lisa said. "Self-esteem comes from years of building a foundation within you. Your parents have been helping you build it since you were born. Your friends and mentors have also worked on it. But most important, as Christians, it should come from the relationship you have with God."

I wish this chick would shut up and put out, Owen thought, and in fifteen minutes she did at least shut up, giving him the floor.

"I want to talk about something that I'm sure all of you have on your mind right now," he said. "Sex." Lisa slanted an eyebrow. Several youth sucked in a bottomless breath; pulses flitted. "The images crowd you," Owen continued. "You see them in school, TV, the movies, the mall. Each of you has physiological changes going on inside you that you can't ignore. I have some questions I want to ask you. Is sex the thrill or source of excitement that you think it is? Will it make your life better?" He paused a few seconds, grinning slightly, politely. "Is sex what you perceive it to be? Is it something you do casually with little thought at all, or does it have a higher purpose?"

Owen's words were drowned out by the thoughts he threw at them on a different plane. Some perceived them as auras; others heard them as clear directives. *Forget about what Lisa said for a moment. At your age right now, whether you're thirteen or seventeen, the most important thing for you to build is self-esteem. I'll agree with that. Without it, you're dead as a dog in quicksand. You owe it to yourself to feel as good about your life as you possibly can. In fact, get as much self-esteem as you can. Go after it. Seize the opportunity.*

He preached to Chance: *Don't be a wuss! There's cherry pie right in front of your face, and you're passing it to that dimwit next to you.*

Chance looked on his other side. Ben Peacock was either scratching the inside of his nostril or fishing for the biggest, greenest bass this side of Texas. Chance looked away in disgust, back to Kimberly. He thought of her smooth, flat belly.

Later that night—or actually during the early hours of the next morning—Chance Bateman crawled into Kimberly Stogner's sleeping bag, zipped it up, and claimed a prize he believed he and only he deserved.

During the Sunday service after the offering, in a little altar meeting of toddlers called children's church, Owen sat on the steps speaking in the softest voice he knew. He held his surprise object in a paper bag, cupping it with both hands, baiting innocent suspense. The flea microphone clipped to his suit caught the waves of sound, however faint and raspy, that were flung from the wet lips of the young.

"How are y'all doing this morning?" he asked the children.

"Good," half of them said.

"Fine," the other half said, mostly in shrills.

The children slouched around the grandfatherly man, knee over knee, along the steps, limber flesh in toddler tank tops, tender bones in dresses, young boys in suits: little people dressed for a big service. Owen noticed one boy in particular, whose curly brown hair and eyes bore more pleasant semblance than the rest.

Wesley Cormieaux lingered on the second step, occasionally swinging his chin to the side like a self-propelled Christmas ornament. His mother had brought him into the service for this portion alone, and Owen could feel her presence in the service, as well as that of the young girl; the mother sitting in the third row to his left, the girl at his feet. He could feel the warmth of Andrea's body, the bright light of her spirit, the density of her hopes.

Melissa Norris had confided to Andrea during Sunday school how she had begun bringing her little girl—like Wesley, also three—into the service for children's church, and Andrea decided to give it a try.

"You all look so handsome and pretty this morning," Owen said. "Most of you are wondering what I have in this paper bag. Is that right?"

One boy sprang to his feet and said, "Yeah!" The others echoed with less exclamation.

"Guess what I have in here," Owen said.

"A rabbit!" the same boy said.

"No, it's not a rabbit," Owen said patiently. It took only a second to look at the little boy, Wesley, son of the traiter, bewildered and taciturn, and lock eyes with him. In this short time he swam in the boy's thoughts, because it was so easy; the boy's mind and soul were so welcoming to alien thoughts and feelings and desires, and Owen implanted his favorite tune and lyrics:

Deep and wide, deep and wide
There's a fountain flowing deep and wide
Wide and deep, wide and deep
There's a fountain flowing wide and deep.

A chubby girl raised her hand.

"Yes," Owen said, pointing to her.

"A toy?" she said.

"No, ma'am," Owen said. "It's not a toy."

The next look into Wesley's eyes planted his message: *Hi, little buddy. Didja know a woman's tummy is yummy?*

Wesley saw an image of a woman's thin, bare stomach, oval navel in the center, lying over the natural slope.

Didja know your momma's got a yummy tummy. You'd like to do something to it, wouldn't you? You'd like to take a knife and stick it there, wouldn't you? I know you would. That's a good little buddy.

"A hamster," a blond boy said quickly.

"No," Owen said laughing. "I'm afraid not. I don't think I could keep a hamster in the bag, either." The people in the front rows found this funny, and a few women from the middle section offered a giggle or two.

Directly in front, inches away from his foot, the girl with the golden hair sat, her smooth face genteel and unwavering. Her eyes showed no fear. Owen recognized that look. Steeled in the blue hue of her irises was a resiliency, even something of animosity; she could do someone harm and, unlike her mother, feel little or no remorse.

"It's clay," Elizabeth said, looking into the preacher's eyes.

"How did you know that?" Owen said in his playful demeanor. "Have you been looking in here?"

Watching from her seat, Andrea wondered the same thing despite the revulsion she felt from the pastor's teasing voice.

The question burned out quickly as Elizabeth refused to answer, and Owen pulled the clay out of the bag, a rectangular slab of gray, then one of white. "Now, believe it or not, each of us is a lot like this piece of clay here. We can be molded and bent to a particular shape, like so." As his fingers worked, at first cleaving the clay in two, Owen quickly shaped a crude walking-stick version of a person. "That's not exactly what I wanted it to look like. Does that look like a person to any of you?"

"No!" said the loud boy, and Owen laughed with the children and parents.

"When you go home today," Owen said, "I'd like for you to think about the shape that God wants each of you to be. Let us pray."

After Owen prayed and dismissed the children, Wesley sat on the carpet in his daze, staring at the preacher, until Elizabeth pulled his arm and led him to their mother, who then took Wesley to the nursery.

Chapter 22

The next afternoon when Andrea was taking a nap, Wesley stumbled into the kitchen on his wobbly three-year-old legs, dressed in underwear and a Bugs Bunny T-shirt with an oval of drool drying down the center.

The seed of thought was knocking on the door like a fruit peddler asking if you wanted to buy what he had planted and picked, begging you to settle for his price, convincing you it was the sweetest and hadn't been contaminated by harmful pesticides. All night, dreams of blood had played in Wesley's head, rewound and played over and over. Pictures of a liquid he didn't understand, except that it came from inside a person and in the dream it was sweeter than anything he'd ever tasted, yet too sweet, too precious, to be tasted. He had to get ahold of that sharp silver object he'd seen in the kitchen, the one that showed his reflection when it was clean, and draw the red fluid from his mother, where everything else he'd known had come from.

He foraged near the cabinet as his little feet planked down beside the oven. Inside, he heard the voice of yesterday, of cold steel and male incrimination. *Did you know a woman's tummy's yummy?*

Mommy's a woman, Wesley. Take a knife and push it in her tummy. A woman's tummy's yummy. Next to the sink, the handle of the knife he wanted projected upward at an angle from a wooden cylinder, dull silver bisecting the slick wooden handle. *How can I get up there?* Those blue eyes roamed the kitchen and located a silver stepping stool leaning against the wall between the refrigerator and plastic trash box. As he walked toward it, he began singing the song that the preacher had given him, humming where he couldn't pronounce or remember the words.

> *Deet and wye, deet and wye*
> *Dare's a fountain foeing deet and wye*
> *Wye and deet, wye and deet*
> *Dare's a fountain foeing wye and deet*

He grabbed the stool with nimble hands, dragged it next to the sink, worked his way up the steps. His insides squirmed with anticipation. Leaning over, he squeezed his hand around the knife's handle and pulled the blade slowly out of the cylinder and clambered back down.

In Andrea's bedroom, Elizabeth leaned over her mother, who slept on her side facing away from the younger blonde, and shook her shoulder. Andrea rolled over slowly, eyes squinting, face red.

"What is it?" she moaned.

"Mom, Wesley's in the kitchen doing something bad," Elizabeth said, eyes wide.

"What's he doing?"

"He's trying to get a knife," Elizabeth said.

"What?" Andrea asked. "Why would … are you sure?"

"Yes, I'm sure," Elizabeth said, taking two steps toward the door. "You better hurry, Mom."

"I'm coming," Andrea said in a chiding voice, pushing off the mattress and pillow, giving the girl a scowl. Her hands were a little clammy, her lower back a little stiff, strands of hair knotted in back, pinching her scalp.

She walked into the hallway, Elizabeth trailing several steps behind. She heard the singing.

"Wesley!" she called as she passed the bathroom. "What are you singing, honey?"

Andrea entered the kitchen, only slightly concerned. When she turned the corner of the refrigerator, Wesley was waiting in front of it, smiling. Before she could make sense of anything, he reached up and plunged the knife four inches into her unguarded stomach. She doubled over, dropped to her knees, where she lay gasping for breath and understanding.

From the edge of the hallway, Elizabeth's scream careened into a deadening squeal.

The blood, wet and rancid and sticky: her own. Andrea looked down at her midsection, at her red-stained hands shielding her sliced stomach, pressuring it. She couldn't remember so much blood filling her hands.

Chapter 23

The Saint Mary's ICU brewed an aseptic smell like its common predecessor, the emergency room, but before Curt could walk all the way inside, the ER doctor on duty, a short, well-built black man with silver-rimmed glasses, motioned him outside. Curt had been called at work while out in the field checking a gas line. Wesley was confined to a room on the second floor. Elizabeth told Curt what had happened, and he had been patient with the staff so far.

Now, an hour later, the doctor in front of him was leading him away from the door.

"How's she doing?" Curt asked.

The doctor nodded. "She's fine. I was a little worried when she came in. The wound was pretty deep. But she coagulated nicely, and we didn't have a problem controlling the bleeding. It will be awhile before she comes out of the anesthesia. She'll be lightheaded."

"Thank you," Curt said.

"No problem."

The door opened, a pencil-thin nurse exited, and it closed before

Curt could get a good look inside. The nurse smiled. Curt looked around, then turned back to Elizabeth.

"Honey," Curt said, "why don't you go get a soda?"

"Okay," Elizabeth said. "I need some money."

Curt dug into his pockets, pulled out three quarters and a dime.

"That enough?" he asked. The fluid rose in his eyes.

"Yes," she said, taking the change into her palm, feeling the clamminess of his. She seemed unfazed by everything, as if she half expected the series of events. When she was ten steps away, with a hop in her step, Curt looked back. He swallowed.

"Wait," he said. "I better come with you."

The first sense Andrea involuntarily made use of was hearing.

"Thanks for coming, Brother Waymon," a voice said.

She waded in and out of the haze, murmurs fragmenting by.

"She's supposed to wake up soon?" A black man's voice asked, gentle and unassuming.

"That's what the doctor said."

"Do you mind my asking where the boy's at?"

"They got him in a room upstairs."

"How's he doing?"

"I went up there an hour ago. He seemed okay to me."

"I wonder what got into him."

"I have no honest idea, Brother Waymon."

After the voices—one of which she was sure was Curt's— came the pain, at first dull, in the center of her abdomen. Then the paranoia and delirium of anesthesia. Shapes clamored into focus: the golden fog of the square light above, the white haze of the walls, the television and IV pack suspended from the stand. Everything fading slowly into focus, then remitting, oblique and blurry, with round edges. A fun house of pain.

"It's in the Lord's hands, Brother Curt."

"I believe it. Doctor said there wasn't much bleeding for as deep as it was."

"It that right?"

"That's what he said. I asked him why she was still in ICU, and he said it's just a precaution."

"I don't know why any of this happened, but the Lord knows. He's gonna take care of your family."

The pain pricked her more precisely, not even an inch above and to the left of her navel. She gasped, and then realized afterward she must have made something of an "uhh" sound, almost a moan.

"Daddy, she's awake," Elizabeth said.

Warm, small fingers grabbed Andrea's hand, the pain subsided, and she moved her head to the side to see her daughter.

"Hi, Mommy," Elizabeth said. Her blonde hair was a little stringy from the long wait, her eyes red underneath.

"Hi, baby," Andrea said.

Curt was at her other side.

"Honey, how you feeling?" he asked.

She turned to him and smiled.

"Sore," she said.

He brushed some of the hair over her forehead with his hand and moved his palm over her cheek.

"They giving you enough painkillers?"

"Yeah," she said, and glanced at the IV pouch. As she turned toward Elizabeth, she saw bits of maroon-colored blood caked on her own fingernails and fingers.

"Where's … where's Wesley?"

"He's on the second floor," Elizabeth blurted.

"He's okay," Curt said.

Andrea's eyes welled up as her breathing labored, and she grabbed the sheets with her right hand.

"How could he … ?" she began, staring straight ahead, at nothing in particular.

Curt moved closer, laid his hand on her shoulder. "Don't think about that, honey. Just get some rest."

Elizabeth moved forward and looked her mother in the eyes, her oval spark of blue so intense Andrea felt compelled to meet her gaze.

"Wesley couldn't help it, Mom," Elizabeth said. "Brother Tisdale told him to."

"What?" Andrea said.

Curt ushered Elizabeth aside. "Mommy needs to rest, honey," he said.

Elizabeth struggled against his guard. "Brother Tisdale told him to do it during church. I heard him! He told him on the steps!" Curt pulled her back more forcefully, but only as a father would his own flesh. "He told him on the steps!"

"Wait for me outside, honey," he told the girl.

Staring ahead, searching for sense, Andrea turned to Curt and said, "Who's that man outside?"

"Brother Waymon," he answered. "From church."

"From church," she said, the dope stretching her already-weakened voice, her eyes closing briefly.

"You remember him, don't you?"

Yawning, she opened her eyes. Outside, Waymon was talking to Elizabeth, who appeared gleefully preoccupied with whatever conversation they were having.

"He's a nice man," Andrea said.

"You feel like talking to him?" Curt asked.

"Yes," she said. "Tell him to come in."

Curt walked toward Waymon and whispered something to him, and the man came inside. He stood just a foot behind where Curt had stood a moment before, hands folded in front of him, wearing a humble look of concern. He leaned closer with his face, eyes intense and full of faith.

"Hi, Andrea," he said keenly.

"Hi." A gentle, labored mutter.

"I don't know if you remember me," he said. "I probably look like some old funny-looking man you ain't never seen before."

"I remember you," she said.

"You sure you feel like talking, because I can come back later if—"

"No," she said. "Don't go. I'd like to talk to you."

"God bless you. It's my pleasure."

Waymon began with the usual: How did she feel? Was she too tired or in too much pain to talk? Were the doctors taking good care of her so far?

Then a void of silence followed, and Andrea sighed, closed her eyes, and glanced with disdain at the IV bag.

"My goodness, I don't know what's happening," she said, looking ahead. "My son's three. Only three ..."

Waymon narrowed his eyes. He'd seen Andrea at church several times during and after the service, as the influx of members flowed— often in small caravans—from their Sunday school classes to the auditorium. He'd never really had a lengthy conversation with her, but he'd done what he could to make her, her husband, and their two children feel welcome and had taken time to compliment Elizabeth. On a few occasions he'd sensed a humble disposition about Andrea; he knew she was wrenching through an adjustment phase, something more profound than the simple transplant from Lake Charles to Dallas, and it was a difficult, painful matrix for her.

"You know, I don't know what all's going on in your life right now," he said. "And it ain't none of my business anyhow, but I know something other than the pain's bothering you. My soul is scarred up from some things happened to me when I was a kid." He glanced at his shoes. "My dad used to drink, and when he did he sometimes felt like hitting something. That something was me. I never thought I'd get away from it, but I guess about junior high I got old enough to outgrow his hand, and I thanked the Lord for delivering me."

Andrea had folded her hands limply across her belly as he'd said this, holding them there as much as resting them, though the added pressure on her stomach might be too much.

"The pain doesn't bother me so much now—not like when I first woke up," she said. "Or maybe I'm just saying that because of the painkillers in my blood." She looked first at the IV bag suspended beside her, then across to Waymon, whose smile put her at ease. "Nurse told me they kill each other on the street for this stuff."

Waymon held his silence, fixing his smile into a softer grin, and let her talk.

"I worry about my children," Andrea said swallowing.

"Uh-huh," Waymon replied.

"I don't know if you'll believe me or not," she said, glancing at him, then back to her hands, "but when I was a girl, I could heal people. With my hands. In Louisiana they called me a *traiter*. Means 'healer' in French." She looked at him steadily, noticing his fervent, narrow eyes. Were they signs of age or distrust? "Too crazy?"

"No no," Waymon said. "God gives some people this power."

She smiled.

"I was seven or eight. When I got older, I started losing it. But lately something's been happening. I've started having dreams. The dreams are real, you know? And I've had these … visions, or something. I don't know what they are."

"What do they show you?" Waymon asked.

"I'm not sure," she said, more weakly now. "They're shaped like people. But they're not people. They're on another planet or something. They're fighting." She paused, looking into Waymon's eyes, letting him dwell in hers as well. "And I only see these things when Brother Tisdale's preaching. I can't stand to hear his voice, you know. It makes me sick, literally."

The old man's hands shook, and he looked away. The memory of Brother Tisdale's startling him on the altar steps resurfaced like something rancid he had eaten. The preacher's blue eyes, cold and fluid and full of a foreign power. No man could convey such a presence.

"Sweet Jesus," he said.

"I don't know why," she said, "but I think he made my son do this to me."

Waymon was prepared for this news and regained his composure. Losing it, he knew, would only make Andrea feel more vulnerable. Plus he felt Andrea was stronger—more powerful, even—than she gave herself credit for.

"You know," Waymon said, in a steady voice, "God sometimes asks us to do things we don't want to do or things we don't think we have the power to do. I don't know specifically what His role is for you, but I think you're a special young woman, and God has an important role for you in this church. Before long, it's gonna be a pretty important one. I don't know what it will be. But there's souls at stake here, and one way or another, the Devil has come into our congregation. I want you to know I love you in Christ, and He's gonna take care of you through this no matter what happens."

Waymon watched as the assurance settled into her conscience, and she closed her eyes and gave in to a peaceful sleep.

Chapter 24

She remembered the quaint smell of dusty mahogany and trampled carpet, the scratched and scarred pews, the decaying backrests of choir seats. She remembered the circular white light above the pulpit, and how, from time to time, one section of it flickered, and at other times went out altogether. She remembered faces, round and warm, and hugs the same, and singing and sometimes clapping of soft hands. She remembered potlucks and baptisms ... backyard Bible school ... and Christmas carols.

But most of all, she remembered voices.

She heard them now.

"We can't bring them into this," the preacher said. "It would be too painful."

A small enclosed room. His chambers. Why was evil so comfortable in the Lord's house?

She saw Brother Hebert's face, darkened with false wisdom, a scintillating shine from chin to forehead, and eyes darker, quartz slabs that peered deeper than you wanted them to. He was talking to deacons or others—it didn't matter whom. His words didn't matter, either. But she could feel his intent, homed in on it as if this eclectic evidence had been in front of her all along, even as a child.

A voice said, "Aren't they members?"

"They're only children," the preacher said. "I sincerely believe they would be better off not being subjected to this meeting. There's no telling what they might see."

"Amen," came a voice.

Another voice: "Whatta ya mean, brother?"

"I don't like these meetings any more than you do," the preacher said. "The children won't have any idea what's going on except that the grown-ups are acting like children, and the parents are gonna be the ones telling them how to vote, anyhow."

"Amen."

In the preacher's heart, the bad place, aglow with fire.

Stomach contorting. A muscle squeezed her navel. Pulling. Pinching.

She opened her eyes.

Darkness.

She remembered.

A lamplight.

Was she gasping?

"Honey?"

Curt's voice.

He started to pat her stomach with sympathy, but he drew it away at the last second, remembering.

She looked at him as he leaned closer.

"Andrea?" he said. "You hurting?"

"Yeah."

Curt disappeared and a minute later was handing her a glass of water and a Vicodin tablet. "Can you sit up?"

Exhaling, she pushed against the mattress with her palms and clinching her teeth a little, threw the Vicodin into her mouth and washed it down with two gulps. She stared at the opposite wall above her dresser. She was home.

"I thought about waking you up for your medicine, but you looked happier sleeping," he said. A gap of silence engulfed them, a strand of discomfort for Curt.

"You have another dream?" he asked.

After a second, she turned toward him.

"What was it about?" he asked.

"My old church's preacher."

More meds.

More dreams.

Revelations.

Her belly pinching. Stinging, as if by one of hell's little winged creatures.

She woke in darkness and reached for the light, which blinded her in the first few moments. She heard Curt's voice, which came and went like the wind, and occasionally, Elizabeth's voice. Had she heard Wesley's?

"Where's my baby?" she asked.

"Hospital. For observation."

She ate only bites of the food he gave her. Bites of what? Chicken? Steak? Cauliflower? She didn't care; it was all the same.

And when it was over, she turned out the light and climbed back through the tunnel into the dark void, which gave rise to her retroactive visions.

"Mommy, I don't want to go to Wal-Mart, I want to go to Kmart," Elizabeth whined from the backseat. Wesley was buckled beside her.

"Well, I'm going to Wal-Mart," Andrea said.

"Wal-maw," Wesley chimed in, smiling and slapping his hands. "Maw-meee."

"Elizabeth, don't start," Andrea said, capillaries flushing her face maroon.

The girl jerked her head away in protest, glaring out the window, reminding Andrea how much of a child she still was.

As she drove out along the gravelly dirt road, her first independent venture in the two weeks after she'd gotten out of the hospital, she couldn't help but look, incessantly, at the rearview mirror, at Wesley's blushing cheeks and beaming smile, and wonder what his intentions were, and if, perchance, he had any thoughts like the ones he had before, of long butcher knives and smiling steel.

"Mom!" Elizabeth said suddenly.

She had run off the road. The brakes jerked them all to a stop. Andrea closed her eyes.

"Sorry," she said slowly. She looked back at Elizabeth. Her daughter's eyes round with caution but not judgment. She backed out onto the road, put the vehicle in drive, and drove more slowly.

Once in town, she stopped at the post office to buy a book of stamps and mail some thank-you notes to friends who had visited her, sent her get-well cards, and cooked meals for the family. Pulling the back door open stretched the stomach muscles on her left side too tautly, forcing a grimace, and Elizabeth pushed it the remainder of the way open.

Seeing people again was a relatively new experience for her; looking them in the eye, one by one, trying to remember if she knew them or had met them once or twice before, and pensively considering their intrusions proved a task she hadn't prepared herself for. Did the short, balding man with silver hair and John Lennon glasses know her, or was he simply donning his Smile of the Year? Or was it Christmas season? She didn't think so.

Did the stocky brunette with silver-capped teeth seem familiar? Or the old woman walking with a cane, grinning? Did these people know what had happened to her, what she'd been through—at the hands of her toddler son, who was walking with her now?

Even the postal clerk—a woman with stringy mahogany hair, grainy skin, and a navy blue bow tie—seemed to regard her suspiciously, acting as if she were suffering an enema, incapable of a full smile. This, and the fact her two children were imitating spider monkeys, made Andrea reluctant to stay a second longer than necessary.

When they got back to the car, as she opened the backseat door for Wesley, Andrea saw Brother Tisdale walk into the post office.

She shoved Wesley into the seat, told Elizabeth to hurry up, and impulsively slammed her door while sliding behind the wheel.

The bank's main branch was only a couple blocks away, but Andrea wanted to put more distance between herself and the self-proclaimed godly man, so she drove, half enervated and recklessly, toward the northern bank branch closest to home.

"Mommy, why are we going so fast?" Elizabeth asked.

"Because the bank's a long ways away," Andrea said.

"But there's one over there," the girl said, pointing over her shoulder. "Did you see it?"

"This one's better," Andrea said.

"Why?" Elizabeth asked.

"Because it's close to home," Andrea said.

"A bank's a bank, if you ask me," Elizabeth said, looking out the window.

Too much TV, Andrea thought.

The car swerved a little, edging just over the striped yellow line. She quickly recovered, however, frightened at the prospect of crashing with her children, and straightened out in the right lane.

There were only a few customers in First National Bank of Dallas when she arrived: two bony old ladies in expensive dresses quacking with each other through lipsticked bills and a balding man in overalls evidently dropping off another load.

Andrea pulled the kids along to a counter opposite the old women, slung her purse on top, whipped out a pen and withdrawal slip, and filled in the blanks. Besides the other daily activities she struggled with, guiding the pen seemed a perilous task. She had to let go of Wesley's hand in the process, and halfway down the rectangular slip she noticed he'd wandered away. Elizabeth was close to her other side, near the end of the counter, looking for something of entertaining value—such as a TV—in the pretentious place.

Hollow with the worst motherly fear, Andrea saw Wesley standing next to Mr. Overalls at the counter, looking up to the man, whose head looked as big as a pumpkin, the little boy's eyes big with trust and the kind of wonder that would make Curious George proud.

"Well, hello there," Mr. Overalls said.

The clerk serving Mr. Overalls smiled.

Wesley smiled up at the big man, put his hand in his own mouth, took it out.

"Well, you're not very talkative, are you?" Mr. Overalls asked in a deep but surprisingly weak voice. His eyes shrank back into blue beads. "Hope you're not looking for money because I done give this purty woman everything I've got."

Wesley repeated the hand in the mouth, but pulled out more juice this time, which he wiped on his shirt. Mr. Overalls saw Andrea coming his direction.

"Here comes the cavalry," Mr. Overalls said. "One of us might be in trouble."

Andrea tried to smile at Mr. Overalls, but she seriously doubted if one came out—especially as she snatched Wesley's hand.

"Where do you think you're going, baby?" she said, guiding him back to the counter. "Stay by Mommy, Wesley. Don't go anywhere without me." Catching her breath again, she grabbed her purse and, children at her side, made her withdrawal at the window next to Mr. Overalls, who by now was tucking his wallet in his pocket, shifting his hips in a peculiar way that suggested he might be passing gas. He walked away.

While the clerk counted her money to her, Andrea heard a voice two windows to her left. A brew of nausea and panic stirred inside her. She tightened her hold on Wesley.

"I'd like to make a rather large withdrawal."

A sonorous voice, dressed with hospitality.

She looked surreptitiously to her left: glanced at Brother Owen Tisdale's profile. She swallowed. Retreated to the cashier. A panging between her ears.

She grabbed the money, did an about-face, and jerked her child's arms toward the exit.

Then she drove back into town to Albertson's grocery store and parked between large Dodge pickups where she hoped she couldn't be spotted. By now, spurned by coincidence, she thought it wouldn't matter. She looked over her shoulder, at the same time taking a deep breath, as the entrance doors opened for them.

She didn't bother to check prices. With Wesley sitting in the shopping cart's child seat, legs dangling, flailing, she wrapped up her shopping in fifteen minutes, a couple of times barking at Elizabeth to stay closer to her. Methodically, but repetitiously, the girl with blonde pigtails always came running or skipping or hopping back to her. The last item Andrea threw into the cart was a package of ground beef. Leaving the last aisle, Wesley yelled "Mommy!" and pointed to a side item—a vertical row of assorted Hot Wheels cars and trucks dangling from one of the shelves.

Andrea slapped him gently on the cheek. "You be quiet," she said with a scowl that, in addition to the pain, made him draw back his hand. Shocked more than hurt, his face contorted in toddler's agony. Andrea suspended her awareness of those around her and what they might think of a parent slapping a three-year-old in the face. You could be prosecuted for such acts in public, she realized afterward, but this was Texas, and more than likely they didn't mind if you punished your child in public, nor in such a manner.

The next moment she doubted herself. *I've spoiled him too long,* she admitted.

She thought about the day Wesley had stabbed her, remembered the very moment he shoved the honed steel into her stomach, and she wondered if slapping him just then in the grocery store hadn't been some small act of retribution (at least in an adult's eyes). *Am I angry at him for that? He couldn't have done that—that wasn't him. Elizabeth has to be right. It was the preacher. But how does she know?*

Wesley's wails sirened around the aisles, but Andrea did nothing to quiet him.

Elizabeth looked on in astonishment; her mother had never slapped her little brother in the face, and she had only taken a light tap once for shouting during the church service.

They proceeded, a young mother and her two children, toward the checkout, unable to meet the requirements of the 10 Items or Less Express Lane. Elizabeth hopped onto the cart's corner for a short ride as the basket slowed. Andrea lowered Wesley from the child seat.

The cashier, a thin, homely brunette with too much makeup, paused as a customer wrote a check, looked at Wesley and Elizabeth, and ushered an ardent smile. Another customer and cart stood in front of them. They waited a minute before the counter cleared and Andrea, with Elizabeth's help, piled the items before the UPC scanner. When they finished unloading the cart, Andrea pulled Wesley along, slung her purse onto the counter, pulled out her checkbook and pen, and started filling out the blank lines to save the next customer a minute. The cashier scanned and sacked the goods, canned vegetables and dairy products, in very little time, and Andrea handed her a check for just less than twenty dollars.

They headed toward the exit. Flinching, as well as disbelieving, Andrea saw what she at first thought was her mind's conjecturing of a recurring image: Owen Tisdale was gathering fruit in the produce section, tying a clear plastic bag of plums at the top.

She paused just long enough for the preacher to raise his head, divert his attention from the fruit, and glare at her, black eyed.

Chapter 25

As finance committee chairman, with funds to watch and new expenditures to review, Rick Pettibone didn't have time to attend his Adult II Sunday school class every Sunday morning. In his thirty years of Baptist upbringing, he'd heard all the stories anyway—from David and Goliath to Rahab's lies to Paul's epiphany—and there wasn't anything new. Some gossip, maybe, but the church crowd often bored him. What lounged in his conscience were business buyouts, bankruptcies, and ventures, and the ideal atmosphere to discuss these was the whirlpool in a friend's backyard. Of course, it didn't hurt if the friend was an executive like himself who knew the insides of deals and mergers and promotions.

At 9:20, he swiped a couple doughnuts and a cup of coffee from the fellowship hall, where Adult III and IV had their general powwow before splitting off into separate groups. He shook a couple hands, trying not to get tied into conversation, but did learn that Vicki Ainsworth was in the hospital, the result of a ten-car pileup on the freeway.

Once he got the full story, Rick barricaded himself at Vicki Ainsworth's desk in the general office complex. He sat there, blond hair sloping over one side of his forehead, in a fancy chair with bigger curves than a supermodel, looking over budget reports, purchasing invoices, and finally, transactions. He swiveled in the chair, scratched his itching scalp. The numbers couldn't be right, he thought; he hadn't seen so much shrinkage since he'd last washed slacks in hot water. He took a drink of coffee that was too dark for anyone to appreciate, folded his hands behind his head, and leaned back in Vicki's chair. He closed his eyes for a second, then opened them.

Owen Tisdale stood in front of him, clad in a black suit, topaz tie, and white shirt. He looked energized, as if, perhaps, this were his first day on the job, his Southern smile wide as any Salvation Army worker's: a pastor for all seasons and occasions.

"There he is," Rick said, trying to hide the fact he was a little startled, a skill he'd learned through owning his own business. He scooted forward. "How's it going, Brother Owen?" He leaned over and shook the stately man's hand, the warmest he'd touched that morning.

"Oh, not too bad, brother," the pastor said. "Just trying to hold down the fort." He laughed as he said this.

"That's a tough job," Rick said. "I guess you heard about Vicki."

"I don't know what we'll do," Owen said. "I can't find my way around without her." The preacher's eyes welled up, and he shook his head.

"You all right, Owen?" Rick asked.

"It's hard," the preacher said. "People like Vicki don't deserve to suffer."

Rick asked if he wanted to pray, and the preacher consented, bowing his head and listening to Rick plead for God's mercy and healing hand. When it came his turn, Owen prayed for five minutes and began coughing. When he ended in "amen," he patted Rick on the shoulder.

"She'll be back soon," the pastor said. He paused. "Rick, it's probably not my place to tell you this, and I really don't want to get involved in anything of the sort, but you're a close friend in Christ. You've helped me out a lot since I've been here, and I feel like somebody ought to tell you, even if it has to be me. There's a rumor going around—and I hate rumors, but you hear 'em—that someone's trying to remove you from your committees."

Rick perked up; his eyes narrowed with curiosity and surprise. "Is that right?" He grabbed his coffee cup and gulped down a half-ounce of the black gook.

"Yeah, and the guy making the dominoes fall," Owen said, rolling his tongue over his lower teeth and briefly looking down, "is B. L. Sherwood. This morning, I heard him talking to Dan Bearden and Luther about it in the fellowship hall, so now I'm sure it's true." Owen cleared his throat. Rick repositioned himself in the chair. "I've been debating whether or not to tell you because I sure don't want to incite anything, you know. But I'd rather you hear it from me than someone else.

"I know how important you are to this church, Rick, and if something does happen and you get bumped from a committee or two, I'm praying—as we speak—that you won't think anything of it, that you'll keep on blowin' and goin' every Sunday in the same manner you always come to church with and with the same service to the congregation you've always given."

Rick tried to smile. "Just a committee."

"You know B. L.," Owen said. "I know him. All I can ask you to do is think about forgiving him and letting whatever he has started come back around to him eventually. You don't have to be on a committee to serve God."

Rick looked half thoughtful, half like he'd been struck by a bowling pin. "It's not that big a deal."

"Let's just pray about it, okay?" Owen said. He reached over the desk, patted Rick on the shoulder, grinned a strained grin, and walked out.

Rick sat in the chair, staring at the wall. And thinking.

Stan Wilcox exited his Adult II class early, so he could gather the Sunday school attendance numbers and draft an outline for the worship service briefing. Everyone understood he had to do this, so his early departure never seemed rude.

He carried his black Stetson and plumped down on a hard metal chair in the Sunday school office, a parlor in the middle of the hallway separated by a counter and a large, thick white pillar. Beverly, the Sunday school secretary, had added the first numbers as they'd come in and now passed them on to him. He was etching out the bulletin when the preacher showed up, standing over the counter.

"Brother Stan the man," Owen said.

"Brother Owen," Stan said, standing up and shaking the preacher's hand. "How's it going?"

"The way it's supposed to on Sundays." They shared a laugh, and

Owen put his hands in his pants pockets. "Well, how'd we do this morning?"

Stan grabbed the attendance notebook, flipped through sharp cardboard pages that could slice your fingers if you weren't careful. "Three-sixty-four. Up fifteen from last week."

"The Lord sure is good to us, isn't He?" Owen said.

"You're telling me," Stan said. "We're about ready to shoot through the roof."

"This keeps up, God will give this church a new building," Owen said.

Stan didn't argue.

"Say, Stan, I've never been too good at this kind of thing," the preacher said. "You know Brother Atwood pretty good, don't you?"

"Probably not as well as some," Stan said cautiously. "I've been on some committees with him."

"I think he's good buddies with Brother Pettibone," Owen said with waning demeanor, looking at the ground. "Brother Bearden came to me the other day and said he'd heard Brother Atwood complaining about the direction of our Sunday school curriculum."

Stan raised his eyebrows.

"I've heard a couple other members talking about it too," Owen continued. "I guess Brother Atwood's been saying a little of this and that. Been saying we need better literature. Been criticizing some of the American Baptist Association pamphlets we have sitting out for visitors, how it should all be Southern Baptist materials, and so forth. Says we need to drop a lot of people off the enrollment, people who haven't walked inside the doors in two or three years. He claims your attendance counts are inflated."

"Inflated?" Stan said with a half smile, wondering, perhaps, what circus had come to town.

The preacher shook his head. "Apparently he's been talking." Owen gave a shrug of the shoulders. "And you know how talk is—it's the root of all evil."

Stan shook his own head, the last trace of smile dissolving into chagrin. "It really doesn't make much sense."

"It never does," Owen said. "People start getting brave with their personal inclinations, and the only thing that happens is someone gets hurt." He paused just long enough to see a slew of needles sink into the gentle cowboy's heart. "I shouldn't have even said anything."

"No, it's not that …"

"Don't worry about it, okay?" Owen said, putting a soft hand on Stan's shoulder.

"I won't," Stan said, and the preacher walked out.

Owen's sermon treaded countless points of view, tones, and unrelenting voices, calling out to those who sat listening patiently.

The voice Sarah Stogner heard swooped down from the pulpit among the guttural pronunciations of the preacher's sermon on Rahab.

"I know there are those of you who think Rahab sinned when she lied about the Israelites," Owen said, pausing while looking at the carpet in front of him. "Beloved, I tell you today, Rahab had never heard the Commandments preached to her. She'd never been taught the difference, in God's eyes, between right and wrong. Therefore, she could not have sinned. But when the Israelites told her about God, she believed, and by lying to the authorities about the Lord's servants' whereabouts, she saved their lives and saved her soul as well."

His gaze fixed on Sarah, eyes a cold cobalt, drawing her closer until, with a heart and mind ready to receive, she knew him to be speaking to her, and her only. He couldn't have been four rows and an altar away; more like four steps. Time stood like a Rushmore stone.

Kimberly's pregnant, Sarah, the preacher said. *Chance Bateman invaded her space at the youth lock-in. Yes he did. He zipped up the sleeping bag and had his way with her in the way that only married adults should.*

Sarah strained to look away, to break the hold of the voice that bound her, but she feared it was merely giving her slack as a predator would a smaller fish. She didn't comprehend the service, or anyone else around her, sitting or otherwise. She lowered her head, heart drumming, drugged to the brink of a blackout. Could she believe these things? Could her daughter be pregnant? And from a youth lock-in? Chance Bateman?

No, he's not that type of boy, she thought.

But Brother Tisdale had just told her, in the most austere voice she could remember, and the preacher didn't lie.

Her forehead and neck began to moisten. She hardly felt in control of her muscles, and even less in control of her will. An unnamable force was holding her, making her listen to the preacher.

Owen's eyes burned indignantly.

Your daughter's going to have a baby, Sarah, he said, *and she's going to have hell to pay.*

After the sermon, eleven walked the aisle as the congregation sang "Have Thine Own Way, Lord." Three professions of faith. One rededicated life. Seven new letters of membership.

During the postlude Sarah sought her daughter in the youth section—the middle second and third row of pews. Perspiration soaked her dress around the collarbone and her eyes reflected a distraught mind. Members asked her if she was okay, but she walked inside her void toward her daughter.

Kimberly stood by Chance, holding his hand. Sarah made her way along the jammed aisle, and when she reached them she grabbed Kimberly's arm.

"Kim, I need to know something," Sarah said.

"What?" her daughter whined, frail under the elder's constricting grip.

Her mouth twitched before the question. "Are you pregnant?"

Not uttered loudly enough for more than two or three to hear, but concise and compact, with solid grit.

Kimberly swallowed, took a small step backward, glanced at Chance Bateman. Sarah followed her eyes.

"Are you?" Sarah asked, noticing Chance's discomfort and urge to leave the aisle.

"Mother," Kim appealed, eyes rolling.

"Is he the one?" Sarah asked, eyes shooting at Chance. "At the lock-in?"

Kim swallowed again.

Sarah moved toward Chance, who turned toward her just in time to meet the hardened palm of her right hand. He flinched from the bitter shock of pain, and his limbs flailed like a jack-in-the-box, his mouth gaping.

"Why couldn't you keep your pants on?" she said. A small group—mostly teens—huddled around. "Was your sleeping bag not big enough for you?" The youth gaped with unease; some trembled with laughter. "I guess you're ready to have a baby, get a job, and support the family?" Chance opened his mouth a crack, as if to say something he wasn't quite sure of, unable to meet Sarah's glare, and leaned back against the pew, the varnished wooden top cold as steel to his hand. His left cheek reddened like a tomato, bubbly and tender. It was all he could do to maintain a normal breathing pattern, something he'd encountered at least a dozen times on the football field—even if it was just the sophomore team. How did Mrs. Stogner know they had had sex? How did she know Kimberly was pregnant? His mother appeared at his side. Short hair blossomed over the slope of her forehead.

"Excuse me," Doris Bateman said, a dark glint in her eyes. "What's the problem?"

Sarah's face peppered maroon. "You bore the problem." She glared into Chance.

"Excuse me?" Doris repeated.

"My daughter's pregnant because your son here didn't stop at the border," Sarah said.

Doris sunk into her shoes with a deep breath. She threw her son a quick, indecisive glance. She gasped and turned back to Sarah. "I don't know everything that's happened, Sarah, but you have no right to accuse my son of something like this here. In *church.*"

"But he had the right to impregnate my daughter here?" Sarah asked.

Doris's face stiffened, and as their voices crescendoed, Waymon Taylor and some of the other deacons moved toward them, talking them into separate corners, restoring, at least temporarily, a sense of calm between the two mothers.

In the hallway outside the auditorium, between scattered clusters of children, Rick Pettibone approached B. L. Sherwood and began peppering him with a series of questions, then four-letter words, forgetting anything about modesty and being in a sanctified place of worship. In two minutes each was a mere three or four inches from the other's jaw, spittle careening, canines awaiting the enemy's flesh. Behind B. L.'s clenched fists came a slew of peacemakers, deacons and otherwise, who, like those in the auditorium, threw water on the fire.

Outside in the parking lot, two sixteen-year-old youths, Brad Whissenhunt and Bo Aiken, slugged it out near their new cars in front of a crowd their own age. They clawed with nails like talons, kicked like bulls, their bodies tattooed with bruises, scrapes, and cuts. The shorter, meaner Brad knocked the bully in the nose against his own tinted Firebird and finished with a combination that shattered several teeth, painted a pint of blood over Bo's mouth, and which would bind him to hours of another place of torture: the dentist's office.

—✦—

After church, when the fights had broken up and Seth Weimer, the finance committee's chairman-in-waiting, had signed $100,000 of the church's money over to Owen, to be deposited in his personal account for what he had termed to Seth "unconventional investment usage," the preacher lay down on his bed with Mehitobel Enriquez, the new secretary, who'd previously worked as clerk for the *Dallas Journal*. The two of them sweated and tumbled the day and evening away.

Chapter 26

Waymon parked under the carport, stepped past the cactus, and knocked on the screen door.

"Come in," Mozelle said. Her voice wasn't as weak as he had feared. It never was.

He opened the screen door, then the other. A burst of sun plodded through in mortar-size holes. The TV was on, a game show.

"Get some coffee, have a seat," Mozelle said, leaning back in her chair, turning down the TV volume.

"How ya been, Momma?" Waymon asked.

"Same ol', same ol'," she said, a touch of complaint in her lips and voice. "Not too bad considerin' the Lord let me live so long."

"Who you telling?" Waymon retorted.

"Who *you* tellin', boy?" she answered, and they broke with laughter.

"Sure can't do the things I used to," Waymon said. "Some days, I don't even want to get out of bed."

"I told ya how hard it was, but you never believed me," Mozelle said smiling. "And for women it's even worse. Once you get past menopause, ya bones git all thin and brittle and start crackin' ever time you stretch or go work in the yard. The doctors get ya on all these pills—calcium somethin' or hormones—and before you know it, you're not yourself no more, and only some of the pain's gone."

"Well shoot, Momma," Waymon said, "I need to get Beula down to the doctor, then."

A second later Mozelle laughed at her son's sarcasm, although not as loudly as she had before. "Well, how's church been?"

Waymon sighed. "You're barking up the wrong alley, let me tell you."

"I wished I could lie," she said, "but from what you told me last time, it sound like somethin' bad gonna happen in that church of yours. Somethin' really bad. You know what I'm tellin' ya, son?"

He met her stare for three seconds, at best. Sighed in self-pity.

"We got kids fighting like animals. Adults fighting like kids." He shook his head. He looked down at the carpeted floor. "Where's it all going?"

"You know where it's goin', Waymon," the old woman said. "In your heart you know. You don't want to listen, but it's tellin' you."

"Some boy in the youth group got a girl pregnant, and their moms got into it after the service. B. L. and Rick started cussing each other out in the hallway. Couple kids busted each other up in the parking lot. I ain't seen that many fights in all the years I've been going to church. Why's it got to start now? I'm too old for this."

"You a deacon, Waymon," she said. "You don't have to work a job no more. You got a roof over your head. You got food, most of your health, and a good family. Lots of folks in that church are working, and all they energy is gone by the time Sunday come around. Even if they got the time, they ain't got the experience you have. Don't worry about being old. This ain't no physical battle, son. This a spiritual war."

Waymon's dark eyes stared at the old woman with an intimate sense of understanding and appreciation for her wisdom. Inside, however, he wasn't convinced. Where would the power come from, the authority to fight a moving source of evil? He sighed again, and the way he slouched in his seat conveyed his feelings of inadequacy and uncertainty.

"Our brothers and sisters are fighting like saints and demons," he said.

The old woman gave him a hard, almost shrewd look. Her eyes glassy and hardened. She kept her position, refused to sit up. "Maybe the demons done come to your church. It's startin', boy. The Devil done sewn his seed. It's time for God's soldiers to reco'nize those seeds and stand against them, make sure they all gone. You always been a soldier for the Lord, Waymon. This ain't no different. Ever time you go against it, you have to look at it like you goin' against the Devil hisself. Because you are."

Elizabeth tapped her mother on the shoulder. "Mom, my hand's hot," she said, touching her face with her free hand.

Andrea sat slumped over the dining room table, writing a letter. "What do you mean, your hand's hot?" she asked in her patient adult tone, without looking at her. "Did you burn yourself?"

"No."

"Better not be playing with matches."

"I wasn't," Elizabeth said.

"Does it hurt?"

"No." The rest of Elizabeth's explanation flittered away from Andrea's stream of consciousness while she focused on the letter: "It's just hot. My face feels cold when I touch it, but only with this hand, not with this hand. My other hand's just as cold as my face."

Andrea, who had never considered herself skilled at multitasking, kept scribbling with one hand and offered her other to Elizabeth, saying, "Give it here."

Elizabeth offered her hand, slowly and cautiously, and as the first fingers touched her mother's hand, Andrea pulled back her own as if having been stung by a scorpion. "Ow," she said, massaging it with the other—she couldn't care less about her writing now. "What ... it doesn't hurt?"

Elizabeth shook her head.

"Let me see," Andrea said, cautiously taking her girl's wrist, which was quite warm. She turned Elizabeth's hand over, studied her palm. "Well, it's not red." With her index finger, she poked the middle of Elizabeth's palm. "Yeah, it's hot all right."

"Why's it hot, Mom?" Elizabeth asked.

For a second Andrea recognized something in her daughter's eyes, something buried in the blue that reminded her of an age-old purpose she once owned, and an ineffable understanding seemed to pass between them, a feeling of uncertain fate and mysterious dreams and their roles in both. Andrea wanted to tell her daughter that fate determined its own course, that it sometimes gripped you and pulled you in one specific direction, and you had to go with it or be left behind. There was no turning back, even if it meant defeat, but her courage remained obscure, and she said weakly, "I don't know."

Andrea looked back at the letter. She went blank—she saw her own handwriting but couldn't get back into the same train of thought. While Elizabeth walked away into the living room, Andrea turned toward her impulsively and said, "Pray about it, honey."

Chapter 27

Chance Bateman toted his football travel bag down the science wing of Mesquite High. Since getting Kim Stogner pregnant, his parents had made him quit the football team, and for three weeks he'd watched his teammates catch touchdown passes that he knew belonged to him. He needed to rededicate his life to God, his parents said.

His shoes lifted off the floor with a spring he hadn't known in two months. He felt good about the things he was about to do, as the preacher said he would. The bag's thick nylon coils obscured the protruding steel barrels inside. He walked to his locker near Mr. Casing's room, fingered the combination, opened the door, shoved the bag in vertically, and sauntered off to class without books, paper, or pen.

The bell that ended his English class and began A Lunch jolted him with the awareness that he was going to go through with it—he was going to retrieve his bag of death's playing cards and start pulling the trigger, and people would bleed and slip in their own blood. He

189

was gripped with equal portions of euphoria and fear. The thought of abandoning the preacher's suggestion never reached him; he proceeded as if some irreversible engine had been turned on inside him and could not be stopped until the death machine had run its course.

Neither Kim nor her parents would consider abortion, so she would be having the child. They wanted Chance to find a job and pay for the pregnancy and birth, at the minimum. Neither they nor Kim had mentioned marriage. His classmates shied away from him as though he had forfeited his status, and former teammates lobbed volleys of "Father Bateman" and "Chance in the Pants" at him in the hallways. His teachers avoided conversations with him.

The world mauls you, the preacher had said. *But in my house are many chambers. Vengeance is good for the poor. It's good warm or cold.*

He strolled patiently to his locker while students skipped past him toward the lunch hall, jostling for position and their cheeseburgers and burritos from the fast-food chains that worked the closed campus. He opened the locker and slung the bag over his shoulder and walked away without closing the locker door.

In the bag's side pockets were a Beretta .357 and a Glock nine millimeter. He'd swiped both from his uncle's house in Fort Worth. His father's .30-06 rifle filled the bag's main compartment.

Except for a young couple necking near a drinking fountain, the halls had emptied. Chance unzipped the bag just enough to slip his hand inside and grip the rifle's stock. He passed behind a vice principal on lunch duty and walked up the steps to the cafeteria. When he walked inside, a teacher gave him a suspicious look but wandered to a table replete with colleagues. He filtered into another section of the lunch hall and proceeded down one side of an L-shaped hallway, easing the zipper along its tracks. Athletes occupied the majority of tables there. A cacophony of joking and laughter bucked from a table of varsity football players.

Chance ignored them, filing past to a table of his estranged sophomore teammates.

"Chance Bateman!" Brad Hobson said. Brad had a bulbous nose, like it had been fashioned out of Play-Doh, and a face to be taunted, but he was the quarterback and wasn't lacking in self-esteem.

"What's up, dog?" Taye Rondo asked, echoing Brad's enthusiasm. He held out his hand, but Chance didn't move.

"How's the wife?" Brad Hobson said. The others howled.

Chance composed himself. "Right now she's a little cold. And dead."

In the time it took for Brad and the guys to spread bewildering looks, Chance had the rifle out of the bag and in front of him. Shots thundered from the barrel. The first hit Brad Hobson in the throat, and a slice of pizza went flying from his hand as he tumbled over in his chair. Chance emptied the rifle on the rest of the students at the table, then grabbed both pistols and turned them on the varsity table. Students squirmed and skittered beneath the tables, hands and feet jerking. Everyone looked ripe for shooting, even people Chance had never seen before. He counted the shots, and when he came to the Beretta's last bullet, he methodically raised the piece, pressed the barrel to his temple, and shot a slug into his brain.

Chapter 28

The judge stood by his office window, looking out at the campus.

"I love this place," he said. "Always tell my wife I have the best job in Texas."

Owen offered a laugh. "Better than the governor?"

The judge looked at him. "He can fry folks. What I can do is send my best young preacher to Huntsville and instill shame and remorse in the inmate before he fries." He turned from the window and took his seat behind the desk. On the wall hung a wooden clock in the shape of a cross, the hands fashioned out of long Roman nails. "How's the flock?"

"Our church is in mourning," Owen said humbly. A day before, he had presided over Chance Bateman's funeral. Before the service, while he was comforting the Batemans, assuring them that Chance's pain had passed and he was sitting with the Creator, he'd noticed Waymon Taylor staring at him. Meanwhile, Kim Stogner was missing, and authorities had issued an Amber Alert. Owen didn't know where her body was, only that Chance may have divided it into two halves and disposed of it as directed.

The evening of the shootings, the church had held a vigil, with members praying and singing hymns. Owen met with the Batemans and Stogners and then with the church deacons, disclosing his plan for healing, which included one week of round-the-clock prayer, with members scheduling shifts to complete each day's cycle, and fund-raising activities for the victims' families. He'd been interviewed by the local and national TV networks and had called for healing and said that only Christ could give the kind of peace the families needed.

"Crisis management," the judge said. "Ought to be a course every pastor has to take. We've got so much of that happening today. Shootings. Bombings. Rape. Terrorism. One of those is bound to happen. You had a run of bad luck."

"If God sees us through this, we'll keep growing," Owen said. "We've got a warm bunch. We'll work this out, and if we keep going the way we're going, you and I will have to trade buildings." Owen didn't smile as he said this, and the deadpan caught the judge slightly off guard, but he sacrificed a hearty laugh for a man of his stature.

"Didn't know they had humor in Mississippi," the judge said and laughed again.

"Lots of surprises in the South," Owen said.

"You got that right," the judge said. "We're gonna give the convention one when their soup cools off a little."

The judge's phone rang. He answered it and told his secretary to hold the call.

"In three months we need to air your services on Dallas television," the judge said. "We'll run a PR blitz. We'll also let everybody know what the liberal Atlanta preacher's all about, and that'll be the end of him." He looked at the clock. "You been on TV before?"

"Once or twice," Owen said.

"Hallelujah," the judge said, tapping his fingers on the desk. "I'm sorry, but I've got some more meetings."

"My pleasure," Owen said.

Owen hated the skin on types like Lisa Etheridge. Pale and white, they thought they were too good for intimacy with anyone save their family or the guy with Hollywood features who happened to hit on them. Lisa had a good shape, but her face could use some work, and her pallid skin made Owen yearn for Mehitobel's chocolate coating. But the mere fact that she thought so highly of herself— even untouchable, with her morals and self-professed commitment to God—made him want to get beneath her all the more.

At the youth lock-in he'd appalled her; he could feel it; he saw it in her mind. And on other occasions she had avoided him or brushed him off as quickly as she could, giving a small-lipped smile, pulling down her skirt, moving past, and avoiding his invitations for more intimate counsel. She'd seen what he wanted, or at least she thought she had, even though he'd sent only the subtlest nuances, and she'd rejected him. *Him.* Turned him away as if he were another worn-out wolf wanting meat. He saw the Spirit in her. Felt it. But he could have her, he knew he could.

So many Christians, so many martyrs. And miserable Yahweh had promised them crowns even he had not seen. But would he have seen them had he followed? He didn't like thinking of that—what he could have had under the control of another—but the thought of loyalty and dependence drove him insane nevertheless. Most people were invalids, he realized. They worked their lives away thirty or forty years with the same corporation, slept with the same woman even longer, ate the same food. Americans were getting smarter, but not fast enough; there remained too many who played by the Book, which is what had brought Owen to Texas and the South.

Her apartment was in a nice part of Dallas. Small willows and short lamplights divided the street lanes, Neighborhood Watch warnings glowed in orange lettering, and smooth black gates guarded many front yards—like that of Lisa's apartment complex.

Something was burning, and black flurries danced in the Dallas sky: a barbecue, maybe. The smell was inebriating.

The preacher wisped through the gate without a sound, seemed to float along the steps to the second floor. The door was locked, but Owen had a way with these things. The doorknob twisted, the deadbolt unbolted. Click. The preacher sauntered inside, the door shut without a sound. The living room was dark. So was the kitchen, but a small light gleamed beneath a door further down the abbreviated hallway: the bedroom.

When he came through the door, he didn't say anything. She was sitting in her bed, legs crossed, reading a book by Max Lucado, one of the nice glam hardcover versions that cost as much as twenty dollars. She wore a white lace gown, which, by itself, would have given sufficient cause for Owen's internal frothing. He locked eyes with her, moved toward her in smooth midnight stride. She seemed to freeze, her white limbs stiffened in front of her. Her eyes, suddenly bloodshot and eggy and green, were devoid of the insouciance she'd shown him at the lock-in; she couldn't ignore him now, she couldn't resist.

He began whistling "Deep and Wide." Moving toward her, between the bed and blinded window, he took off his jacket, casually, as if all alone, and tossed it onto the bed's corner.

Lisa tried to talk; what came out was a garble in her throat.

Shaking limbs and scalp, she was, Owen thought, the best kind of virgin. One who thought herself pure, beautiful, incorruptible. Not that her flesh was smoother than a model's, but that the mind that commanded it did so with tightened reins, so that they were off-limits to everyone save her future husband.

"Always wanted a Sunday school wench," he said grinning. He continued to whistle his song.

He lowered himself, knees on the floor, moved his hands over her.

She couldn't yell; her mouth locked up, teeth grinding, in an expression of cold and shock. She stared past him in horror, spitting consonants from her frozen mouth.

Moving on top of her, he finished the deed amidst her horrified gasps. He rose up and raised his hand. His index fingernail grew into a six-inch scalpel. An epiphany seized him: He relished earth's playground, where his crimes went unpunished.

He could overpower almost any Christian. Those with faith either under- or overestimated it or didn't know how to use it. If Owen ran into trouble he could outwit them. Those with promise slaved away in poverty and obscurity, shunned by their own churches and religious establishments, which were too elite to recognize them.

Yahweh rarely seemed to intervene, especially when only the body, and not the soul, was at stake.

Only now, as Owen's handiwork grew to greater proportions, the girl stood in his way. At first he had thought perhaps she was only there to confuse him. But now the thoughts of Elizabeth Cormieaux—a cute blonde child with untampered soul and unrealized power—intruded his mind. As the anger mounted in his heart, on his face, and in his raised hand, he dove at her, stabbing the scalpel into Lisa Etheridge's abdomen.

Chapter 29

Figuring Lisa Etheridge's body wouldn't be discovered until the next week, when she would fail to show to work, Owen resumed his Sunday pastime, pelting the congregation with Scripture, words Justin Collier didn't care to hear. The skinny, nail-biting fourteen-year-old was thinking of the Cowboys-Redskins game he would attend that afternoon. He sat in the middle third row, with an open space between him and Amanda Lathrop, a buxom blonde who avoided him like the West Nile virus. His medium-length brown hair slashed just over his eyebrows, like a skater's, although he didn't own a skateboard. His parents woke him up each Sunday morning no matter how late he stayed up or what he did the night before, fixed him breakfast, and trucked him to church. Now he sat listening to a man with a receding hairline speak of a foreign story in what seemed a foreign language, and in a Southern drawl.

Brother Owen Tisdale stood tall as always, belly protruding more than usual, in a gray suit that would make most Southerners proud, preaching about Ruth and the blemish—or as he put it, "mark of the Lord"—that saved her from childhood sacrifice.

"When God has a purpose for you," he said, "nothing can stop you from carrying out His plan. God is all-powerful. He knows everything. He knows everything about you. Man, I wish I had that kind of power. Don't you?" A hoard of smiling faces beamed back at him. "Wouldn't you like to have complete dominion over everything? I know I would." He chuckled and the congregation laughed. "He loves us unconditionally. Is your love unconditional? I know I have a hard time with it. If you blindside me at an intersection, am I gonna love you? Probably not. If I blindside you at an intersection, are you gonna love me, even if you know I'm a preacher?" Again the chuckles. "Probably not. You might forgive me, but you might not love me. At least not at that moment. God, on the other hand, will love me every minute no matter what I do."

Justin thought about the game. Until he heard a sermon on a different frequency: an alternative channel.

He locked on to the preacher's eyes, of a vast blue ocean. His lips, moving like the waves. And then the voice, clear as saltwater.

Follow me, the preacher said. *Follow me. I'll take you to a better place. Follow me. I'll give you what you want. You can have everything I have. The books are lies, the Bible's a lie, a billion lies bound together. Follow me. I'll worship your choices. In my house are many chambers. Your house has many chambers. Follow me. I'll take you home.*

Justin fumbled with the words in his adolescent head. What was this sermon about? Loyalty? To whom? Was he imagining this? Was this a panic attack? The words resounded personally, as if the preacher were speaking directly, and only, to him. They penetrated with greater volume during the beats when he met the preacher's roving eyes.

What's there to think about? the preacher continued. *My house contains multitudes of which no one has ever seen! Have the angels seen them? Has God seen them? Has His army seen them? No one has seen them but me and my servants! And one of them can be yours. I've prepared a room for you, Justin. Come and be a part of my house.*

Justin bent over so that he could breathe a little easier. His face, a reddened flush in a crowded chapel, effused with sweat. Did the preacher tell him this?

It was an uncomfortable feeling, like being cinched in a vise-grip, but Justin couldn't block it. He couldn't find refuge from the voice; he couldn't stand up and walk away. All he could think of, as the voice thumped his conscience like a pulse, was turning away, fighting, or walking the aisle and kneeling at the altar.

"No," Justin pronounced with his tongue against his palate, but hardly audible. He glanced at Brother Tisdale's face. The eyes. *No. I won't go there. My home is not in your home. Your house is not a mansion. No.*

The preacher stopped his sermon, glared directly at Justin.

A few heads turned.

I hope you can live with the consequences, the preacher said in his thoughts.

Not five seconds later, trying to relax in the pew's cushions, Justin felt a knife in his side, and he doubled over on the carpet beneath the pew, hollering. The right side of his belly burned with his body's natural red fire.

Owen ranted in the pulpit while members scrambled to the youth. Everyone in the congregation turned toward the commotion, but the preacher found no reason to stop his sermon; he stood above the top step, stared at the blonde-headed girl in the white dress.

Elizabeth stood from her seat in the third row, looking at him, meeting his force with her blue eyes. Her lithe, bony frame paled compared to the preacher's, but she didn't blink. The preacher's lips didn't move. She moved to the boy, edging around the legs of the adults. Something in her eyes knew. Wanted something. Wanted to give.

"Justin, what's wrong, buddy?" a man with thick black hair was asking.

The boy's face, red with asphyxiation.

"Let's move these pews back," B. L. Sherwood said. Stan Wilcox, Casey Atwood, and some new members muscled back the benches.

His mother, Brenda Collier, held his arm. "Justin! Justin!"

His world, blue and blurry, shards of blackness. Burning. Burning.

A cool hand on his side, on his lower ribs. He started to push it away, he didn't want to be touched. A small hand, a child's hand, roving over his side, and the cool pulsing that it brought, as if, by nature or command, searching for the inflammation. Cooling. Cooling the searing fire. Cooling the right side of his belly, the muscle and beneath, down to his pelvis.

He let the hand remain, his own hand gliding over the girl's small fingers.

They sat around him, dozens of members, family, friends, waiting for an emergency team to arrive, watching the girl hold her hand on him.

"What are you ..." Brenda started to say. The girl looked up at her with the humblest, bluest eyes.

"It's okay," an old voice said above her.

Bending over them, Waymon Taylor laid a hand on Brenda's shoulder.

James Robertson, who'd come from the hallway, said, "Ambulance will be here in a minute."

Justin had stopped struggling, stopped wincing; he was lying calmly now, Elizabeth's soothing hand on his bare side. The burning had subsided. But something was coming from her hand: a pulsing. Almost shooting from it.

"I don't think we need no ambulance," Waymon said and looked up at the preacher on the podium.

Chapter 30

The room was so white and stained with aseptic smell it almost drove Andrea back out the door. Her own hospital room hadn't been as white, as plain. As doomed. Hadn't smelled as bad. Had she looked as bad as Vicki Ainsworth looked right now?

An emaciated face hid behind a blanket's seam, perched on a pillow. Vicki was hooked up to an IV and separate tubes crawled into her nostrils. Two thin limbs dangled over the blanket, resting on her torso. Blue bags draped her eyes, and her breathing was rough.

Andrea leaned backward on her haunches, looked over her shoulder as if to plead to the nurse who had led her to the room, but the nurse was gone. Andrea had left Elizabeth and Wesley two doors down in the waiting room—the nurse said she would keep an eye on them. Deep within she felt the guilt of not having visited sooner, but it had been difficult getting over her own ordeal: the wounds, physical and mental, the bad nerves. This is what she had become, someone afraid to step inside another room of white walls, so she allowed herself the excuse.

She stepped forward.

The hardened heels of her shoes made a dull, resonating clunk against the floor, a sound that seemed to affect the whole room as though a greater entity were swallowing it up. She walked closer, edged alongside the bed, waiting for the face to reveal itself in greater detail. Vicki's breathing, a rough, staccato train of wheezing and phlegm-filtered gasps. How could she be in this shape? How many weeks had she been here? Here she lingered, worn thin and lifeless, on a sturdy mattress for the undead.

Is this the best Dallas has to offer? Andrea mused.

"Vicki?" she said.

Vicki's eyes opened weakly, fluttered. She moved her hands, struggled to move her arms. She managed to at least turn her palm over, open it. Andrea patted her palm over Vicki's, laying it there softly as if laying clay on clay. She felt the cold knobbed heel of the woman's hand, heard the rush of war in her lungs, and, trying to make sense of this, tightened her hold, caressing the soft flesh of Vicki's thumb and her reddened knuckles.

Andrea's eyes watered. "I'm sorry." She looked into her friend's eyes, searching for the woman's former resemblance. In a couple minutes, Vicki seemed more at peace. "I'm going to pray for you, Vicki." Her voice barely audible.

Andrea stood in silence for several minutes, praying her prayer, unsure when it would end. Their hands clutched tightly, like strands of rope, locked and interwoven, pulling against the other's strength. Finally, the movement of her lips stopped while, coincidentally, Vicki's began to move, uttering something of a whisper. Andrea floated her hand onto Vicki's head, touched her hair.

"What, Vicki?" she asked.

The sound washed up from her throat. "Ehhh."

"Vicki, maybe you should try to rest," Andrea said.

But Vicki's eyes bulged, the blue in them brightened like a flame. "Eh-eh-eh-eh-eh," she said. Her hand squeezed death out of Andrea's. "Ehhhh—" The latter grated more from the mouth, from her tongue, forced there from inside her. The last words motored through, and Andrea heard them clearly. "Red," Vicki said hoarsely. "Red."

When she stepped out of Vicki's room, she saw Waymon Taylor spinning a yarn with Elizabeth and Wesley, who sat in their seats as they were told, laughing, legs swinging.

When he noticed Andrea, he saw the anguish in her face.

"Andrea," he said. "Didn't know I'd see you here."

She managed a tender smile. "Just came to see Vicki."

"Well, that's why I came," he said. A less than optimistic look overcame him. "How's she doing?"

Andrea's eyes welled up. "Not much better." She told Waymon what she thought Vicki had been trying to tell her: that the church was unraveling at its financial seams. She described Vicki's condition before Waymon changed the subject.

"What your girl did yesterday …" Waymon said. "You weren't there to see it, were you?"

"No," Andrea said. "I was in the nursery."

"I stayed after to talk to Justin and his mother," he said. "And some of the deacons. I know there are doubters, but I'm not one of them. You see, the heart don't lie." He placed the fingers of his right hand over his heart as he said it, looking into Andrea's eyes, which sparkled like crystals. "My momma always told me us black folks were more superstitious than anyone else. But I know what I saw."

"She touched him?" Andrea said. "She told me she helped him."

"It was something from heaven," Waymon said. "The boy was in all kinds of pain, and when she put her hand on him, he was fine. It was a miracle. That kind of thing don't happen in Dallas, Texas.

"Do you remember what you told me about your childhood?"

She nodded.

"Your daughter has the same gift, doesn't she? This—what did you call it? That old Cajun name for it."

"Traiter," she said.

"Traiter," he repeated.

On the way to her car, Elizabeth held Wesley's hand, and on a couple occasions, when he tried to pull free, she grabbed tightly, and he started to whine.

"Hold my hand, Wesley," she said. "And watch for cars."

Andrea couldn't help but look at the ground. She compared her recent turn of events to Vicki's, and the juxtaposition appeared incongruous: She had been stabbed, yet her pain had been quelled— almost too easily; Vicki had been in a car wreck, and there she was, stuck in a Dallas hospital bed, confined to unbearable pain.

"Mom, why didn't you want me to go in there?" Elizabeth asked.

"I just … I didn't want you to have to see her," Andrea said. "She's very sick, and she's hurting, and … I don't know." She realized the poignancy of her daughter's words were adding to her stress, making her look one way, then the next, fidgeting like a neurotic.

"Why can't we help her?" Elizabeth asked, her little face

scrunched up in wrinkles, looking up to her mother. She had so much power for a young age, the kind that made her feel an adultlike responsibility for others, as if they were under her care and she alone could help them, could cleanse them of pain, of mental and physical and emotional suffering, and of the scarring it sometimes left. "Didn't you hold her hand?"

"I held her hand, honey," Andrea answered, "but she was in a bad accident. She almost died." They reached the car, and Andrea paused with her hand on the door handle. "And it's like the preacher was feeding her poison or something. Can you feel it? The badness? He hurt her body, and now he's poisoning her spirit, and that's all we can do for her right now because the poison has been festering inside too long." As she said this, Andrea brushed back her hair with her hands, squinting through the sunlight.

Chapter 31

James Robertson stepped behind the flimsy black lectern in the fellowship hall, where the congregation often gathered on Wednesday nights. The air was hung over with coffee and spicy lasagna.

"Because of some concerns about church finances," James said, "the deacons have decided to hold an emergency business meeting." His mild, beneficent demeanor invited instant criticism.

"This meeting isn't sanctioned," said Seth Weimer, sitting next to Dan Bearden. "How can we have a business meeting when the church secretary isn't present?"

"That's right," a woman said.

B. L. Sherwood spun around and said adamantly, "The *real* church secretary's in the hospital."

"Our pastor's not here, either," Seth said, turning to the others around him.

"Does he even know about this?" another member, a beefy cowboy, asked.

"You and Dan are here, aren't ya?" B. L. answered.

"Excuse me?" Seth said.

"Wait a minute," Dan said.

"You're excused," B. L. said quickly, getting in the last lick.

"He knows about it," Waymon said, turning to the cowboy.

"Who was it, exactly, that thought of this?" Dan asked.

James Robertson, starting to break a sweat, looked weakly down at the lectern, then out at Dan Bearden, not knowing how to respond. B. L. started to get up, but Waymon patted him on the shoulder, motioned him to keep his seat, and rose instead. He and James whispered something back and forth, and James pointed to the papers on the lectern and took the seat Waymon had been sitting in.

"I'm a member of this church," Seth continued. "It's my right to voice my opinion."

"And you've voiced it," Waymon said matter-of-factly. He unraveled a crinkly paper from underneath the finance report and looked at it a moment, holding the members in suspense. "Guess I better read this, just to let you all know for sure that we will, one way or another, be having this business meeting. This is from the church rules, Section three under Rights of Members and Church Conduct. It says: *Anyone who obstructs either the formal or informal proceedings of a vote to hold a business meeting or the proceedings of the business meeting itself will be asked to leave the meeting, or, if necessary, dismissed and/or escorted by lawful authority.*

"Why do we need this meeting?" the cowboy asked.

"First off," Waymon said, "the last business meeting we had was almost four months ago. Now, you can ask anyone at our sister churches or anyone at the state or national convention, and I think they'll tell you the same thing: that's too long."

"That doesn't mean anything," Dan Bearden said. "We're not Missionary Baptists!"

"You better thank the Lord we're not," Waymon countered, glaring at Dan. "If we were, hell would have froze over three months ago."

"Excuse me!" Carol Tinsley said, glancing at Dan and Seth. "But can we conduct this—whatever you want to call it, business meeting or talk show—like adults? Just so you know, I've been writing down everything everybody has said, and I'll be keeping the minutes when we actually get into the meeting."

Upon Waymon's suggestion, a motion was made by James Robertson to go into the formal meeting, and B. L. seconded the motion. When Waymon asked if any were opposed, Seth Weimer, Dan Bearden, the cowboy, and a handful of others—mostly newer members, but some older, as well—raised their hands, and Carol wrote their names down in the minutes.

Waymon paused while James and Carol passed out copies of the church financial report. Studious eyes balked at the numbers, whispers flitted between the pages.

After reading over how much was listed on the bank statement—officially, $162 in the church account—Waymon summarized the amounts owed from the report: $235,866. The majority of it loans from various banks and mortgage companies.

"It's a wonder we have the lights on in this place," B. L. quipped.

"Now, I know we had some preexisting loans and mortgages dating back five years ago," Waymon said, "but it's inexcusable—maybe even criminal—how this debt got out of hand, and we need to find out what happened. We weren't in this bad of shape under our last preacher."

Seth's face hardened. "Well, I am the finance committee chairman, and I don't know where you got those numbers, but they're not right."

"I know who you are, Seth," Waymon said in a tone neither derogatory nor complimentary. "But there's over three hundred active members in our church who deserve to know what's happening with the money they put in the plate each Sunday. It's their money. Not the finance committee chairman's. Nor any committee's. And only a small amount of it is the preacher's."

"We've been growing," Seth said. "I have kept a close watch on the accounts, and there's not a remote chance we could be that far in the red."

"Well, we are," Waymon said. "And this is the official bank statement, and what you have are the copies of what I have up here."

"And where did this so-called church financial statement come from?" Seth asked.

"The church secretary's notes," Waymon said.

"Then it's not official, is it?" Dan asked.

"Vicki Ainsworth is as accurate a secretary as there is in Dallas," Waymon said. "And it was during a visit to the hospital the other day that she alerted me to the financial situation."

"But we don't know that," Seth said. "She's not here. And she's not the one who produced the financial statement. You just admitted that."

B. L. turned to Luther and said, "We need to get that skinny carrot-topped boy off the committee." Luther chuckled through a web of wrinkles.

Waymon lowered his eyes to the papers, tried to laugh off the assault. Just below his esophagus, a patch of heartburn told him maybe it hadn't been a good idea to organize this business meeting, take the podium from James, and try to fend off these piranhas, but inches away his heart told him that in the end everything would be golden. *Keep the end in mind. The rewards are waiting there.*

Waymon began forming words with his mouth but not with his mind. He was about to say something—he didn't know what—but the words would be catapulted at Seth Weimer and Dan Bearden and maybe even the cowboy and whoever else wanted to listen or take offense or absorb them. New members. Old members. It didn't matter. And the words wouldn't be nice. But as the first word was almost halfway out, from the hallway, clothed in casual denims and a green polo shirt, Owen Tisdale walked into the fellowship hall and stood behind the last row of chairs.

Waymon looked at the newcomer, and several members followed his gaze.

"Thank the Lord," Seth said.

"Come on in, pastor," Waymon said, neither cordial nor defensive. He didn't have to ask someone to give the preacher a copy of the information; three people in the back offered him the material, and he scanned over it quickly as the eyes cast on him waited for a response.

"Sounds kind of high, don't you think?" Brother Tisdale said.

"Yes it does, Brother Tisdale," Waymon said. "But if there's one medium that can't lie, it's paper. I think most of the people present, and even those who aren't, will believe the numbers they see on these statements."

"The numbers sound high, but I'm sure they're at least in the vicinity of what we owe," the pastor said. "I would, however, like to remind the church that a big portion of what the members have been giving has been placed into the building fund account, and because we continue to grow, and if, in addition to a larger building, we are looking at a more visible and accessible location, some sacrifices will be necessary in the short run."

Waymon didn't know what to say, and there was an awkward gap of silence.

B. L. finally turned in his seat and said, "Bank statement don't say nothin' about a building fund."

"The building fund is in an account at First Federal," Seth said.

"Why the heck is it there?" B. L. asked.

"They had better interest rates," Seth replied.

B. L. turned away in his seat, faced forward, and behind the scar on his forehead, muttered, "Aw, bull."

"It's all right," Luther told him. "They're not going nowhere." Several paired members turned to each other in their seats. Husbands and wives. Children and parents. Longtime friends. Whispering.

"Got the dadgummed mafia running our books," B. L. said.

"We checked around," Seth said. "First Federal had the best rates for a nonprofit organization's saving fund."

Shaking his head, sucking in one side of his cheek, B. L. said to Luther, "I guarantee you, someone's making a profit off this."

Chapter 32

Revival air swept through Mesquite on a Friday, the third of a five-day event that was to conclude on Sunday. Overhead, gray and white clouds frothed low over Dallas behind a malignant-looking thunderhead, moving northeast as they usually did, heading to some greater front.

On the Crown of Thorns Baptist program was listed one Reverend B. Hank Henshaw of Crane, Texas, affiliated with Paul and Timothy Ministries. He preached the first two nights, filling the seats with 318 and 359 people, respectively, and was scheduled for Saturday and Sunday as well. He'd brought his own organist, a crinkled old woman who wore squared granny glasses, and looked, Andrea thought, like something rehashed from the fifties, and who smiled and played notes at the reverend's exclamations as if it were a baseball game.

On this Friday night, Brother Tisdale had prepared the congregation for what he said was "God's gift of the Holy Spirit," the redheaded stepbrother version of a faith-healing service.

"We need not be ashamed of what our Pentecostal brothers

and sisters are doing," Tisdale had said the night before to the reverberation of amens. "When the Spirit infiltrates the building, when It gets inside of you and shakes your bones and soul, there's nothing you can do about it. You can't control It. You can't tell the Spirit what to do. The simple fact is, you have invited It in, and It's gonna do what It wants."

Brother Henshaw, a small but stubby man with thick Southern jowls and curly hair, stood on the steps in his black suit, delivering his charismatic oration through the microphone on his collar.

"He heals because He wants you," he said, sidling the steps, making his presence felt to each member. "He heals through my hands because I chose to be His servant, and He chose me just the same. There are a lot of quacks out there. A lot of them want to take your money. They don't quote the Bible as we have these past couple a days. They want you to believe in their outer coats for profit."

"Amen!" came a loud voice from the third row, the cowboy donning an amber Stetson.

"They want you to believe for their own sake, even though their hearts are clogged with sin."

"Amen!" the cowboy said again, in a deep, husky tone.

"He said, 'I am the way,'" the reverend proclaimed, pointing a finger above Brother Tisdale's head at an angle that may have been intended for heaven.

"Amen!" the cowboy said.

"I am the truth."

"Amen!"

"I am the light."

"Amen!"

"And whoever enters will have eternal life."

"Amen!"

"And He said, 'In my house are many chambers,'" the reverend said.

"Amen!"

"And I'm gonna take you to one of 'em right now," the evangelist said.

"Amen!"

A minute later the guest preacher was one step from the front pew, holding an elderly woman by her gaunt shoulders, professing their faith.

"I'm gonna heal you in the name of Jesus, amen?"

"Amen," the old woman said.

He looked at Brother Tisdale, who nodded solemnly, then placed his hand on the woman's head and pushed her backward. An usher guided her as she stumbled short of falling down, short of the full Pentecostal routine, and she took a seat in a front-row pew, disconcerted, leaning her head back, but failing to shake like those she'd seen on the *Praise the Lord* TV program.

"In His name you are healed."

Apart from the ushers, the healing service lacked format: the sick stepped forward, the sick were healed. There were no wheelchairs. And the crowd—even the deacons, longtime members, and hard-core Baptists—stood in amazement at what they saw.

An old humpbacked man, Mac Weatherford, wearing the thickest glasses in three Texas counties, lumbered down the aisle. Everyone held their breath. The members knew Mac's story, and those who were visiting could clearly see the declivity in his posture, the way his head bent forward and down—like a bird's—from a deformity caused by injury and disease. He'd suffered a back injury in World War II similar to JFK's—and on a ship, as well—only he hadn't had the president's medical staff to help him walk upright. Now he was old and could barely see, could hardly steer his wobbling white Impala straight to go to Sunday school.

"Howdy there, brother," Reverend Henshaw said, laying a hand on the old man's sloping back.

Mac didn't wait for a question asking what the Lord could do for him. "I'm a World War II veteran, and I hurt my back in the war. It ain't been right since, and it nags me worse than my first wife."

"Brother, there's not a wound on this planet that God can't heal," Reverend Henshaw said.

"Amen," the cowboy said.

The evangelist placed his right hand on Mac's back, the left on his forehead. He whispered into the old man's ear, at a level the microphone didn't pick up. This went on for thirty seconds, and the people in the crowd—especially the women, who held their hands over their mouths, their stomachs, or someone's shoulder—awaited the act of faith.

Henshaw impetuously raised his whisper into a loud voice, saying, "I heal you in the name of God." Mac lapsed unconsciously into an usher's arms. His head and shoulders jerked like a puppet's as the usher held him in a seated position on the floor. Women's eyes widened at the old man's convulsion, and Henshaw waited a few seconds until Mac's jerking settled into a light trembling.

"Take it easy, Mac," Henshaw said. "God's not finished with you."

The usher lay Mac supine on the floor.

"Who else wants to bathe in the Holy Spirit?" Henshaw asked.

A middle-aged man stricken with moles on a paralyzed face wobbled on a bum hip toward the reverend, and Henshaw was soon placing his hands on him and healing him, too. While he lay on the carpet, others followed, and finally Mac Weatherford woke from the spiritual hold and, with the usher's help, rose to his feet. He stood erect, straight as a pole, moving his head in circles, disbelieving his own range of flexibility in his spinal joints.

"My—" Mac muttered. "My ... my ... my."

"What is it, brother?" Henshaw asked smiling. "Spirit got your tongue?" Witnesses were seized with the dichotomy of laughter and crying. "What back injury?" He gave Mac a tight hug. "Oh, I love you! I love you in the Lord!" While Mac hugged friends and family, Henshaw turned back to the crowd. "What sick story does your life hold? How long have you writhed in misery? Ten, twenty, thirty years? Maybe all of your life. I got news for you. Good news. The news of Paul, John, and Jesus. You don't have to put up with it any longer. Give in to the One who can whiten your dark world. In His house are many chambers, and there's one wrought with your name in gold. Step forward with faith."

The man with the bum hip rose and walked with less effort, and the healing continued.

Waymon Taylor watched from the back.

What he saw was slightly disconcerting, less than hopeful. Had Mac Weatherford just been healed? By an evangelist from Crane, hundreds of miles down the road, south of Odessa? Was Mac standing upright, something he had failed to do in the twenty-plus years Waymon had known him? How did Owen Tisdale know Reverend Henshaw?

He hoped Mac was really healed. He hoped he was healed and free from pain, and he prayed for the others, that they might be genuinely healed, however bizarre the notion sounded, instead of playing to the tune of some kaleidoscopic carnival. But something about it—like many endeavors Owen Tisdale was associated with—made Waymon's knees shake. *Even when the picture looks beautiful in the eye and mind,* Waymon thought, *it's the feeling in the spirit that counts.*

As he watched the reverend heal a blind retarded boy, Waymon saw, from the corner of his eye, Andrea Cormieaux and her daughter enter from the back. Andrea was covered with a dark green skirt, the daughter decked in denims and a light blue short-sleeved shirt. He immediately left his place at the pew and went over to them.

"How you doing, Andrea?" Waymon asked. "I didn't expect to see you here."

"Well, I wasn't planning on coming," Andrea said. "But she wanted to come." She looked at Elizabeth.

"She did?" Waymon said looking at the girl, then back at Andrea. "Where's your boy?"

"Home," Andrea said. "Curt put in a long day at work and didn't feel like coming, so I left Wesley with him." Waymon looked at Elizabeth, seemed to study her wonderingly. "Yeah, for some reason she wanted to come."

Waymon bent his knees to be at Elizabeth's eye level. "Is that right, honey? You wanted to come here?"

Elizabeth looked determinedly into his eyes, then nodded.

"Well, let's grab us a seat," Waymon said. He led them closer than where he'd been sitting, to a small open space, and they stood like the others.

Elizabeth peered between the bodies in front of her at the preacher, who was sitting to the left of the pulpit, at the organist to the preacher's right, drumming keys with witchy fingers, and finally, below the cross-shaped podium at the Reverend Hank Henshaw, whose black eyes met hers and quickly bounced off.

Andrea and Elizabeth watched as the evangelist laid his hands on the participants: a deaf teenage boy, a bald woman suffering from cancer, an enormous man with an eating disorder. Sending all to the floor in a spiritual stupor, his eyes incessantly homing in on Elizabeth.

Sweat streaked down the reverend's brow. He started to lay his hands on an old man with quarter-sized cysts streaking across his balding head, but stopped short, pulled out a white handkerchief. Patted his face. Stumbled over words, making excuses, his eyes finding the blonde girl.

"And God said," Henshaw said, "that we … ought to glove—*love*—each other and care for each other, and the laying on of hands is, well, through faith, one way we can show our love."

He looked back repeatedly at Brother Tisdale, who, at one point, appeared to glower back with disapproval. When he touched the balding man on his head, Henshaw drew back his hand as if receiving a sizable electric jolt. He massaged the hand in the other. Looked at Elizabeth. At the preacher. Paced side to side, then stormed toward the side hallway exit.

Brother Tisdale followed.

A few in the congregation were looking at Elizabeth, talking and asking questions.

Waymon and Andrea exchanged looks.

"Come on," Waymon said, leading them to the foyer behind the pews. "I think she knows something."

Andrea bent to her knees, looked into her daughter's glassy eyes. "What is it, honey? Why was that preacher looking at you like that?"

Elizabeth glared out the glass doors leading into the parking lot. A mature look—the look of knowledge—glazed in her eyes, the look of a prophetess staring into a distant world. "He's healing them." She looked up at Waymon. "He's healing them with the preacher's power."

"Which preacher's power, baby?" Waymon asked.

"Brother Tisdale's," she said.

Andrea looked at Waymon. "What's he doing this for? What does he get out of it?"

"I don't know," Waymon said. "I don't know unless it gives him more power over our church or something. I mean, if you think about it, every good thing he's done, he done ten things that was bad."

Elizabeth walked toward the glass side door.

"Where you going, Elizabeth?" Andrea asked. The girl didn't answer. "Elizabeth, where are you going?"

Elizabeth came to the door, looked through it, and, with what seemed like a normal child's effort, pushed it open with her small arms and hands. Andrea and Waymon hurried behind her, and together they stepped outside. The sun had set minutes before, and the night sky still possessed a filmy radiance about it, one that let you view dim objects above and obscured some of the stars and most of the Milky Way.

Brother Tisdale and Reverend Henshaw were meandering through a parking lot crowded with SUVs and new pickups and Toyotas. They veered around the side of the building and out of view.

"That man's afraid of you, isn't he?" Waymon asked.

Andrea turned in front of her daughter and took her by the shoulders, stopping her. "Elizabeth, honey, where are you going?" she pleaded, her voice breaking.

The little girl looked up at her mother, her blue eyes awash with faith.

"Let her, Andrea," Waymon said. "We're with her."

She could have argued with him, and for a moment she felt like telling him that Elizabeth was her daughter, not his, but she remembered the regret at not having done more when she was a child herself, when her power climaxed as a traiter, when she could have rid her church of the old preacher and kept the families together. She realized there wasn't enough time. She let go of the girl's shoulders, and they stood on each side of her as they walked around the building. Behind them, people sauntered from the hallway exits.

When they reached the back parking lot, they saw the two preachers talking a hundred feet away. Something about Henshaw's face looked different. Andrea and Waymon instinctively stopped, but Elizabeth continued walking toward the preachers.

"Elizabeth?" Andrea asked. "What are you doing?"

"Making him go away," the girl said.

Waymon caught up to her. "Why?"

"One less preacher," Elizabeth said.

Henshaw, looking suddenly spooked, truncated the conversation with Brother Tisdale, whose eyes, like those of wolves, glowed cobalt in the evening light and struck a sharp chord within Andrea. When Elizabeth came within twenty feet of them, Henshaw backpedaled, skidding on dark dress shoes across the asphalt. Seeing that she wouldn't stop, he turned and ran.

Elizabeth kept her gait, kept walking, passing Tisdale, refusing to meet his eyes. Tisdale started walking back to the building. Waymon and Andrea stayed a few steps back, watching what transpired. It was clear what happened, yet unclear. Thirty or so feet into his run, Henshaw moved his arms in a manner that suggested he was trying to shake off his coat. The more his arms shook, the more the coat flaps lost their shape, lengthened, spread out, and took on a peculiar thin form. At forty feet he lifted off the ground, descended a foot or two and nearly bounced off. The coat, slacks, and shoes dropped to the ground, while the darkness concealed his naked body as it swam into the black sky. Spiraled in a slow wide circle in the air, with a dreamlike slew of webbed wings.

Flapping.

Whirling.

Flapping into the night.

Chapter 33

They gathered around the heavy conference table, seven of them, like Knights of the Round Table, minus the armor. Old men, mostly, searching for the Holy Grail.

It was Saturday, the room was sweltering, some were already breaking a sweat, and Luther kept complaining about the heat, saying, "You sure that air conditioner's on?" A convenient day to meet for most of them, but for B. L., taking time away from the oil field for even an hour was a lot like pulling teeth: It was hard, and it hurt.

Luther asked the question again, and Waymon, who with James Robertson's consent and help had called them together, assured the older man it was on. "We're all hot now, brother," he said.

"It's hotter than a Chinese chicken shack," Luther barked.

"Well, let's kill some chickens, and we won't have to worry about it," Waymon said, toying with the buttons on his polo collar.

Officially, Crown of Thorns Baptist had twelve deacons, and it was this detail that Waymon had talked about with James, specifically, who to include and exclude. He'd originally thought of asking all twelve to be there, but after reconsidering and talking to James, he decided, at least preliminarily, to ask those he knew the best. These deacons had been at Crown of Thorns for several years, men he thought would listen objectively to what he had to say. Those who trusted and believed each other enough so if evidence were presented, they could take an active, unanimous stance against the presence that had infiltrated their spiritual home.

"I'm glad you all could make it," Waymon said. "There's something I've been wanting to tell you—and tell the church—for a long time. Brother James and I asked you here because we think you should hear it first. I have a copy of the church financial statement if you need one.

"But what I really want to tell you is this: Ever since our current pastor set foot in this church, and especially as of late, I've felt in my heart and seen with my eyes an evil seed growing. I know some of you have experienced it."

Luther was nodding, although looking a little confused, unsure. Perhaps he hadn't been prepared for Waymon to go on the offensive.

"Could I take a look at that?" Casey asked, his face tan from playing golf.

"Why sure," Waymon said and passed it down.

Rick looked away, set upon the realization of Waymon's words weeks ago. "I remember when we went to Oxford, when we first heard him preach," he said, folding his hands over the table, interlocking his fingers, his eyes rimmed disconsolate and showing nothing of his previous arrogance. "You could feel it then, couldn't you?"

"I reckon I did, brother."

"I'm sorry, Waymon," Rick said. "The majority isn't always right. Now we're paying for it."

"The past, Brother Rick," Waymon said. "That's all that is. Only one way to go from here."

"Amen," James said.

"He sure could preach," B. L. said.

"Devil can do a lot of things," Waymon said. "He can do just about whatever he wants. He can preach the Word of God if it serves his purpose. He can preach, play the organ, sing hymns. He can kill Christians."

"You don't think Tisdale's the actual Devil," Casey said. "As in Satan?" He drew one eyelid higher and away as he said the last part.

"I'm not sure what he is," Waymon said. "But I know it ain't good."

"But the Beast himself?" Casey said.

"The Devil, of the Devil, an associate, it don't matter," Waymon said. "The seed's the same. All I know is we're waist-deep in the red when we shouldn't be. Our church workers are being hit by cars and raped. Our youth are getting pregnant and killing other students."

"Why would he misappropriate so openly?" Rick asked, studying the financial report.

"Because he doesn't care," Waymon said. "He thinks we're dumb. And powerless. Actually, he knows it."

"But there's not really any proof he was involved in any of that, is there?" Stan asked. Although he'd left his cowboy hat at home, a long-sleeved checkered shirt wrapped him in Western style.

"That's what his supporters will say," Waymon said. "But we have a young mother in this church whose three-year-old son stabbed her with a kitchen knife, and her daughter claims she heard Owen Tisdale, our pastor, tell him to do it. And last night that thing—that evangelist, whatever it was—just jumped up in the air and flew away. The Cormieauxs saw it, too. Now as bizarre as that might sound to some of you, you can't ignore that Andrea Cormieaux was stabbed by her own child, just as we can't look the other way at all the other violent acts that have been thrown at our church family.

"You're right, Stan. We can't prove any of this. We have to stick to what we know: We're a lot deeper in the hole than we were before this preacher came here, and we shouldn't be."

"Are these numbers right?" Rick asked, staring at the statement.

"Does the bank lie?" Waymon asked, drawing laughter. "Got it from the secretary's desk."

"If that ain't authentic, I don't know what is," B. L. said, scratching the scar on his forehead.

"I can't believe it," Rick said, looking at the figures and shaking his head, shifting in his chair. "Tisdale's screwed us every which way."

"We got to connect him," Stan said. "We got to show proof."

"How do you take personal testimony into evidence?" Waymon asked. "There's something about Tisdale. When I'm around him, especially when it's just him and me, I feel … I don't know … spiritually threatened. That's probably the best way I can put it."

"Our pockets are threatened, that's for sure," B. L. said.

"So is our air conditioner," Luther added.

"We need to find out where this money's going," Stan said.

"Or where it went," Luther said.

"That's right," Rick said. "Then we can show the church it was misappropriated."

"And we can bring the church to a vote," Waymon said. They looked at him as realization set in at the depth of everything.

"The damage is done," B. L. said. "We can't afford no more. We ought to run his butt out of town, is what we need to do. Save the church some grief."

"Amen," Luther said.

"Now hold your horses, brothers," Waymon said. "Take your fingers off the trigger. I don't think any of us should confront him about it. That's not our place. We're not the ones to do that."

"No telling where he's put the money," Casey said.

"That's what we need to find out," Waymon said. "When we do, we'll have what we need to vote him out."

The lights in the small room flickered. Something was burning.

"You smell that?" Casey asked.

"I guess it's time we got out of here," Waymon said.

Chapter 34

In the small, square Adult IV Sunday school room, along the hallway next to the fellowship hall, Luther stayed after class talking to Morgan Lathrop. The door was cracked open. There were still fifteen minutes before the service started.

"It just doesn't make sense how we run up a debt like that, you know?" Luther said, his voice loud and whiny.

"Yeah, I know," Morgan said with an expression that bordered on a smile. A tall man with parted, graying hair, he stood bracing a thick Bible and lesson book against his hip. "That's a lot of money."

"Shoot yeah, it is," Luther said. "I could maybe see if we were a few thousand dollars over budget or something. Then he and his dummies could say what they want. Ten, twenty thousand, even. They could say that's because of the building fund. But hundreds of thousands?"

Morgan nodded his head; he held his mouth open, almost smiling, listening. "In the old days, there wouldn't be no business meeting. If the church saw a debt like that, why they'd all go to the preacher's house, tell him to pack his bags and get out of town. And those were the lucky ones."

"Yeah," Morgan said. "A lot of churches have had some nasty fights."

"Well, if we don't watch it, there's one afixin' to start here," Luther said. "You went to the business meeting, didn't you?"

"Yeah," Morgan said.

"What did you think?" Luther asked. He held his paper coffee cup to his lips but found it empty.

"I don't know," Morgan said, shifting all the pressure onto the toes of his dress shoes. "Seems a little funny."

"I tell you what, most churches would've been talking to lawyers and would nail his butt up on charges," Luther said.

"They might," Morgan said. He sidled a step toward the door.

"A lot of funny stuff has happened since this pastor's been here, and it's starting to look like it's not just coincidence. People getting knocked off committees. And people who haven't been members but one or two weeks getting nominated to committees."

"Sure have seen some new faces," Morgan said.

"Well, I guess we better go if we're gonna be on time," Luther said.

They walked into the hallway and saw, in addition to three children playing by the drinking fountain and seven adults heading toward the auditorium, Brother Tisdale, walking the same direction down the hall, in even strides, in his fine dark blue suit.

After the service, long after everyone else had left, B. L. showed up in the hallway. He'd gone home and changed clothes and driven back in his Conoco company pickup truck, shoes scuffed and sleeves rolled back, hanging around like he had done in high school.

He peered down the hallway, waited by the drinking fountain, took a drink of the foul-tasting water, took another, put his hands in his pockets, thinking. It was ridiculous, he decided, wasting time in a vacant church, thinking the preacher himself would be there. He took his hands out of his pockets, preparing to walk out, when he saw the familiar form at the end of the hallway: the dark shape of a suit.

The suit walked toward him, and the clear contour of Owen Tisdale's features emerged behind it. His shoes clumped on the tiles.

B. L. stood erect, his chest pushed out like a cannonball. Suppressing his sentient side, he met the preacher's eyes with antagonism as they zeroed in on his.

"Brother B. L.," the preacher said.

"Owen," B. L. said.

"What are you still doing here?"

"Thought I'd find you here," B. L. said. "Guess all this is yours, idn' it? This building. This church. Everything that belongs to the church is yours now, idn' it?"

"Brother B. L., we—"

"Don't *brother* me," B. L. said, his face and fists hardening. "I don't know what you did with the money, but I know you didn't put it in no building fund."

"Well now," the preacher said, feigning surprise. He slipped his hands into his pockets. "B. L., I would have never expected this from you."

"Oh, shut up," B. L. said.

"Not only shocking, but lacking tact," the preacher said. He looked down at his shoes, polished and obsidian, then calmly back up. "Did you come here to accuse me of something?"

"I'm not accusing you," the brawny man said. "I came here to kick your butt."

"My butt?" the preacher said, suddenly amused, chuckling. "Not that I haven't had it kicked before, but you gotta understand these things are not drawn to scale. It's a lot like chess, you know?"

The preacher's sudden change of personality was a little disconcerting for B. L., and a level of discomfort settled inside him. Nevertheless, he couldn't control his anger. As an oil field foreman, he was used to chewing out his roustabouts, used to talking down to someone. He was rarely called in to answer to his superiors. He knew his job's requirements, and if he fell short it only roused his anger, which he vented by spewing it on someone beneath him. He raised a finger, pointing it at the preacher, who looked at it like a foreign object.

"You need to sell your stuff and get out of town," B. L. said, his finger swiping away to underscore the "out of town" message. "You've cheated our church enough, and if you don't leave, I *will* kick your worthless rear end."

Owen had stopped laughing and now seemed full of thought. "You wouldn't happen to know a good lake in the area, would you?"

"What?" B. L. said.

"Well, I was just wondering where in the world I could dispose of your corpse once I'm finished with you."

"You crazy ..." B. L. said, backing away. When he reached the door, he pulled against it and found it locked. He pulled again.

Again. Again. Big biceps flexing. The harder he tugged, the more it rattled against the bolt.

The preacher walked toward him as he struggled with the door.

"You're very mistaken about something," the preacher said. "I don't work for you. This is a proprietorship. I work for me." When the taller man came a few feet within reach, B. L. strained to pull his hand from the handle, but it held him, and he couldn't even move his fingers, grimacing with impatience and fear.

The silver metal frame of the door reddened with a copper glow and little rings of smoke swirled from its surfaces. The features in B. L.'s face admitted defeat: the angles of his eyes, the shallow blue irises, the wrinkles, the way his jaw ground helplessly. The look of pain. He fell to his knees, beads of sweat rolling down his face.

He turned toward the preacher and muttered, "I rebuke you."

The preacher bent down a little, leaned in closer to hear him. "What's that?"

"I rebuke you ... in the name ... of the Lord," B. L. said.

"Why, sure you do," the preacher said. "As I was trying to explain to you before, you're just a little out of your league. Just a little."

The door handle's heat singed the skin on B. L.'s hand, and he let out a whimper that gave rise to the preacher's short chuckle.

"You whining, crying little Christians," the preacher grunted. "Think you're worth the tiniest microscopic piece of dust. You rebuke me?"

Owen pointed his finger in the direction of the wall opposite the doors, turned it around in a twirling motion. B. L.'s body involuntarily jerked away from the doors, his hand still attached to the handle. He yelled out like he hadn't since he was a boy. His arm broke from the rest of his body, blood sprayed the preacher and the glass doors, and B. L. flew with brute force against the wall, the bones in his back grinding out a sonorous sound like the popping of knuckles, but amplified a hundred times. He crumbled to the hard floor. Two shallow trails of blood streamed from his nose as he sat there, head dangling forward, staring into oblivion.

Later that night, Luther slid into the sheets in his boxer shorts, hid his shaking hands under the pillow. The coolness calmed him only a little. Betty, his wife of thirty-four years, sat on the other side reading a Sue Grafton mystery. Even with her reading glasses and her age, Luther found her attractive, but he had no plans of getting physical.

"What are you so nervous about?" Betty asked.

"I'm not nervous," he argued. "Quit asking."

He'd always been nervous, twitchy like a little boy, and tonight he was especially nervous about something, but his temper was even worse than his anxiety, so she let go of the questions.

"All right," she said, folding her book, laying it and her glasses on the side, and turning off the lamp.

Luther rolled over a couple times: the first time facing away from Betty, the second facing toward her. Then he turned over onto his back, looking up into the dark. A couple seconds went by. A couple minutes. He was relaxed, close to falling asleep. Breathing steadily, calmly, as a child.

Something clamped inside his chest, jerking him fully awake.

"What is it?" Betty said.

The lamp came on, and she was staring down at him at a forty-five-degree angle.

He caught his breath. Then he felt it again, a tug inside the chest. He tried to breathe, but it came again.

Betty yelled.

The phone fell to the floor, its bell banging.

It came at him again, something that felt like a barracuda biting his heart, sinking its salty jaws into the muscular organ from four sides, biting with each last beat, until the lamp went out for good.

Four days later, a Thursday, on the eleventh floor of the Dalburton Building, Rick Pettibone was working late. He sat at his desk in a black leather chair, slightly bent over, filling out paperwork. His office was dark, but the lone security light near the door allowed him just enough clarity for a few more signatures. A few more, then he'd shove the papers in the drawer, lock up, and go grab a beer. A few feet behind him, through the large glass windows, the Dallas lights glowed and blinked, a starry abyss of business deals past and present.

"What do you know, Rick?"

Rick jerked up. A trail of ink where he'd begun to sign his name snaked down the acquisition document through the lines and print.

Owen Tisdale stood twenty feet away, hands in his pockets, wearing a navy blue suit that looked black in the dark.

"Didn't scare you, did I?" the preacher said.

"Just finishing up," Rick said. "Thought I was the only one here."

"You are the only one here," the tall man said.

Rick gave Owen a bewildered glance. "Anyway," he said, pushing the papers into the drawer, "it's no big deal. Just papers."

"Is that right?" Owen said.

Rick shifted in his chair, started to say something, held it, then relaxed. "Brother Tisdale, did you want to talk to me about something?"

Owen smiled. "Yes, as a matter of fact I did," he said. He leaned over the desk, drummed his fingers on the polished surface. "I came to give you a message."

"A message?" Rick said.

"Yes," Owen said. "I came to tell you that your pampered life as you know it is coming to an end."

Even in the dark, Rick saw the preacher's pupils, how they dilated, how the boundaries of blue opened, swam with what seemed like waves of the same, or was it the blue of fire? Rick swallowed, looked down briefly, couldn't believe he was hearing this.

"If you want to threaten me …"

"I don't make threats," Owen said. "You see, contrary to popular belief, papers and signatures are never required when you deal with the Devil. You belong to me."

"Who do you think you are …" Rick began.

"Gone to church your whole life, haven't you?" Owen turned from Rick to peruse the office's features. He ran his hand over the smooth front of his head. "Sang the songs, did the dances, served on committees, did your deacon's work. You did everything you thought you were supposed to do."

"Brother Tisdale, I'm getting a little tired of this," Rick said.

"Your mommy and daddy walk with Him," Owen said. "But you don't. You're my kind of man, Rick. You walk with money."

"Get the hell out of here," Rick said.

"You even use my kind of language," Owen said.

Rick leaned back in his seat, blew out a stressful breath. "Okay. I'll just call the police." He reached for the phone. He tried picking up the receiver, but it wouldn't budge; it seemed fastened by steel bolts, and he picked up the entire phone, struggling with both hands to pry the receiver off.

"You know, I could smell your heart from the South," Owen said. "Sour as urine. You're as selfish as I am. But unfortunately—at least for your sake—you don't have good judgment in choosing sides."

The phone crashed on the floor, bell jingling.

The next instant, an ineffable force uprooted him from the black chair, throttled him against the glass wall, and through the shards that broke from the impact of his body. The voice that carried past each story carried a high pitch—not a shriek, but a boyish off-balance gargling yell.

"Telecommunications," Owen said. "The wave of the future." Bits of glass suspended in the air outside, and with the brushing motion of his hand, he summoned the pieces back into place, the shards seamless, part of a whole, forming the perfect glass pane as it had been before.

Chapter 35

Owen had to get out of Dallas.

It wasn't the heat. Or even the petroleum-polluted empty sky.

He didn't mind the suit and tie—he'd worn them for years.

Nothing could grow in this dry stink.

Only stupidity and tumbleweeds.

And rednecks.

He sped south in a green Jaguar, zipping past pickups and the state pen in Huntsville that had sent more than one toasted convict to Owen's fiery playpen. In Houston he swerved east, revved it up to 100 miles per hour, and set it on cruise.

He rolled the window down, turned to look outside. "Houston, the dark crotch of Texas!" He laughed hysterically.

He didn't worry about state troopers—he had a way with them. He chuckled at car wrecks. In front of him, a Dodge pickup and Lincoln Navigator slowed, careened out of his way. Possessed by his own laughter, his face purpling, his hands now beautiful, fingers swallowed by 24-karat gold.

In a month a Dallas TV station would roll the cameras into

Crown of Thorns Baptist to televise the services. From there it was downhill: people would fall in love with his sermons, and in six months he would be president of the convention.

Straight east on Interstate 10, past rest areas and exits and cheap gas and hick towns. Faster. Faster. The world didn't move fast enough. These stupid ingrates—the way they looked over your shoulder, monitoring your every move. He couldn't leave Texas fast enough. *Get me out of this state,* he thought.

Once he crossed the border into Louisiana, a whirling sense of inertia spun inside him. The trees loomed greener, taller, thicker. The air smelled cleaner—his kind of clean. Moist. It was true, the rumors. Roaches with wings. Mosquitoes the size of dragonflies. Buxom country babes with bodies more supple than Hollywood starlets'. Bigger game for hunters. Something could live—could thrive—in this environment, more so than anywhere else.

The road was bumpy, but he didn't slow down. He stomped the gas pedal, the Jag's tires thumping, the suspension coiling. He drove thirty or forty miles until he hit Lake Charles. He took the Westlake exit, circling around a loop, passing industrial plants. Then he saw the enclave of carnival buildings and, behind them, the river boats: the Isle of Capri Casino. A procession of cars and pickups clocked through the semicircular entrance. He trailed behind, stopped in the middle, left the engine running, gave the valet a hundred-dollar bill.

"Thank you," the valet said. "I'll take real good—"

Owen waved him off, opened the casino door, and entered.

The cool air swallowed him at once, bathed him, replenished his borrowed body, and of course, his spirit. He walked past the escalators and stood in front of a large waterfall. He closed his eyes and breathed in the sound of rushing water crashing against and into itself, the aroma of its foaming white minerals.

"I love the South," he said.

He rode the escalator upstairs, walked down a hallway crowded with walking flesh, past a little restaurant called Everything Shrimp!, and stopped at the Rewards counter before the security checkpoint.

A blonde behind the counter nearly jumped toward him, her face beaming, blue eyes indicative of Owen's own.

"Mr. Tisdale?" she said.

"The one and only," he said, offering a small grin. "How's business, Tammy?"

"Booming," she said. "How've you been? Where did you scoot off to?"

"Texas, unfortunately," he said.

"We're so happy you came back to us," Tammy said, smile glowing. "Doesn't seem like the same place without you." She reached over and hugged him. "Anything I can do for you, let me know."

"I will," he said, walking toward the casino checkpoint.

Other attendants acknowledged him.

"Hey, Mr. Tisdale!" a beefy black security guard said. His name tag read Kendall. "The Gumbo Man is back!" He held out a thick, eager hand, which Owen shook. "It's been too long! Where you run off to?"

"Texas," Owen said, making an angle with his lower lip.

"Aw, now that's bad business down there," Kendall said. "Don't you know not to go down there?"

"Bush left, so I figured it's as good a time as any," Owen said.

"No kiddin'," a female attendant said, laughing heartily. "Last I heard, they changed from frying folks to quartering, so there's always a bright side."

"That there is," Owen said.

"Hey, if there's *anything* I can do for you, you know I'll do it," Kendall said.

"I know, Kendall," Owen said walking through, onto the large casino boat.

He passed through a set of doors, whisked by the front bar. A spread of tables divided the vast rows of slot machines, which sang *ding-ding-ding-ding-ding-ding-ding* with everlasting breath. An escalator traipsed down to the boat's first floor, where the slots were more numerable. He remained on the second floor.

A dark-eyed blonde cocktail waitress brushed past him, looked back, and stopped, circular tray in hand, a look of shock and disbelief.

"Owen!" she said, hugging him with her free hand. "How are you? Can I get you anything?"

"Oh, I guess I might have a margarita," he said.

"Blink and I'll be back," she said.

"I'll do that," he said.

"Mr. Tisdale!" a black coin attendant yelled, a bag of quarters in his hand. "What's going on?" Owen nodded while the young man, whom Owen knew played football at nearby McNeese State University, emptied the coins into the slot machine, biceps bulging with each shake of the bag. "Glad to see you back!"

"Same here," Owen said.

Cool air wove around the room in an invisible wraithlike dance, diluting the smoke-infested atmosphere with one less toxic—even to Owen's lungs. People smoked and drank, said whatever came to mind, especially when they won but also when they lost. Lushes and drunkards were born: college dropouts, deadbeats with scuffed-up empty wallets. A man at the craps table rolled a winner and pumping a fist yelled, "Yeah baby!"

"Want to try some keno, Mr. Tisdale?" a brunette asked from behind her table.

"No thanks, I'm a blackjack man," Owen said.

He walked into the dimmer VIP area. There he ambled toward a full table where another blonde in a white uniform dealt the cards, where the minimum bet was one hundred dollars. A manager, a middle-aged man with thick reddish-brown hair and a mustache, came over and stood at her side.

"Mr. Tisdale, would you like to play at this table?" he asked.

"Yes, I believe I would," Owen said, standing up straight, sticking his belly out.

The manager walked over to a Latino-looking man at the end, bent over, whispered, and the man moved, taking his chips and drink with him.

"Why thank you, Chris," Owen said, taking the seat.

"No problem, Mr. Tisdale," the manager said.

A vintage VIP glass snapped onto the table in front of him.

"Here you go, Owen," the cocktail waitress said, her fingernails reaching around his shoulder, over the collarbone. She whispered, "I'm free tonight if you have some time."

Owen smiled back at her.

A stack of chips clinked in front of him before Owen could draw cash from his wallet, and when he fanned out a row of one-hundred-dollar bills she ignored them for several rounds until he insisted she take them.

"Go ahead," he told her, sipping the margarita. "Got plenty of it. Let's keep it honest just this once." His smile lightened the table's spirits, and the others returned his fervor, smiling, delivering compliments. A woman sitting next to him wanted to know where he was from, to which he said, "Why, the South, of course." A port worker told a blonde joke, and the dealer blushed.

Owen won at first—quite a bit, in fact—and the chips piled in front of him. But after an hour the dealer changed, and an older, thinner wiry woman shuffled behind the table; she knew the rules backward and forward and made you aware of her knowledge. Owen began losing and several at the table quit playing, got up and left, until it came time to rotate and the blonde came back. Then the seats filled up faster than Wal-Mart. But Owen continued losing, and losing, won a couple bets, then lost a big one. And lost. And lost. And kept losing, until he didn't care.

"Oh, Owen, I'm so sorry," the dealer said, stopping short of scraping his chips.

"Can't always win," he said. "But the fun's in the playing."

"I'll make it up to you," she said.

"No no," Owen said, holding up his hands. "I don't want any favors. Just wanna play. You and I both know these are all my chips anyway." He laughed a single hearty laugh.

"Yes they are, Mr. Tisdale," she said laughing. "Yes they are."

He remained in his seat at the table, in the casino, up all night, playing, concealing the cards. Seeing which card he was dealt, studying the spades, waiting for another card, a better hand. Studying the spades. Dealing his hand. He lost more than he won, he didn't care. He played the cards, and kept playing, talking to fellow gamblers (no doubt poorer in the pockets than himself), telling the dealer to deal, until he was tired of the game … for now.

He stomped upstairs to his suite, reserved for him and no one else, flopped onto the bed and the clean, handmade comforter with embroidered lilacs and azaleas, and waited for room service.

Chapter 36

"Did you have it?" Andrea asked her mother.

Jean and Calvin had driven up to Dallas from Lake Charles for an extended visit. They were sitting in the trailer, the six of them, in the living room. The smell of baked pork chops—the supper they'd already eaten—wafted in the air. The television was on, the anchor on CNN telling of another terrorist threat and the bombings in Israel. Elizabeth was playing with Calvin on the couch while Curt minded Wesley on the floor, occasionally tickling him under the arm.

"No," Jean said.

"Then why do Elizabeth and I have it?"

On the couch, Elizabeth hopped onto Calvin's leg, and he gave a playful yell.

Andrea and Jean turned to them.

"Baby, be careful," Jean said. "Your grandpa's getting old and cranky, and so are his joints."

"Who's gittin' old and cranky?" Calvin said.

Laughing, sitting on the edge of the cushions, Elizabeth leaped and again landed on Calvin's thigh, her blonde hair flying as she did.

"Oww," Calvin said, mouth wide open, nose to the roof, holding his leg in facetious horror.

The girl giggled.

"Elizabeth," Andrea said mildly. "Behave."

"We all have unique talents," Jean said. "We're blessed differently."

"I know," Andrea said. "But is there any reason why some people have one specific gift and someone else has another?"

Jean laughed. "It's okay to start asking why," she said. "The atheists and humanists think Christians are against it, you know. Like in the garden, as if the moral were that people should never consider why something happens or why God gave someone a particular command. There's nothing wrong with the question, even though it can drive you crazy." The older woman sighed, looking straight ahead, and Andrea looked down at her lap. "We don't always understand God's plan, but it exists. And it works. I think He chooses some of us to fight bigger battles. That might be one reason."

Elizabeth, hopping on Calvin's leg, but less forcefully now, jerked her head around. "What do I have, Grandma?" Calvin jabbed her with underarm tickles, and she burst out giggling and turned back toward him in her frenzied manner.

Andrea scratched her stomach where it itched between the scars; where the scar traipsed into her navel was the worst, but nothing her nail couldn't get to. She looked away from the television, but not at her mother, pondering something.

"Mom, how much power does a traiter have?" she asked.

"I think it depends on the person," Jean said. "No one's the same." She leaned forward, folding her arms, her eyes austere in the lamplight, watching Elizabeth. "That girl is loaded with power. You really don't know how much power you have, do you?"

"We don't have modern-day prophets," Andrea said, with something of a question mark in the tone.

"But we have modern-day workers," Jean said. "Not much has changed when you think about it. We're still fighting the battle. We'll keep fighting it up until Armageddon and the Apocalypse."

"So we're just trying to hold the fort, Mom, is that it?" Curt chimed in nonchalantly.

"Curt, don't be a butt," Andrea said.

"Curt, don't be a butt," Elizabeth repeated, laughing.

"Elizabeth," Andrea reprimanded.

"See what you did, babe," Curt said to Andrea.

"She doesn't need to mimic adults," Andrea said. "And she knows better."

"I'm sorry, Mom," Curt said to Jean. He lay back across the floor, perched on his elbows. "You were saying?"

"I was about to say it's a little more than that," Jean said. "We're very important to God. He didn't create us to be inferior to the Devil. Our sin made us susceptible to Satan, but with faith we can overcome him. And death."

"Jean, are you preachin' again?" Calvin said.

"Yes, honey, I am," Jean said.

"See what I married," Calvin said softly to Elizabeth.

"What if God gives you power and you don't know what to do with it?" Andrea asked.

Jean pushed out her upper lip, raised her shoulders. "You just have to be willing. And do what you can with whatever you've been given."

For a minute Andrea and Jean watched the television. Andrea beckoned Wesley toward her, scooped him up, hugged him. He reached with blubbery arms around her sides and grabbed hold of her shoulders, and she said soft words to him. When she let him down he ran back to Curt and, from behind, smiling treacherously, wrapped the same limbs around Curt's collarbone, and Curt pulled him over his shoulders, carefully, and gently wrestled and tickled him.

"Andrea," Jean said, leaning toward her daughter, closing off their words from the others. "I did a reading the other night. She's going to go up against something."

"Mom," Andrea said accusingly. "You and your cards." She shook her head in mild reproach.

"I like to know what's happening in the other world," Jean said. "There have been other Christian mystics, even in the Bible. King Solomon was a mystic. I don't like to pray and leave it at that. I have to know."

"And what secret knowledge did the cards give you?" Andrea asked superciliously.

"They said," Jean answered nodding, glancing away at the TV, "Elizabeth will be confronted. Or rather, she might be the one doing the confronting."

"Mom, you're speaking in riddles," Andrea said.

"That's what the cards give you, honey," Jean said. "You ask questions. You have to interpret them."

"That could mean a thousand different things," Andrea said. She made a face. "This TV psychic says *this* is going to happen to *you*."

Jean smiled in curtsy. "Well, I guess that's what most people think about them."

Curt had rotated toward them, listening. "Jean, is there a dead chicken anywhere on the agenda?"

"Chicken!" Wesley said jumping up.

"Curt," Andrea said.

"All right," he said.

"I think I'd rather just pray and leave it to God," Andrea said. "I'd rather not know. All it does is scare me." She lingered with the thought a moment, then cast a reproachful look back at Jean. "Now I know where Elizabeth gets her stubbornness."

"I wouldn't doubt it," Jean said. In a whisper she said, "How do you think I put up with your dad all these years?"

"You would have given the apple to Adam, wouldn't you?" Andrea asked.

"I would've shoved it in his face," Jean said grinning. "After taking the first bite."

"Mom," Andrea said with a hint of a scowl. "I know you're not that bad."

Jean smiled.

Curt had pulled off Wesley's shirt because of the heat and the fact that it was nearing his bedtime. The boy had crawled away, found something behind the lamp table, something to marvel over, and now stood naked except for his underwear holding the thing in his hand.

"Hey, what you got there?" Curt asked.

Wesley looked at his discovery, then looked at Jean. He seemed intrigued by the colors, the art. Jean saw the outline of a tarot card. Then, through the lamplight, Wesley held it in plain view for her and Andrea to see, as if he were showing it off.

A skeleton in a chariot.

Death.

"Oh heavens," Jean said. She reached over, snatched the card. She swallowed anxiously. "It must have fallen out of my purse."

Chapter 37

Beula Taylor didn't understand such matters. "Church people," she always said, shaking her head as if those two words made it perfectly clear how alien and pitiful they were. Spilling the goods to her, even under such circumstances, in such dire times, did Waymon little good.

"Somebody botherin' ya, why don't ya just go sock 'em?" she said.

Go sock 'em, Waymon thought glumly. *Yeah, that'll solve it.* He thanked the Lord for patience—it was a blessing, he was sure of it, a valuable skill that came from an outside source—the ability to withstand Beula's personality for so many years. They had had good times; yes, they'd had those. But there also seemed to be an odd relationship between them, as if much of the time they hadn't been husband and wife, they hadn't lived in a marriage, but a partnership. Waymon felt it first after the birth of Tabby, their second child, yet he had endured. Nowadays people—some near his age, even—were procuring divorce papers as fast and conveniently as cups of coffee from the 7-Eleven. Maybe times were just changing, he often thought.

As usual, an uneasiness compelled him out the front door, into his sedan, to his mother's house. He never seemed to regret it, either.

Once inside, sitting on the sofa at the end nearest his mother, he noticed a glint of sunlight, gold and spotted with an asteroid field of dust, streaking from the doorway of his mother's room, which was just on the other side of the living room wall. And then, perhaps because of the silence, he pictured himself as a scrawny thirteen-year-old sitting on the carpeted living room floor watching an older, now-outdated Curtis television.

"Come 'ere, Waymon," his father said. "I wanna show you somethin'."

Waymon measured four feet from head to foot, if that. Reluctantly, he walked into his parents' room, which was dry and baked with sunlight. A quilted comforter coated the queen-size bed. The room was small and carried with it a scent of iris.

The top drawer of his father's dresser was open, tilted downward, and he'd already pulled out what he wanted Waymon to see. He stood there in the room, by the dresser, holding a scratched brass pocket watch in his hand, admiring it.

"Your grandpa give it to me, and his grandpa give it to him," he said, opening it up and looking through the glass, at the spindly hands. "Your grandpa's grandpa was a slave. A preacher slave. The white man owned him was good. Treated him better than my boss treat me, that's for sure." He laughed, and the child Waymon chuckled, staring at the watch. "The white man give it to him. Handmade. Gramps used it

for sermons. Don't work, but it sure looks pretty." He shook his head in *last-second admiration* and then handed it to Waymon and said, *"Here you go."*

———

"Waymon, you gonna drink that coffee, or you gonna let it turn to mud?" Mozelle said, eyes big as a frog's.

"Huh?" he uttered, turning dazedly toward the voice.

"Your coffee," she said.

He looked to the side, noticing the cup for the first time.

"Didn't put no wine in it," she said. "Fermentin' won't help it none."

"Okay, Momma," he said, remembering how she used to coach him at suppertime—*Aren't you gonna eat some salad? Here, put some good broccoli on your plate. Meat loaf never hurt nobody.* "You don't have to be grouchy."

"Grouchy?" she said laughing.

"Now you know I get enough of that at home," he said with levity.

"I wasn't being grouchy," she said, hitting her knee.

"Yeah you was," he said. "You was being grouchy enough for both of us."

"Well, I'm sorry," she conceded. "I guess I forgot what it was like at your place."

He tasted his coffee, looked over the cup, into the room where he'd taken more than one beating from his father, and the smell of alcohol, toxic and nauseating, returned in a hot flash. For a second he saw the belt, the palm, the fist. The next second, the belt again. Felt it.

God take it away, he thought, and shook it off.

"Your coffee don't ever change, Momma," he said, looking at her. "It's as black as me. Why you got to make it so strong?"

"How you think I lived so long?" she asked.

"Always thought it was the Holy Ghost," he said, taking another sip.

"Shoot," she said. She straightened herself in the chair and grabbed her own cup.

"If there's one strength you had, it was waking me up," he said.

"Yeah, well you needed waking up."

He stared into the guest room, taking in the light and dust.

"Momma, you think there's a chance Daddy was saved?"

"How many times you asked that question," the old woman said. "We're not Buddhists. You can't pray for someone who's dead, Waymon, you know that. The Mormons and Catholics do."

"I know," he said. "Just curious."

"I feel your wanting," she said, meeting him with her dark eyes. "You wish there was something you could do about his soul. It's a waste of your emotions. You gotta ask God to take it off your conscience. How you think I made it in this house? Everyone thought I was a loon for stayin' here after he died. 'You gotta get out the house,' everybody said. I prayed for hours, boy, and never did look back."

They talked over other issues, a little about politics, the Bushes, corporate scandals, how Texas was setting records for killing convicts, and when it was time to go, Mozelle walked him to the door and asked him where he was going.

"Down to the church," he said. "But the preacher's probably hanging around."

"Don't let that stop you," Mozelle said, the incipience of prophecy in her eyes. "The church is God's rock. Good a place as any for battle. The Devil wants to find you, he'll find you. You can't hide from him. It's what you do once he finds you that counts." She talked about Job and how Satan had entered heaven freely to debate with God about Job's allegiance. Standing there by the screen door, Waymon listened to the words, absorbed them as he had as a child, even though he knew the story.

He knelt in front of the altar, in front of the This Do in Remembrance of Me sign. The sanctuary's dead air chilled the nape of his neck.

"Are you standing behind me?" Waymon asked.

Silence. He thought he might be imagining things.

"Why I certainly am," Brother Tisdale said.

Waymon got up off his knees and twisted around.

Tisdale's white crewneck glowed faintly in the dim auditorium.

"Come on, Brother Taylor," the preacher said. "Let your guard down. There's nothing you can do to me that I haven't done to myself. If you hadn't facilitated this, someone else would have. My quarrel's not with you. In fact, you're one of the few folks I enjoy calling brother every Sunday."

Waymon didn't flinch, gulp, or retreat, nor did he look down. His eyes pierced the preacher's.

"I know what you are," Waymon said. "Or I should say, who you are."

The preacher smiled. "I'm glad a member of the African-American race knows something."

Waymon readied his heart and mind for whatever pain might knife him.

"Your people have slaved for the white man, who has slaved for me," the preacher said. "That should give you some sense of where you stand on my totem pole."

"I just slave for God," Waymon said. "But it's funny, He treats me like a king."

"Like He treated Luther," the preacher said. "Your deacon brothers."

"They died in the flesh," Waymon managed to say, little more than a mutter. It was all he could do to look Tisdale in the eyes. He was going to play this game by the Book; the truth couldn't hurt him, only his anger could. "Yes, their bodies are dead. But their spirits are alive."

The preacher looked at the ground, grinning. "You're the cooking fat I use in the grease pan." The grin subsided and was replaced by a look of insouciance. "I've never been thwarted by one of your kind yet."

Waymon closed his eyes, took a breath. "It's never man who brings you down."

The preacher studied him. "Do you think I'll do the same to you?"

In the awkward silence that followed, Waymon nearly lost control of his bowels. He closed his eyes briefly, opened them. He didn't know what lay ahead, whether he would be bleeding on the floor the next minute, minus his bowels, head, or both. All he could think of to put the notion aside was his faith—and the Scripture that emptied from his mouth like habitual breath.

"In my Father's house are many chambers," Waymon said. "My dead brothers have the largest rooms, and I hope I'll get one too."

The levity emptied from Tisdale's face. His eyes danced with blue fire, and he leaned forward on his tiptoes. He glanced at the engraving on the table, then at the baptistery.

"I admire you, Waymon," Tisdale said. "You give a good fight. Most people don't know how, even when they can. Your mother's a wise woman. She raised you better than most. I almost wish she would be around a little longer than she's going to be." He stared at the deacon, waiting for a response.

"She's lived a long time," Waymon finally said. "I guess it's got to happen."

"There's no guessing from my point of view," Tisdale said. "The sad thing is, it's not when, but how." Again he glared into the deacon's eyes. "Looks like you're gonna play the onward Christian soldier. Good for you, brother. Good for you."

Waymon considered attacking, or at least fighting off the impostor. He'd nearly said something about Satan's tongue and the lies that shot from it like a perpetual fountain. And why not? It was the truth. In this case, the truth would be his best defense, but he had little to measure it by. He couldn't ask B. L., Rick, or Luther—they weren't around to recount their methods or plans, whether cool or warm or belligerent. Waymon doubted any of them had been warm, especially B. L. Even if it were the truth, such a statement was visibly inflammatory, and he deferred to a more diplomatic approach. Another thought stirred inside him: Was this what it had been like in the desert? Forty days, forty nights, Satan baiting anger, luring a reaction, Jesus fighting it off, controlling his emotions? A war of words, riddles, philosophy, and attrition?

"If you could hear your daddy's cries," Tisdale said, looking up as if seeing the very image he was speaking about. Waymon's eyes narrowed. "Man, is he in pain." He gently shook his head. "Crying in my backyard. Not for alcohol or even for his family. Not for you. Just crying. Kind of hot out back, you see? And back there, ain't nothin' gonna help anybody. No sunscreen. No fireman's suit. The River Styx is real, Waymon, and your daddy's sailing through it in a boat of flesh."

Waymon looked down briefly, took a breath, raised his head.

"He might be," Waymon said, eyes a little watery. "But there's nothing I can do about that. If that's where he's at, it's because he chose it." He felt hollow immediately after he said it, as if his soul and innards had been pumped out in an instant, but he used every ounce of his sixty-five-year-old energy to harness himself, and he stood there at attention, struggling to hold the altar's ground, waiting for the next blow.

Spiritual warfare, he realized, was the maintenance of actions reflected from inside. He didn't feel triumphant, he felt humble. He knew he'd done the best he could, maybe even a little better. At the same time, he questioned how much he could protect himself or, for that matter, the church.

Chapter 38

"Mommy, me and Wesley want to go to KaleidoScoops," Elizabeth said from the backseat. Her voice reverberated off the car's interior, repeating itself, as in fact it did. "You said we could go get some ice cream when—"

"I know what I said, Elizabeth," Andrea said, turning left on a green light. "Now if you're quiet, we'll get to the hospital and the ice cream place in one piece."

Leaning into the front seat, Elizabeth said, "But Wesley and me—"

"Get back into your seat," Andrea said, seeing her daughter in the mirror, trying to keep her own eyes forward. She regripped her hands on the steering wheel. "Put your seatbelt on. *Now.*"

"Mawwwm," the girl whined.

"Elizabeth," Andrea said, scowling in the mirror.

The girl didn't sulk. She snapped on the seatbelt and held her silence.

A few seconds later at the light, Andrea said, "We're going to the hospital first. To see Vicki. Then we'll get some ice cream."

When they reached the hospital, Elizabeth was more cooperative, helping remove Wesley's child-seat restraints, helping him out of the car, and holding his hand while they walked inside, where visitors crowded the lobby and hallways. Babies were crying, patients coughing and sneezing.

Bleeding season, Andrea thought morosely. *This is where everyone dies while their family and friends are waiting.*

She led the children to Vicki's room and, before entering, sat down with them in the nearest seats in the hallway. She took her daughter's hand, looked into her eyes that seemed to know what was coming before Andrea put it into words.

"Elizabeth," Andrea said, "now it's your turn to touch Vicki. If we go in there and she's still sick, do you think you can help her?"

Andrea knew she could have given Elizabeth a peremptory command to go into the room and heal Vicki, something along the lines of "Get in there and clean your room" or "Wake up, it's time to go to school." She remembered, however, the dozens of rooms her mother and others had told her to enter, regardless of her energy or the fact that she was young and could scantly bear some of the sickly sights writhing with disease—whose face was uglier than any witch's or devil's—and she remembered the feeling of being used, called, whatever the right term was, and not having a choice, even if her choice would always be yes. This was why she didn't load her daughter in the car like cargo and drive her to every sick person's home, telling her to touch this nice old man with MS or that woman with diabetes or this child with scarlet fever. She wouldn't do that. No.

Elizabeth took hold of Andrea's hand and, smiling, said, "Let's go inside."

They walked into the room, the three of them. The bed was high enough so that Wesley couldn't get a good look at Vicki, and at his age, he wasn't too concerned about how she looked anyway. The room smelled like Mr. Clean, at least. The white walls seemed like a border to another dimension; if you stared at them long enough, the corners disappeared and the whiteness lost any semblance of shape. No doubt Vicki must have had many such thoughts, especially when awakening, that she was moving on from her bag of bones.

She was awake, immobile and tucked beneath the hospital blankets, and when she saw Andrea she managed a weak, pained smile. The IV infused amber electrolytes into her arm, tubes still ran to her nose. Her face was fuller than before, her eyes weren't bloodshot like they had been, and the symmetry of her cheekbones and eye sockets was resurfacing. Even with the improvements, a dampness draped her skin, paled it the color of ivory. She had been sweating out the pain, the disease that had come with the car wreck.

Elizabeth walked around the bed and stood at Vicki's right. "Hi, Vicki."

Vicki faintly lifted her head off the pillow and rolled her eyes toward the girl. "Hi, sweetie," she managed in a voice that rubbed against the sides of her throat.

"How are you feeling?" Andrea said.

"Oh, some days are manageable," Vicki said, grunting out words. "Where's your little one?" She tried to look over the bed although the strain forced her head back down.

"He's down here," Andrea said, moving behind Elizabeth, steering Wesley with her hand on his shoulder.

"How's he doing?"

"Fine," Andrea said. "We're all fine."

Elizabeth stretched her arm over the bed, placed her palm on Vicki's forehead. She looked back at her mother.

"A little warm," she said. Vicki smiled, laughing what little she could, and Elizabeth giggled, keeping her hand in place.

Andrea wondered if Elizabeth was playing around or if she was working, focusing on the dissemination of Vicki's disease. A minute later Elizabeth's smile had emptied, as had the chuckling back and forth between her and Vicki, and a fierce, resolved look burned in her eyes, settling on her hand, the woman, the array of pain, and all the badness that came with it. Andrea wondered what Elizabeth saw. Did Elizabeth perceive the pain as a big block of red as she had? A sea of red, a mountain of red, a planet of red?

Vicki closed her eyes.

"I can feel your hand now," she said. "Warm. So warm. What are you doing, honey?"

"It's okay, Vicki," Andrea said. Elizabeth looked at her mother. "Here, give me your hand." Andrea took Vicki's hand. It was warmer than her own, softer, the muscles and bones zapped of strength. With her other hand she steadied Wesley, making sure he didn't wander off or bump into something.

She didn't want to tell Elizabeth what to do—not in this matter—or how to do it. She could feel her daughter's power, and it may not have been any more powerful than her own, but something inside Elizabeth, her personality or early maturation perhaps, gave her a greater command and understanding of it. Andrea felt it, the spiritual aura of something greater than herself, greater than Elizabeth, greater than humanity, hanging in the air, ripping waves through the particles and shades of light, distinguishing between right and wrong. And she trusted her daughter to wield this life force into effect, knowing the result would be good.

Andrea closed her eyes, praying silently, guiding the warmth through her hands.

Wesley jostled behind her, to her left, and then said, "Mommy, da dice cream—"

"Shhh," Andrea said. "We're almost done, baby."

In seconds Vicki's breathing quickened, and she was moaning, but not from pain.

"Oh," she said in what sounded like a bland voice, though the easing look on her face suggested otherwise. "Oh, what …"

"It's all right," Andrea said.

Elizabeth placed her other hand between Vicki's neck and shoulder and closed her eyes like she saw her mother doing. Three minutes later Vicki opened her eyes. Her face told nothing of anxiety or pain, and her breathing leveled off.

"Andrea," she said.

Andrea opened her eyes. Vicki turned to get a good look at the child traiter. Elizabeth opened her eyes. She had a cautious look in her eyes, which matched well with Vicki's own confounded disposition. Vicki looked back at Andrea.

"It's gone," Vicki said. She squeezed Andrea's hand tightly. "What did you do?"

"*We* didn't do anything," Elizabeth said, eyes and mouth wide.

Vicki reached out to Elizabeth, squeezed the girl close to her, pulling her halfway up onto the bed, buried her face in her shirt, wailing.

Chapter 39

THE NEW TESTAMENT IN 3 MONTHS.

Waymon remembered the sign like one of the cactus plants in his mother's flower bed. It hung out front on the Crown of Thorns Baptist bulletin post, letters big enough for the Dallas elderly, visible for all who drove past the front entrance. An advertisement for a bare-bones reading course beginning with Matthew and ending with every diehard Baptist's favorite, Revelation.

It gave rise to Waymon's latest thought when he heard the news of Rick Pettibone's death: *Three dead deacons in three days.*

He knew, technically, it was five days—three deacons in five—or at least that's what everyone was led to believe. But it felt like three days.

He didn't accept the news of Rick's death as casually as the day's weather, but it also didn't come with the same shocking intensity as Luther's or B. L.'s. Especially Luther, who most members regarded as harmless. Grouchy, yes, but still harmless.

With three of the seven-deacon ad hoc committee members dead, he felt that calling a meeting with the remaining deacons or anyone else might jinx the collaborative effort to remove the preacher. It wasn't just a question of achieving what they wanted; he didn't want to end up dead anytime soon. So instead, he used a more indirect method that couldn't be easily traced: the telephone. All it would take to spark a word-of-mouth war—which the preacher had himself waged—were three or four calls. Three or four calls to the right people. Of course, he'd spent a good portion of the past three days and nights on the phone, listening to the details and the grief, asking questions, consoling Luther's widow, Betty, and Theresa Sherwood. There was no answer from the Pettibone house. Between calls, Waymon sat hunched over in his recliner, feeling like the old man he knew he was becoming, but he was deep in thought, meddling with philosophy and faith, asking himself if God would allow his life to be taken like those of his brother deacons. The information the Dallas Police Department had wasn't enough to blow their noses with: neither Rick's nor B. L.'s death had been ruled a homicide. And though Waymon and the remaining deacons knew better, everyone else believed Luther's sudden ascent was because of natural causes— which is how it was officially filed.

Now he found himself lodged on the edge of the same seat, a resting tremor in his hands like he'd had Sunday night when Luther died, when he'd tried to steady the receiver against his ear. Beula was in the kitchen. He'd told her he was okay, everything was okay, just not to bother him. He closed his eyes, gritted his teeth, thought of Jesus in the wilderness, the temptations, Jesus on the cross, and said, "God, give me strength."

Slowly, he settled down and made his first call—to James Robertson. They recounted the deaths, then discussed what to do, what not to do, which options were available. Waymon sensed the same stress in James's voice that he heard in his own, and there were little gaps of silence that hadn't marked their previous conversations.

"I don't know if calling the deacons together will do us much good," James said.

Waymon tried to lighten the mood. "Ain't hardly any of us left to call."

James gave what sounded like the hybrid of a grunt and a laugh. "Getting that way."

With that, Waymon felt a valley running inside him, a vast hollow valley where nothing grew, and his heart burned a little, and he clenched himself there with his free hand, rubbing away the pain. He thought about the initiatives he'd taken, the decision to call the seven deacons together, and how three of them were dead, and how James sounded now, and he pondered his status among his peers now, his spiritual brothers, and asked himself if it hadn't been diminished in the wake of the tragedies.

He told James of his plans to call other members, and James agreed that it was safer than meeting in person.

"What are we going to tell them?" James wanted to know.

"Let's call a vote."

"A vote," James said pensively. "You reckon we have enough votes to win?"

"If we don't, the Lord will provide them," Waymon said.

"We've had so many new faces that I feel like a visitor sometimes," James said.

"I know," Waymon said. "Some change is good, but the thing

is, this preacher ain't no good even for the new faces. They're on a sinking ship, but they can't see it's sinking. The Lord will provide. Don't worry about the numbers."

"If we waited ..." James said. "Now seems a little soon."

"It didn't take two minutes for the Lord to split the Red Sea," Waymon said. "We give this preacher any more time, and we won't have a church anymore." He heard James give a long and steady exhale, the kind that required some labor.

"When did you have in mind?" James asked.

"Sunday."

"Sunday?" James asked.

"Sunday," Waymon said.

"Well, I don't know, Waymon," James said. "We have services, and some people might not be as willing to hold a business meeting on top of it."

"That's true, brother," Waymon said.

"We've usually had them Wednesday nights," James said.

"Yeah, we sure have," Waymon said. "I'm worried not everyone will show up Wednesday."

"Hmm," James said.

"But if we hold it Sunday night, after the service, we can tell everyone in church on Sunday to be there. Tell them how important it is. I think we'll have a better chance of making sure everybody's there."

After a few smaller considerations, James went along with the format, and they agreed on the number of vote counters: four. They would select them from the ushers, two older members and two rookies, to appease Owen Tisdale's camp. They dangled around names of people they would call, to get the ball rolling, to spread the news, and following a brief span of silence on both ends, before they agreed to go, James again asked Waymon the question that haunted him.

"What do you think happened, Waymon?"

Waymon knew James was referring to Luther, B. L., and Rick.

"I can't tell you," Waymon said. "If you believe in the Devil like I do, I think you know."

Waymon called Andrea, explained the plans for Sunday night, and told her not to worry, but to be there and they would stand together—and, if possible, to bring Curt. He didn't mention her children—nothing with regard to Elizabeth voting—except to ask how they were doing. When they discussed the deacons' deaths, Andrea sounded frantic, on Waymon's behalf as much as anyone's, and told him to keep his distance from Owen Tisdale. Waymon told her that Satan approaches you at his own leisure, on his own schedule, and you're going to face him sooner or later.

When they were done with the conversation, Andrea called Vicki Ainsworth. Vicki was up and moving around. She said she would look for additional copies of financial ledgers and check with the banks for further records of church transactions, including those related to the building fund.

Then Andrea called Carol Tinsley, who called a number of families and everyone in her Sunday school class.

Stan Wilcox also received calls from James and Waymon. Stan, in return, gave Casey Atwood a ring.

James called Craig McManes, who went down the list at the front of his songbook and called everyone in the choir, including the pianist and organist.

Mostly what pulsed across the phone lines were the already-established evidences and speculations of the preacher's financial misappropriations, and the plan to vote him out, to fire him, after the Sunday evening service. Over a few of the lines, however, darker suspicions burned: three deacons' deaths in a week couldn't go ignored, not with the other mysteries of Owen Tisdale's tenure.

On Saturday, the day before the vote, autumn crashed its blitzkrieg on Dallas. The willows and oaks lost their leaves, cooled into stale skeletons. Patchy cumulus clouds streaked across the sky, threatening something worse behind them; the sun dimmed, floated farther away. Even the lawn, hedges, and trees at Texas Baptist Seminary, watered daily by an institutional army, bowed to amber. Crown of Thorns Baptist Church took on an abandoned look.

On Sunday morning, downtown Dallas stood somber and glassy, telling everyone to stay home. No building was more exemplary of this than Crown of Thorns Baptist, whose drying daisy petals spilled onto the hardening garden, the remnants of roses shrinking into crunchy beetle bits. The glass doors iced over and, when they closed against the metal rims, grated with the scream of something fighting to be let loose, or killed. The cumulus clouds fatter, closer to the church.

Three hundred ten people attended the second worship service that morning, a significant number, as always, compared with the eighty or ninety who attended the early service at eight o'clock.

Because he stood in the pulpit as much as the preacher, Craig McManes slipped in the announcement of the business meeting that would follow the evening service, repeating it twice. Word of the meeting had already spread like an oil-well fire during Sunday school, especially during the first ten or fifteen minutes of class unofficially designated as gossip time, and the news continued to be passed around during the service, as if carried on the offering plate. The program bulletin, however, made no mention of it. Craig had been leery of trying to slide it past Mehitobel's eyes. He'd been careful with his wording during both services, alluding to the authority which instructed him.

"An urgent matter will be brought before the church," Craig said of the meeting.

Brother Tisdale eased through both sermons, talking of Paul and his first letter to the church in Corinth, how the great apostle stood and delivered his messages amid flurries of beatings and stonings. The second service concluded peacefully, without event, only rumor, and the great void of time between noon and night resembled a football team's locker room hours before kickoff: a silent gorge.

During the evening service, Brother Tisdale continued preaching about Paul—the sermon anchored in Ephesians—of the infidelities and trials of the church at Ephesus and how Paul labored mind, body, and soul to keep the church together.

Waymon felt the jitters during the preacher's rants, where he talked about "churchbusters" and their lack of scriptural knowledge and the damage they did, unknowingly, apathetically, to families—to victims—of church breakups and splits. He felt the preacher's eyes on him, cool and truculent.

Craig McManes scratched his head. Stan Wilcox put his knees together, pulled them apart; repeated the process. Curt Cormieaux yawned. Elizabeth sat in her pew—pen, paper, and hymnal in hand—drawing a picture of the preacher.

James Robertson looked across the congregation, discreetly watching faces and reactions.

Dan Bearden sat up in his seat, straight and solemn, nodding.

The big cowboy leaned back into the pew's oak, hefty arms crossed, sawing amens from the pulp of his throat.

Seth Weimer, who sat in a pew behind Dan Bearden near the front, tilted his head to one side, occasionally whining high-pitched amens like a little lamb.

Andrea remained in the nursery, where she helped Wesley make friends, until Emily Wharton, a fifteen-year-old, came in and told her that the invitation was being given. Emily took over for Andrea, who walked through the hallway and waited in the foyer until the invitation ended.

No one walked the aisle. The music faded.

Brother Tisdale thanked everyone for coming to the service and said he would see them on Wednesday. He closed with a short prayer. Shortly afterward, while the piano pranced through the postlude, whatever hopes the preacher's supporters had of getting the congregation to disperse and go home were dowsed when Waymon climbed the pulpit steps, lowered his face into the microphone, and proclaimed that the business meeting would now begin.

A few people going out the back—new faces, new members, who obviously hadn't heard of the meeting or of its importance—stopped at the doors, donning questioning dispositions, and meandered back toward the pews, converging with the confluence of others.

Hearing the preacher's faint, murmuring voice through the wooden doors panged Andrea's stomach, and a prelude of nausea pelted her. She closed her eyes, palm on the handle.

"Jesus, help me get through this," she prayed. She stood there in meditation, pondering what she would do if certain uncompromising situations presented themselves. "Please, God, don't let this be like my old church."

She leaned against the doors, and they acquiesced with some movement of their own. She saw the maroon carpet, the pews, the stained-glass windows, and the smell hit her as well: a clean house of worship, a lively auditorium. Waymon was standing in the pulpit; people were sitting and standing, some walking to their pews.

"If we could get started," Waymon said. He glanced at Andrea, smiled, and nodded. "If everyone would please have a seat."

Andrea found Curt and Elizabeth along the right side, five rows from the front, and slid inside the pews to join them. Upon seeing her mother, Elizabeth showed her one of her sketches: a diminutive church building fronted by a large, sharp steeple; a fence around it; people standing inside the fence against what looked like a gate with little minarets, and a figure looming outside the gate, hands grabbing the top post.

"If we could get someone to motion us into meeting," Waymon said. He looked slightly uncomfortable, craning his neck toward the microphone.

After a couple moments, Matt Berringer raised a hand and said, "I motion."

"We have a motion," Waymon said. "Do we have a second?"

Stan Wilcox lifted a couple fingers—a peace sign.

"We have a second," Waymon confirmed.

On the front row, Vicki Ainsworth was taking notes.

Seth Weimer and Dan Bearden were sitting side by side now, in the third row. Directly in their path, in the front pew, sat Brother Tisdale, and when Andrea noticed him, he was looking directly at her, head cocked over his shoulders, studying her with a semiscowl, eyes large and austere. Her stomach flipped and she clutched her belly, staring down into the hymnals on the rack. Curt's hand slid behind her neck, squeezed, and the tension melted on one side. She turned to him and smiled.

"Vicki, if you'll start the minutes I believe we'll go ahead," Waymon said. Vicki nodded. "We've asked you to remain here tonight, *we* being the deacons, to act on a matter that is paramount to our survival and progress as a church of God.

"During the last business meeting, we brought up the subject of our massive church debt. To our surprise, it is larger than it's ever been. The question of possible misappropriation arose. We've had financial problems before, but not of this magnitude. Where did all this money go? Our finance committee chairman, Seth Weimer, along with our pastor, Brother Owen Tisdale, informed us that most of the money had been transferred to the building fund for a new church.

In the last couple days we've discovered that the building fund does exist, but that it's nearly empty. Transfers have been made from the building fund directly into Brother Tisdale's personal account."

A scant moan washed through the crowd.

"We have documentation for all this," Waymon continued, "and we'd like you to take a look at it."

Waymon cued James with a nod of the head, and after James took a stack of copied papers, four ushers came forward and distributed the mass around the room. Waymon waited patiently, allowing the congregation several minutes to look over the egregious subtractions and transfers of money.

He saw their faces, the pinching mouths, heard their whispers, sighs, groans: dismay, disappointment, awe. Among Owen Tisdale's supporters, resilient tongues were restrained behind gates of teeth.

Stepping out further along a narrow ledge, Waymon continued. "We have asked you here to call a vote on this matter. This is something Brother James and myself and the other deacons have been praying about for some time. I believe, with the information on these documents, that the Lord is sending us a clear message."

Dan Bearden stood up in haste, pointing his finger at the ground in front of Waymon. "What gives you the right to call this vote?"

"Mr. Bearden," Waymon said, "we, the deacons, represent the church body. We're here to serve the church body, we're acting on their behalf. We're their representatives, and by bringing this to a vote, the members have the final say on this issue. Do you not want them to have their say?"

Dan Bearden waved Waymon off, as if to say *Aw, shove it!* and sat down, only to give rise to Seth Weimer.

"I don't believe the church wants to vote on retaining Brother Tisdale," the redheaded man said. "No one's raised this issue except the deacons, and the deacons don't have absolute authority. We should vote on whether to have this vote."

There was some agreement in the congregation, some yeahs and amens.

Waymon took a breath, then said, "First of all, Seth, it's not in the church rules to do that. All that's required to vote is a motion and a second. And it would be a waste of time."

Lorie Pizzalatto, a new member, stood up and said indignantly, "Why are you so set on running off Brother Tisdale? He has done nothing but good work for this church, especially during the hard times and losses we've had since he's been here."

"Amen," the cowboy bellowed. "We're doing good things here!"

Casey Atwood jumped from his fifth-row seat on the left side. "Since when is killing people and wrecking the church a good thing?"

A lurid look of disbelief wrenched Lorie Pizzalatto's face, and from her mouth leapt incoherent mutterings of defense and assault. Then, after a matrix of shouts between Casey Atwood and the cowboy and Dan Bearden, it appeared Casey and the cowboy were seconds away from crossing the aisle, going at each other's throats. Members stepped between and talked them down into their seats.

Mothers began herding the children through the doors, hurrying them as if sheltering their weak bodies from starving, snarling wolves. Carol Bishop was walking her two sons down the aisle; Jeffrey was seven, like Elizabeth, and Brett was nine. When she passed the Cormieauxs, she saw Elizabeth and held her boys up for a second.

"Andrea, do you want Elizabeth to come with us?" Carol asked, the plague of concern marking her face. "We're going outside to play." Her voice beckoned with an adult's singsong maturity.

Andrea paused. She put her hand across Elizabeth's belly. "No, thanks, Carol. It's okay." They watched the remaining children—none of whom were older than twelve—filter through the exits.

The preacher bent his head forward, and at that second Elizabeth's face sloped with sadness and she whimpered.

Curt and Andrea turned to her at the same time, their heads bending close to hers. "What's wrong, babe?" Curt asked.

The girl glanced at her father, then looked up at her mother, sniffling. "He wants us to die."

Andrea looked at Curt, then back at her daughter. Until now Elizabeth had seemed undaunted by the preacher's power; she had resisted his incantations, his spiritual hold over others. Andrea had witnessed the girl's resistance: the incident in the church parking lot, the way she chased away the faith-healing demon.

"You can feel it, can't you?" Andrea asked. With her thumbs, Andrea wiped Elizabeth's dampened eyes. "Baby, don't worry. I'm here, and your daddy's here. There's no way we'd let anything happen to you." The instant she said the words, she doubted they were the right ones. A realization stopped her heart: *Owen Tisdale, the Devil in human form, was strongest inside the church.* Behind the pulpit, he could destroy a church from within. Like some undercover fiend. Like the Antichrist donning the mask of peace.

When Andrea turned back to the pulpit, she noticed Seth Weimer standing again, mouthing off to Waymon, trying to resurrect his dead argument. But Waymon would have none of it, and he warned the scrawny man that if he didn't sit down he would instruct the ushers to remove him from the auditorium and, therefore, the vote. The little redhead, seeing two ushers take a step toward him from the foyer in back, pursed his lips and relented to the pew.

It was a new member, Glenn Rodriguez, who took the next initiative. "I move we vote and that we do it by secret ballot."

Before anyone could argue, James Robertson slid a hand up and said, "Second."

"We have a second," Waymon repeated. "All opposed."

An army of hands stabbed the air, and Vicki Ainsworth looked back and started writing, but Waymon rolled on, the meat of Psalm 23 turning in his mind: *Though I walk through the valley of the shadow of death, I will fear no evil: for thou art with me.*

"Ushers in the back," Waymon said, "if you'll pass out the ballots." Four men in long sleeves and ties walked forward along the aisles, passing out rectangular slips of paper. "The directions are there on the ballots. It's a yes or no vote. Check yes if you want our pastor to remain pastor of this church. Check no if you believe Crown of Thorns would be better off with a new pastor and ministry."

Men and women dug in pockets and purses for pens and pencils, made checkmarks and *x*'s in the proper boxes. Dan Bearden and Seth Weimer and others voiced their displeasure in short blatant slurs, but, nevertheless, made their marks and deposited their slips into the circulating boxes.

Curt gave his pen to Elizabeth, and he and Andrea watched the girl mark her selection, and then they marked their own. When everyone had finished, the ushers carried the boxes to the back and kept the congregation in suspense while they counted, an endeavor that lasted five minutes according to Waymon's watch. One of the veteran ushers, Hugh Lassiter, walked down the center aisle and brandished the tally across the steps. Reaching, Waymon grasped the paper, looked at the numbers, and spoke into the microphone.

"One hundred fifty-eight yeas to retain our pastor," he said. "One hundred sixty-five against."

An eclectic stream of sighs and disbelief hissed through the pews.

A few members blew single shouts in triumph, as if it had been a miracle football-game finish, while others expressed their disgust or dismay.

"Bull!" the big cowboy said, tossing an imaginary fist of dung at Waymon.

Waymon looked into the crowd. "According to church rules, a majority vote is all that's needed."

Seth Weimer stood shocked and lost, like a boy badly needing to pee. Just when Dan Bearden stood, Owen Tisdale himself rose and climbed the steps.

Waymon stepped aside as Brother Tisdale rounded the pulpit, its armor shielding priests, prophets, and preachers through the centuries. The preacher's fingers slid around the horizontal plane of the cross-shaped structure, as if searching, his eyes on the center aisle, meditating.

The crowd quieted until there was nothing but the sound of humming lights and the oblivious shouts of children playing outside.

"You think you can vote me out?" the preacher said. Again, the humming lights. He scanned the congregation. "You can't vote me out of my own house! This is *my* ministry! This is where I work. Where I've always worked!" He gripped the varnished middle of the pulpit, lifted it as if it were made of paper, hurled it from his hip toward the side wall near Andrea, where it crashed against a stain-glass window, gutting a rainbow of glass.

Curt and Andrea shielded Elizabeth from the flying shards. The large pieces didn't fly very far, but bits of glass sprinkled the pews and carpet nearby. Brother Tisdale strode behind the choir loft and exited through the back door leading to his office. Members scurried to those nearest the glass to check for injuries. The glass hadn't hurt anyone; it had only nested in Rita Peters' hair, and she sat in her pew shaking it loose.

Dan Bearden and Seth Weimer stood gaping. Brother Tisdale's behavior had been violent and inexcusable. His supporters would never come back but might take up somewhere else, join another church, another movement, with someone else to rally behind.

Everyone was okay. The preacher had left without a fight.

Chapter 40

Andrea saw her childhood church: white pillars, chipped paint, haloed lights, the smell of old pews and carpet. Friendly faces, large hands enveloping her small hand, soft hugs from big women. She heard their voices, and she remembered home. It soothed her to the brink of lethargy: her fears were gone.

In the dark, as she slept beside Curt, his hand on her bare, scarred belly, her eyelids fluttered, pictures reeling past.

Somewhere in the voices, she heard that of the old preacher, Brother Hebert, and it gradually rose, a crescendo, until it was all Andrea heard. Suddenly the voice retreated into a vacuum and lost its volume completely, and new sounds replaced it.

New voices: people from Crown of Thorns Baptist. Carol Tinsley's empathic, consoling tone. Vicki Ainsworth's. Waymon Taylor's. She heard those of her family: Curt's, Wesley's, Elizabeth's, and she reached for them, trying to summon them toward her, as if with a fishnet: cast and pull.

She was standing in the trailer, the living room, flimsy floor beneath her. She heard a laughing, squealing voice from outside, that of a child, and when she looked through the drapes she saw Elizabeth spinning in circles in the yard as rain soaked her, her mouth wide open, catching the drops. Lightning flashed behind her daughter, not more than fifty yards away. She heard the bear's roar of thunder, as if right above, clawing toward them.

"It can't hurt you, Mommy!" Elizabeth said, arms outstretched, her body spinning. "Come outside with me!"

She opened the door.

The day was bright with sunshine, yet it was raining. Elizabeth was smiling in the foreground of darkness.

The next second she was standing in Crown of Thorns Baptist Church. Alone. Darkness pervaded the aisles, and she felt cold, construed thoughts telling her arms to hug her own chilling body, which she could not see. She could faintly make out the rounded shapes of pews, squared windows, the cross-shaped pulpit.

And she smelled something. What was it? Stale carpet, books? Something old? Something burning? Smoke.

A smoky smell that made her want to vomit.

Flesh. Hell's smoke.

A moan billowed from the pews. It broke into something like laughter.

She recognized the tone. The voice could never deceive her, not since she'd become an adult.

"Traitor," the dark voice said. "In my house are many chambers."

"You're not God!" she screamed into the dark, in the direction of the voice.

In the baptistery, above the water, she saw a light that burned with the charged static of electricity: her daughter's bare body, white and *glowing, hair rustling behind her shoulders with omnipotent wind, eyes open, glaring, the color of fire.*

———o———

The storm buildup started at four o'clock in the morning.

When thunderstorms came in November, they were led by a cold front, the kind that swept into town unannounced, during the dark hours of the morning. Thunder growled with congestion, lightning glowed in the gray, but the wind hardly amounted to more than a strong breeze. As dawn came, the thunder eased, and by the time Sunday school classes started, the sky was all but clear, with harmless white popcorn clouds falling off in the distance and the sun beaming modest rays.

Since the pastor had been removed and the church was officially in a transition period, Crown of Thorns Baptist reverted to a one-service format on Sunday mornings. Only one week had passed since Tisdale's ouster. Surprisingly, it seemed a comfortable distance between the present and the past, even though Tisdale's supporters, especially Seth Weimer and Dan Bearden, had threatened legal action, calling the church office every day of the week, sending out flyers to members in an effort to reinstate Tisdale to the pulpit. The Lord's Faithful Servant, they labeled him.

Waymon was scheduled to preach, something he hadn't done in nearly a year. James Robertson recommended it, and he'd capitulated. Because of this, his mother had decided to attend, and she sat, tidied up and grinning, in the third row of the left section.

Andrea and Curt sat with Elizabeth in their usual place. Andrea had considered bringing Wesley into the service, but at the last minute, fearing a struggle to keep him quiet and still, she had decided to put him in the nursery.

While the piano and organ were playing the prelude, Waymon walked from pew to pew, welcoming members and guests. He came over to his mother and kissed her on the cheek. Earlier in the week, he had sought her advice on the sermon he should deliver.

"People been slaughtered," she had said. "Souls been wounded. I reckon anyone following that act gonna have their work cut out for 'em."

He hadn't told her of the threat Tisdale made on her life. The way he saw it, they were all threatened. Still, it lay in the back of his mind. With words of Scripture, however, he fought the idea of her dying violently. He told himself that Tisdale was lying and that the root of all sin lay first in believing the Devil's lies.

Waymon had talked to Craig McManes about the service format, and Craig had agreed to tone down the "contemporary" aspect Tisdale had implemented, but not to completely abandon it, as some members—especially new ones, and guests—had found it fulfilling. Craig welcomed everyone and opened the service with "Onward, Christian Soldiers." When the music segment ended, Waymon stepped behind the pulpit and launched into a sermon he titled "Responding to the Lord's Call."

"Moses was called to do something for the Lord," Waymon said. "And when he heard what it was God wanted him to do, he thought he was too small or inadequate to do it. He asked God, 'Why do You want me to do this? Can't You get somebody else?'

"Some of you here today have probably thought the same thing. You've asked God that same question, haven't you? And then you convinced yourself that it was only your conscience. You told yourself that you were imagining the Lord's call. You said to yourself, 'Oh, He ain't telling me to do anything.' Well, I tell you one thing: If that thought was in your head in a church service or where two or more were gathered for the Lord's sake, then what you heard was a call. It wasn't your imagination."

He wiped his brow with his sleeve. "I'm sweating worse than a black preacher."

The congregation shed a gentle laugh, the kind reserved for meetings and holy days.

Outside, the two fronts danced leagues above the church steeple, circling each other as they spliced down in symbiotic union. Silently, the swirling mass funneled down.

Waymon thundered on. "The Bible says, 'Do whatever you can for Christ's sake.'"

A couple hard thumps on the roof interrupted him. The lights flickered.

Waymon ignored them. "Just as Paul proved later on, even while he was dodging rocks, the men and women of Christ, His servants, will persevere—"

Clinking came from the sides—something tapping against the stained-glass windows.

Baseball-sized hail punched through the glass, spraying rainbow shards and panes. Women and children shrieked, old men hollered. A ball of hail beaned Norma Greenway in the ear and the aging woman covered the gushing wound as she knelt to the floor. Todd Wallach, who'd founded Wallach Insurance and had even run for city commissioner, turned to the windows, to the source of commotion, and satisfied his curiosity in the most painful of ways, taking a fastball dead-center in the nose. A stream of blood stained his suit and tie.

Three young children—two girls and one boy—stood close to the only window that hadn't been busted, crying with defeated looks on their pink faces.

Curt leapt from the pew and ran toward them, shielding them as the last glass pane exploded, but he felt a diamond-shaped fragment slice across his arm. Vicki Ainsworth saw this and crawled toward Curt. The children were crying, and Curt braced them with his bloody arm against the wall between broken windows, fearing something else might come through them. Vicki took off her blouse and tied it around his injured arm, cinching it just above the cut.

As Curt's bleeding ebbed, the ground trembled. Sheetrock poured down in slices and ripped clumps, dusting the faithful with its white powder. The lights blew out above, and plastic ashes swarmed upon the pews and people, burning wood and skin. Rafters stabbed through the air: some as if catapulted, others as though shot downward from hunters' bows. Slots of gray knifed above and the roof opened up, but without rain.

What sounded like a train from Hades roared above them, chewing away at the church, sucking a few members to the roof, where they disappeared into an angry funnel's churning, dark mouth. As the roof opened and the twister sliced into the orifice, the steeple tumbled across the remaining rafters and wobbled miles into the bleakness above. It sucked up the pulpit, vacuumed a few more people. The bodies rose as if falling upward, sucked up, forgotten.

The faithful held on to the pews and hymnal racks with legs, arms. Waymon locked his hands around a chair bolted to the floor in the choir loft, kneeling at its side. Only Elizabeth stood unattached, unclenched to anything of the world. Holding on to a pew by its book rack, Andrea shouted at her in the slush of storm, unable to hear her own voice. Elizabeth looked back at her, calm, unfazed by the events, pondering something else, blonde hair blowing behind her.

"Elizabeth!" Andrea repeated, feeling the ligaments in her fingers tire like old rubber bands stretched to their limits. "Elizabeth! Grab on to something!"

Anchored to the foundation without apparent effort, Elizabeth looked at her as though she knew a secret and did not need to tell it.

"Grab the wooden seat!" Andrea said.

Elizabeth stood still, waiting out the storm until it slowed. When the rain filtered into a drizzle, then slowed altogether, she looked to the ceiling, through the hole that now revealed a thick layer of gray, even though the clash of fronts had passed.

While most members of Crown of Thorns Baptist lay on the carpeted floor, holding on to wooden limbs and parts in the weakening storm, they heard a series of *clip-clops*, short and hollow, at the front-door entrance. After a dozen syllables of the staccato notes, a dark figure emerged, walking confidently through the mist.

Owen Tisdale, dressed in black Armani, strolled down the center aisle, where members sprawled between pews for protection, hiding under wet wood, pressing their cuts with servants' hands.

Andrea thought of Elizabeth standing in the open. She wondered if Wesley was okay in the nursery. Had it also been torn apart? She uncoiled from the floor and rose to her feet, steadying herself with the aid of a pew. At first everything was blurry. She heard Tisdale's footsteps, hurried toward her daughter, who glared patiently in his direction. A bitter blend of disgust and wrath stirred inside Andrea. If only she could do something to oppose him. She thought of hitting him with something ... an object ... anything that might hurt him ... a pew.

The pew nearest her hefted itself toward Tisdale, striking him in the chest and knocking him down. He rose slowly, bleeding from the mouth. Craig McManes whacked his head with a hymnal before Tisdale shooed him away, lifting the song leader onto the piano with a banging of keys.

Andrea conjured similar telekinetic thoughts: flying pews, chairs, hymnals. At once, they obeyed her orders and rushed toward the man in black. He diverted the pews with a wave of his hand, and they spun off to the side, but a few of the hymnals got through and jabbed his face.

Sensing an opening, Matt Berringer darted toward him, lowering his head as he increased speed. Owen gestured toward the far wall, and Matt grunted as the force propelled him fifty feet into the air against the wall. Bones twisted and cracked in the same instant, and Matt's body revolved, spinning to the ground with a thump. Women shrieked.

Casey Atwood spied the former preacher from his vantage point at the front entrance. Sporting a goatee and mustache, his hair smashed from the wind, Casey resembled the Devil more than the Devil himself—the goat-man image taken from the Greek god Pan. His eyes blazed a red glow. He'd grabbed a fallen steel beam, one that narrowly missed him in its flight. He stood squeezing it hard enough to make his hand bleed. The blood streamed down his right hand, lubricating his grip. He crept behind the preacher. When he was within ten strides of landing the blow, Tisdale, without looking, flashed his palm behind him toward Casey, and Casey's head torqued halfway around against gristle and bone, breaking cervical vertebrae. He floundered to the floor. The beam clanked against wet, carpeted turf, painting yet another blood stain.

Ginger Atwood, Casey's five-year-old daughter, darted from underneath a pew toward the body of her father. She hugged his face, whimpering.

"Ginger!" her mother, Alice, said. "Ginger!"

Ginger turned to Tisdale, her face burning with hatred. "I'm gonna kill you!"

Tisdale paused and turned to face her. "You can't kill me." He looked up through the roof into the gray sky. "It's not my time."

Bunched against an overturned pew near the front corner, Mozelle Taylor twisted her way from the floor to her feet. She searched under the nearby pews for other members.

"Git out from under there," she said. "You ain't gonna let that ol' snaggletooth win, are you? He knows where you are, anyway. Come on, git out from under there." When they saw the old woman unafraid, they crawled from the corners and hiding holes. "Now, start prayin'." They prayed loudly and grabbed Bibles and quoted Scripture. The woman pointed at Tisdale to denounce him.

Tisdale paced to the front of the trashed sanctuary, then stepped up to the metal square where the pulpit had been anchored. Now he stood with his head bent. When he raised his eyes and the fallen members saw that they were entirely black—not blue at all—a dull, empty gasp spilled from them, as though they were saving their screams for what they already knew: the Devil was in their house.

"This is my house," Owen said in a deep voice that rattled the building's crumbled remnants. "And in my house are many chambers."

Waymon listened to the words, wondered why God's adversary had quoted Scripture. Crawling from the choir loft, he looked anxiously, comprehensively, at the members below him, searching for recognition. The philosophies and doctrines and Sunday school lessons and sermons melted into one pot: the damage done to God; the violence of mankind; the pain that scarred the divine. He understood now that he and so many other Christians had underestimated this foe since the beginning, and an image flickered in front of him, a vision: Christ on the cross, spear in his side, struggling to breathe, his belly rising in quick, failing bursts. He could see it clearly as if he had been standing beneath the cross. A series of epiphanies formed in his mind: *With the first temptation in the garden, the first sin, Lucifer himself had brought about Jesus' death. A parent will give her life for her child if she loves that child. Through sin and an understanding of God's nature, the dark angel killed Christ Himself, knowing God loved humans enough to exchange His life for their own. The power of ransom burned bright in hell. How much more power would be needed to topple God's kingdom, if not for the Scriptures dispelling such ruin?* Waymon lowered his head. His eyes watered in disbelief; fluid streaked down the grooves of his nose.

He searched the congregation for the eyes of his brothers and sisters, until he saw a pair that reflected his pain. Andrea struggled to her knees between the aisle, watching his reaction, and weeping. Had she seen the same vision?

"That was the first sin," Waymon muttered. He turned to the congregation. "He tried to steal the Lord's kingdom! That was the first sin! Now he's stealing the words! We can't let him take this church!"

Elizabeth sidled from pew to pew and drifted toward the pulpit steps, locking eyes with Waymon.

"Don't that make any sense?" Waymon asked, as if making a plea to the girl.

Elizabeth's dress was wet, and at that moment she looked like a miniature replica of a jilted bride, eyes attentive, humble.

Waymon narrowed his eyes, ambled toward the man in black. "He ain't about to steal anything else."

"My purpose is greater than the Light, my existence more renowned," Tisdale said, black eyes roving. "I have no creator, nor do I create. My purpose is honorable. I balance the world. Yahweh sits on my throne, in my kingdom."

"Liar!" Waymon grunted with creased face, and moved toward Tisdale to push him from the platform.

"No, Waymon," Mozelle cried.

Waymon heard his name, but not the warning. When he was a body length away, Tisdale waved a hand at him and the deacon grunted from a force that rocked him into the air and slammed him into the high wall behind the organ. Something snapped in his back and his eyes stilled. He crumpled to the carpet. Andrea led a chorus of screams. Mozelle Taylor bent over in agony.

Contiguously, a child's angry, commanding voice split through the cries.

"No!" Elizabeth roared from her tiny mouth. She thrust up her hands and a cannon force lifted the man in black off his haunches. He emitted a profound, awkward grunt, his head rocked back, and he kicked as he sailed over the choir loft into the baptistery, where his skull crushed the glass frame and his body tumbled into the water. Red swirls spilled from his head, his body gave way to the liquid.

Concerned and awestruck, Curt ran toward his daughter. He was hesitant to touch her at first, but then his hands found their way to her small shoulder blades. He remained silent. Brothers and sisters came out from under the pews, all eyes on the baptistery. They followed Elizabeth up the steps, some holding hands, until they stood together on the platform watching the opening. The water swallowed Tisdale's body. Bubbles emanated to the surface, the water fizzed. They stood silently, doubting, disbelieving.

Carol Tinsley stood beside Elizabeth. The girl looked up at her.

"He's still here," Elizabeth said.

Gretta Mullins and Curt exchanged looks of uncertainty.

When a few minutes had passed and some had turned their heads, an aurora of light, amethyst and green and blue, spewed from the baptistery's red water, tendrils and tentacles flurrying from the tail end. The light danced away, as if with wings, toward the shattered stained-glass windows and tore through to the outside.

Behind the organ, Andrea knelt over Waymon's body, making greater noise than Mozelle, who sat shaking beside her. When the life had left Waymon, it had done so with his eyes glazed and half-closed. Red rivulets eddied from his mouth and nose. They didn't listen to his breathing or take his pulse—they knew he was dead; no one could have survived that kind of impact. Andrea touched his shoulders, pressed her palms there, clutching, hoping. She felt nothing.

"Elizabeth," she said.

They made way for the girl. Accompanied by her father, she traipsed toward the organ and met her mother's pain.

"Help me, baby," Andrea managed.

Elizabeth bent to her knees. She touched his forehead with both hands, leaning over him. Her hair hung in front of her, brushing Waymon's face as she poured her power through her palms. She closed her eyes, and when Andrea saw this, she did the same, praying, seeking different shades of light while she moved her hands to the old man's chest, envisioning his heart.

Brothers and sisters had gathered around them now, holding hands and praying.

Elizabeth moved her hands to Waymon's neck, massaged the neck bone, reaching with the cup of one hand along a few vertebrae beneath. His skin warmed from her hands' heat, muscles and tendons twitched, bones shifted and cricked. She palmed up over his neck, cradled his head with her tiny arms, smoothed her face against his cheek. She remained this way for several minutes, working together with her mother, feeling God's power in the dark of their closed eyes, until she felt something beat beneath the man's skin. She felt his breath on her wrist. She smiled, opened her eyes.

Waymon's eyes showed recognition but hardly moved. After a couple of minutes, his eyelids slowly raised, and he looked as though he were trying to smile.

"Mommy," Elizabeth said excitedly.

"I know, honey," Andrea said.

The witnesses started wailing. Carol Tinsley embraced Vicki Ainsworth, and the two rocked in spirit. The traiters continued their work, pushing life into the deacon.

James Robertson had broken his arm when the twister had thrown him—at least it hadn't sucked him up—and his wife and a few members were tending him, bracing the arm, searching purses for painkillers. Since the lines were dead, Stan Wilcox had run across the street to call for an ambulance. Sirens whined blocks away.

Some of the congregants were walking around, dronelike. Others labored as they could, picking up sheetrock and bricks and rafters, pushing back overturned pews, the piano, already pondering rebuilding. Of those standing near the platform, half of them stared at the blonde girl, bewildered by her power. The rest, like Gretta Mullins, reached down and hugged her.

Waymon's eyelids opened further, and his Adam's apple bobbed down his throat as he swallowed. He opened his mouth. The way his head was positioned, he saw Andrea first; then he looked up at Elizabeth, who giggled. She repositioned his head, lowered it slightly from her grasp, let it fall onto the little cushion of her thigh.

"Y'all must be the angels," Waymon said.

Everyone shouted.

When Waymon regained enough strength, they moved him against the wall a few feet away, where he braced his back. Elizabeth scooted toward him, and he pulled her into a thankful embrace. A new drizzle of rain, warm and sweet, washed the congregation, while the deacon tilted his head, looking up through the hole in the ceiling.

The EMTs had entered and were tending to James Robertson, Todd Wallach, Norma Greenway, and others: bruised bones, cuts, dislocations. Stan Wilcox returned. He walked around the organ, past the others, and stood over Waymon.

"You all there, Waymon?" He appeared more nervous than a man of his country-western style should. His hands shook, and he kept swallowing.

"About as 'there' as I ever been," Waymon said.

"Want to stand up?"

"Better take a rain check on that," the old man said. Andrea, Mozelle, and Elizabeth stayed with him while the others, despite the flashing lights outside, stood on the platform holding hands, singing and thanking God for the rain.

... a little more ...

When a delightful concert comes to an end,

the orchestra might offer an encore.

When a fine meal comes to an end,

it's always nice to savor a bit of dessert.

When a great story comes to an end,

we think you may want to linger.

And so, we offer ...

AfterWords—just a little something more after you

have finished a David C. Cook novel.

We invite you to stay awhile in the story.

Thanks for reading!

Turn the page for ...

- **Discussion Questions**
- **An Interview with the Author**

Discussion Questions

1. How does Owen Tisdale differ from traditional and biblical depictions of Satan? How does he adhere to them?

2. Can faith explain Elizabeth's courageous stand against Tisdale, or is she simply more gifted than the other characters?

3. What role does church politics play throughout the work?

4. Of the protagonists, which character achieves the most? Why?

5. Whose story is this—Waymon's or Andrea's? Does it matter?

6. In what ways is Crown of Thorns Baptist Church similar to your own church ? In what ways is it different?

7. Which of the secondary characters captured your attention? Why?

8. How does knowing early on that Tisdale is Satan affect the manner in which you read the story?

9. What were the different ways Tisdale manipulated and influenced the church members? Why wasn't he able to do this with Waymon? Andrea? Elizabeth?

10. In what ways did Tisdale endear himself to the church?

An Interview with the author, Darren Dillman

What was your inspiration for this story?

I have an aunt who lived in southern Louisiana for many years, and she told me about the traiters and their characteristics in the churches there. I was intrigued by their unique characteristics in comparison to the typical faith healer you see everywhere else. That was how I came up with Andrea and Elizabeth. Then there's the aspect of Owen Tisdale. I suppose the influences here are numerous. For one, of the classics, I always admired Hawthorne and how he portrayed both the preachers of his time (*The Scarlet Letter*) and the Devil ("Young Goodman Brown"). As my students in English 102, Composition and Literature, know, I am crazy about the latter story, which I teach in the course. While many of them sit doe-eyed in class after having read the story the night before, wondering what it was all about, I revel in the occult details of the piece. What can be more romantic—literarily speaking—than walking with the Devil at night, discussing with him both your fate and that of your ancestors?

Do any of the characters come from your own life?

Bits of Mozelle Taylor are modeled after my grandmother, just as pieces of Waymon reflect my dad. But generally, no. My life is much more boring.

What was your writing process for *The Preacher?*

I did some character sketching before the actual writing. I also wrote down some possible directions the novel could go, plotwise. I typically did a day's work longhand before I went to the computer. I wrote half of it before heading into a graduate MFA program. From there, it kind of stalled until my third year in grad school, when I pulled it back up on screen and finished it. Then I let it sit a year before revising it.

What were the greatest challenges you faced as you worked on the story?

Finding more characters to kill!

Juggling the yin and yang forces—in essence, playing God. Deciding to what degree Owen Tisdale would succeed, how much he could take away, in terms of the damage done, and vice versa, with Waymon Taylor, Andrea, and Elizabeth.

Deciding when to disclose information was challenging, because I had to determine what kind of novel this was going to be. By withholding more information about character identity, I could have molded it more into a mystery, but it also risked less action up front and in the middle. What I intended—at least from the reader's viewpoint—was to make it a brawl fairly early and maintain that tension to the end.

How did you make decisions about the manner in which Brother Tisdale would act in the story?

Tisdale is all about appearances. I wanted to portray someone who was effective, personable, and even likable as a preacher, someone who met the expectations of the common churchgoer. His other face, however, the one that flies beneath the radar, reveals a prankster, a hedonist, a lawbreaker, someone who hates the creation of man and will try to destroy him via politics, religion, etc.

Why did you choose to present a story with such a boldly drawn Satan instead of opting for a more subtle character portrayal?

I don't view Satan, by nature, as a subtle type of character. As his exit from heaven demonstrates, he's not boring—he's dramatic. He's a bad boy, and he would have flown under the radar had Waymon, Andrea, and Elizabeth not opposed him. Besides, it makes a better story. Does anyone want to read about a Satan who sips tea with the crocheting club on Sunday afternoons and volunteers to help with the youth group bake sale?

Was any of this prompted by your own real-life experience in church?

Yes, somewhat. When I was six or seven years old, the church my family attended had a nasty split. Everyone liked the pastor, but he had been taking off several Sundays for reasons most didn't find acceptable, from what I remember. The pastor caught wind of an impending vote to dismiss him, and he called people who had rarely attended the church in an attempt to bolster his support. It worked, and he won the vote. I had just become a Christian, had been baptized, and could have voted as a member, and the vote would have won the case for the pastor's dismissal. However, my parents, as well as others, decided to shield the children from this type of belligerence. As a result, many of us left the church and ended up starting another one in our own small community.

How much research did you have to do for this novel? How did you go about that?

Not much. My dad is an ordained deacon who has done his fair share of preaching and song leading in the past. He gave me some information about committees, procedures, and written records, all from the perspective of a small church, of course.

What do you hope readers come away with after reading *The Preacher*?

I hope they feel they've read something interesting, a work that held their attention and didn't waste their time. I don't feel there's a lesson for them to learn or message to come away with. If there is a particular theme, I think the readers know it already—the book simply confirms their convictions.

Where do you go from here? Is there a sequel in the works? And if so, how do you top Satan's preaching gig?

Yes, I am planning a sequel, but that is up to the publisher. I'm not sure anything can really measure up to Owen Tisdale, although the Devil and his muse can be very creative.

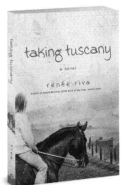
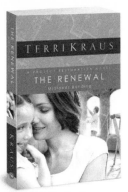